ZILA'S EYES

Charron Plumer

Pizote Press

Zila's Eyes/Plumer
ISBN

For Kaila
With her beautiful eyes

Zila awoke to the sensation of something moving softly over her outstretched arm. She opened her eyes and kept her body still. Without moving her face, she glanced out of the corner of her eyes to her left arm and settled her vision on a large purple and yellow morpho butterfly sitting on her hand. If she wanted, she could have closed her fist over the exquisite creature. Instead, she slowed her breath and studied the fine markings and colorings of the insect.

Finally, the butterfly lifted itself and fluttered away. She stretched her long, slender body on the soft blanket laid over the bed of large palm leaves and soft earth, and slowly lifted herself into a crossed knee position. It was a beautiful morning. She looked up toward the streaks of sunlight filtering through the multi-layered canopy of treetops and gave a silent thank-you to the gods above, below, and in every living thing for another day of life. She had much to accomplish this day.

It had been many days since she had been in contact with anyone. She was supposed to meet up with Grandmother just as the moon appeared over the crest of the tallest peak, at their usual spot. She wanted to gather some special gifts for her beloved mentor, so she had a long day ahead of her traversing over the mountainous region to find the rare and potent items. She also sensed that there was a need for her presence in the lower village.

She rose from her sleeping space and brushed away any remnants of her presence, slung her satchel over her shoulder and headed off to find the nearest stream to freshen herself.

Chapter 1

Simone Jenkins

Her body felt warm and tingly. She wanted to just lie in bed and enjoy the sensation of feeling refreshed, well rested. Simone stretched her long, thin limbs out and wriggled her toes. She felt good. It had been so long since she had felt this good. The god-awful pain that had held her skull in a vise was magically gone. The constant cramping of her limbs and intestines had disappeared. She had slept well. She felt at peace. She felt alive.

Something was different, very different. She glanced over at the clock and was surprised at the time. It was 9:10 in the morning. She couldn't remember the last time she had slept past 4 a.m. Brad's side of the bed was empty and cold. Of course, he had been up for hours, gotten the kids up and dressed for school. Fed them breakfast, packed their lunches and walked them to the corner to catch the school bus. Was he still in the house or had he already left for work?

She hoped he had left. These last seven months had been torture for him. Though, in a way, she hoped he was still in the house. Wouldn't it be lovely for him to peak in at his wife and see her with a smile on her face, see her not scrunched up in her persistent fetal position, hands clawing at her head or wrapped around her gut trying to hold the pain at bay. Wouldn't it be lovely for him to walk in, sit next to her on the bed and notice her legs, her long, slender, beautiful legs, relaxed, stretched out, toes happily wriggling?

The house was quiet, though. He was gone. He had escaped the sad house. Oh, if only he was here--just this one moment, this one peaceful moment. One could almost believe that the illness, the dying was over. Ah, maybe that was it. Had she already passed over? Well, if that was the case, so be it. She was deathly sick of being sick. Sick enough to die. Ah, but her little ones, her little darlings—too young to be motherless. God, please don't let this be a dream, don't let this be the other side. Simone smiled once again—a big, wide smile. She felt so good.

She gingerly pulled the covers back. Her gown was dry. Usually, by morning time, it was a ball of damp, sour smelling sweat. She carefully turned on her side and lifted her body up, pulled her legs over the side of the bed, and sat on the edge of the bed, long legs dangling pain free. The sun was coming in the window, a soft breeze danced in the folds of the light curtains.

San Jose, Costa Rica

Dr. Ferdinand Olivera was pleasantly surprised as he examined his patient. A month ago, he believed that she had just a few weeks to live and had prepared her and her husband. And he had stopped the grueling chemotherapy regimen. Instead, in front of him sat a young mother who was smiling, not grimacing with the pain that had previously lined her beautiful face. He returned to his desk to look at the blood test results and found the numbers to be significantly changed. He believed that Simone Jenkins was in remission. Her husband, Brad, an executive on loan from a company based in Houston, Texas, grinned.

"How long have you been feeling well, Simone?"

"Three weeks to the day. The headaches are gone, the constant pain in my legs and stomach are gone. I've been walking in the park every day. My appetite is back and I've gained three pounds. It feels like a miracle, Doctor. The chemo must have worked."

In Olivera's mind, this did not seem possible. He knew the drugs had a slim chance of altering the woman's fate and more of a chance to kill her more promptly than the actual disease. But often, an oncologist will do the treatments as a way to offer a sense of battle being done, and of course, miracles were possible. It appeared that was the case here. This beautiful young woman had suffered too much. It had been a fast moving disease.

He could not make sense out of the situation presented in this moment. Possibly the body was rejoicing in being free from the onslaught of the chemo drugs and had rebounded in health. If that was the case, he knew this would be temporary. But he was not going to say anything about that.

"Tell me Simone, have you added any new vitamins or supplements?" He noted a questioning look between Simone and her husband and saw Brad nod.

"Well, I hope you don't mind, Doctor, but a couple of months ago, on the advice of a friend, I went to see a naturopathic doctor over on the east side. I've seen her a few times and she gave me some tincture to mix in my tea. The idea was to boost my immune system in order to better handle the chemotherapy. It's probably not related; I'm guessing the chemo has done its job. There's no denying that I feel better and I'll take this feeling for however long it lasts." Simone said this with a wistful glance to her husband, both of their eyes filling with tears in gratitude for this reprieve.

"What is the name of this supplement?"

"Gosh, it doesn't have a name. Just a small bottle with a dropper and instructions: 'two small drops in a cup of herbal tea three times a day'. The doctor said to not, under any circumstances, take any more than she prescribed."

"Did you feel any side effects?"

"Yes, some nausea, vomiting, and diarrhea for the first few days. Leslie told me to keep taking it and that those symptoms should pass. And they did."

"Leslie?"

"Oh, yes – Leslie Goetz, the naturopathic. Her main office is in Bribri and she goes into Puerto Viejo a couple of times a month where she has a second, smaller office. I have a cousin that lives over there. She's the one who referred me to her. She said that Leslie had helped another patient who lived in Limon who also had cancer."

Dr. Olivera jotted the name down in Simone's chart and smiled at the couple. "Well, of course, I don't mind. There are many things that can contribute to healing and a sense of well-being. Sometimes, just taking things into your own hands can shift the course of disease. You keep up whatever is working for you and come back and see me in a month or sooner if you start experiencing pain and other symptoms of the cancer."

"There are some new drugs that are coming down the pike and if you are in remission and the cancer returns in the future, we may consider using these new protocols. It's good to give your body a rest. Your blood test looks remarkably good right now. Here's an order for you to get another blood test in two weeks; the results will be sent to me and I'll get in touch if I need to see you if anything significant has changed."

He stood up and came around from behind his desk and shook the hands of Simone and Brad. He watched as they walked out of his office arm in arm. He wasn't sure what he felt. Sadness, possibly, because he knew the cancer would be back. More so, though, he was curious. Simone had mentioned another patient in Limon. He would call around over there, speak to some of his colleagues and see if any of them had a similar situation develop.

He thought more on this subject, and then went to his computer and began an email. He would contact the pharmaceutical company that provided the chemo drugs he was working with on this difficult blood cancer. Maybe they could tell him something about any cases of spontaneous remissions.

He also had three other patients that he was giving the experimental oncology drug too. One of the pluses of this drug was that it was only given once a month. His patients came to his office for an infusion of the drug over a four hour period. Then they rested another two hours, then left.

He pulled the charts of the other three patients to see when they were next scheduled. One this week, and the other two next week. He looked forward to these visits. Maybe they were all turning the corner, but he didn't want to get his hopes up.

Now he needed to figure out who the patient was in Limon that Simone had mentioned. Maybe he could track down the naturopathic doctor in Bribri and have a collegial consultation. Olivera was open-minded and believed in a holistic approach to healing. Who knew? Maybe, by Simone taking things into her own hands, she *was* altering the course of her illness.

Seattle, WA

Dr. Zachary Walker reread the email, stretched back in his chair and put his hands behind his head, and gazed out the window. Was it anything? He wondered. He then sent a quick email back thanking the doctor in Costa Rica and asked particulars about the patient, such as age, duration of treatment, vitamins, and supplements. Dr. Olivera had not given the name of the patient nor too many details. Dr. Walker said that he would check into their database of physicians using the new chemo drug and would get back to him if he learned anything about other cases that might be similar.

He received an email back from Dr. Olivera the very next day. He learned that the patient was a young woman, 30 years old, that she had been diagnosed nine months ago with a rare cancer of the blood, and due to her age and excellent health prior to becoming ill, she was a candidate for the experimental drug, RX-T38, developed in the Biogenesis labs.

She had been on the drug for the last six months. Dr. Olivera added that his patient had reported that she was also being treated by a naturopathic doctor who had provided her with a supplement. Dr. Olivera had no idea what the supplement was, and didn't think it was related to the improved health status of his patient, but thought he should mention it.

Walker pondered this. There were about 50 trials with RX-T38 currently going on around the world, but not in the U.S., as it hadn't yet been approved for trial use. To protect patients, their names were not known. Only the treating oncologist had the name and demographics of the patients. To date, there had not been any cases of spontaneous remission, and in all honesty, there had been little improvement in the patients' health. Plus, the drug had serious side effects. He then picked up his cell phone and called the only person he knew that he could trust implicitly.

"Hello, Zack."

"Gretta." They were old friends and never wasted a lot of words. They had gone to college together, had a brief stint as lovers, until they both agreed that their fortunes were best acquired along paths that did not include them as a couple. "I need something done."

"Of course. What is it?"

"I need some information and possibly an extraction."

"What and where?"

"Costa Rica. Can you do this? I think time is important."

"Of course, darling. I have a couple in Brazil. They can be in Costa Rica tomorrow."

"Are they discreet?"

"They're so discreet, they don't even exist. I've never met them; but without fail, they have performed successfully. I only know their first names. Tell me what you want done and it will happen."

San Jose, Costa Rica

Dr. Ferdinand Olivera was the first to get to his office that Monday morning. He usually was. His nurse and office manager both had long distances to travel to get to the office. They were sisters, Rosa and Marcella, twins actually, and they had been working for him since he had relocated his practice in San Jose over fifteen years ago. Olivera was a bachelor and the two sisters had taken on many of the caretaking roles one might receive from a spouse, except for the romantic ones. They fussed over him, did his laundry and invited him to their homes for holiday meals.

Though, they tended to be late reporting in each morning, they made up for this small infraction in many other ways. They ran a meticulous office and engaged each and every one of the doctor's patients. Dr. Olivera was an oncologist and had a good reputation with patients and his colleagues.

He chose, though, to keep a small practice, and did things the old-fashioned way – taking time with each patient, getting to know the whole person and his or her family. Rosa and Marcella had the same approach. The office was warm and comfortably furnished. Generally, the doctor only scheduled five patients a day.

He also had the reputation for trying new and cutting edge treatments for serious cancer diseases, especially cancers of the blood. He was often invited to the States and Western Europe to meet with researchers from the larger pharmaceutical companies and he had been treated to symposiums, and occasionally, he presented at these events. In truth, though, he preferred the quiet, small practice he had built and preferred taking care of those patients in Costa Rica who had few other options for treatment.

This morning, when he came to his office door, he noticed that it was already unlocked and slightly ajar. He quietly pushed the door open and peered into the waiting room. Nothing looked disturbed. He wondered if he should call the police before entering, but as he stood slightly inside the doorway, he could not detect any sound or movement.

Maybe the sisters had not pulled the door fully shut the previous night; though another voice told him that was very unlikely. The sisters were extremely cautious about security. He decided on the side of safety and quietly stepped back out into the hallway of the building and down the stairs to the outside. There he used his cell phone to call the local police, hoping they wouldn't take hours to show up.

To his surprise, two officers showed up within ten minutes. He indicated what he had found, feeling a bit foolish in the moment as the officers looked at him quizzically. They asked him to wait in the building hallway and went inside his office. A few minutes later, they came out and beckoned him in. They advised him that it appeared that there had been a break-in and pointed to the wall of files behind the front counter. Dozens of patient files were strewn all over the floor and counter. Many were open and pulled apart. He stared at the mess in disbelief.

"It appears that whoever broke in here was looking for something in the patients' files. Your medication room and the treatment rooms look undisturbed. Can you come in and look to see if anything is missing?" one of the officers requested.

"Good grief! What a mess! I don't understand this! What would anyone want with patient files?" Olivera responded, while following the officer into his medication and treatment rooms. He opened some cupboards and the refrigerator, checking his supplies. "Nothing seems missing here." Just then, the front door opened and Rosa and Marcella walked in.

"Buenos Dias, Doctor. !Los siento..." They stopped in mid-sentence. "!Dios. Que paso aqui?"

One of the officers put up a hand and then asked the two women to remain by the front door and looked over at the doctor with a questioning look.

"They're my nurse and office manager, Rosa and Marcella." And speaking to the sisters, he said: "It appears that we've been broken into. Some of the patient charts have been pulled down and searched."

The ladies clucked under their breath. Rosa responded, "Well, Doctor, we will get this cleaned up. As we clean up, we'll try to figure out what, if anything is missing from these charts and if it has anything to do with particular patients. But, we need to get working as your first patient this morning will be here in just about one half hour."

The officers took some pictures and made some notes and gave Olivera a card and asked him to contact them if he could figure out if any patients were in any danger due to their files being tampered with. The doctor nodded with a big sigh and promised to get in touch if they found out anything once they cleaned up.

Though Simone felt so much better, she was still fatigued. Every day, after she had walked the kids down to the bus stop, she took a leisurely stroll around the neighborhood. Her husband had reluctantly returned to full time work, which was good, as his company was becoming a bit impatient with his absences and part time work. He hadn't cared though, nothing was more important to him than Simone and the kids. The walk tired her, but each day, she was able to walk a few additional minutes.

After her walks, she usually worked in her studio for an hour or two. She was a fairly adept painter, mostly working with water colors, which sold quite successfully back home in Texas. She had become inspired by the bright colors of the tropical plants, flowers and birds of her temporary adopted country. They had been living in Costa Rica now for almost four years. Their youngest child had been born here.

When she had become ill a year ago, Brad had wanted to take her back to Texas to get treated. Simone had resisted this; she loved their life here and how her husband was more relaxed and happier. Plus, she trusted Dr. Olivera and was grateful to be a candidate for the experimental drug he was able to provide.

After working in the studio, she had a light lunch and then crawled into her bed for a much desired nap. Most days, she would sleep up to two hours and wake just in time to walk back to the bus stop to meet the kids after school. Today, she followed a similar schedule. After working in the studio, she grabbed her favorite soft blanket, lay down on her bed and pulled the cover over her face to block out the light and immediately fell into a deep afternoon sleep.

During her naps, she often had vivid dreams; and today's was no exception. This dream held the roar of a cascading waterfall, and the smells and loud sounds of jungle life. She brushed up against colorful foliage and felt as if she was running away or towards something. Then she felt a soft breeze and sensed a soft flowing whiteness hovering over her. Abruptly, Simone's eyes flew open. A noise woke her and it wasn't a noise that carried over from her dream. It was the click of a door closing.

She sat up still waiting for her body and legs to hold her back from the ease of movement. No, all was well with her limbs, though she felt as if she had been running, fragments of her dream still lingering. She got up and walked out to the front room. The front door was closed, but it wasn't locked. Strange, she thought. She always locked up when inside and especially when going in for a nap.

She opened the door and stepped out onto the porch. She glanced down the street and saw a dark SUV pulling away about a block down the street. Since she lived on a dead end street, she watched the car maneuver a U-turn and drive back by her house slowly. The glare of sunshine made it hard to see inside, but she thought she saw a woman in the driver's seat and possibly a man in the passenger's seat. Both were looking straight ahead, seemingly unaware of Simone standing there. She did notice that the woman had long very blond hair or something light and flowing from her head. A scarf?

She became aware of the time and realized she needed to hurry down to the bus stop to meet the kids. It was Friday and the family planned to take a weekend trip over to Limon to visit her cousin. Simone had also scheduled an appointment with her naturopathic doctor in Puerto Viejo on Monday. She was planning to keep the kids out of school and give them some much needed play time with their parents.

She was looking forward to a relaxing interlude on the Caribbean coast and hoped to spend some time swimming in the warm sea. Plus, she was just about out of the tincture that Leslie provided her. She was a bit superstitious and didn't want to stop taking it; she felt so well and healthy right now and didn't want to change anything.

Later, when she and Brad were packing, gathering swimsuits, towels, sleeping bags for the kids, some toys and games for the drive over, Brad asked if she had packed her medications. She still needed to take extra vitamin B supplements and some fairly strong anti-inflammatory pills, she responded, "Yes, oh and please grab the tincture for me."

"It's not in here," he yelled back. "Do you have it out there in the kitchen?"

"No, check the bedside table. I took some just before my nap. Maybe I didn't put it back." She usually kept in a cool dark cupboard.

"Not here, sweetheart."

Simone walked out of the kids' room into her bedroom with a frown on her face.

"Hm, what did I do with it?" She wondered out loud. "Strange." Her heart began beating a bit more rapidly. Simone prided herself on her efficient, organized nature. Everything had its place. It was one way she could have some control over her life.

"Well, good thing we are going over there." She tried not to panic about the thought of not having her doses over the weekend. God, it's probably all in my head. But, even so, even if that's the case, I wouldn't want to go without it. "Let's call Leslie and leave a message, maybe she'll be in her office tomorrow."

Seattle, WA

The package arrived in Express mail on Monday. Dr. Walker received it and took it down to the lab himself. Though he trusted his lab personnel, until he knew what he might be dealing with, he thought it best to work on this himself. Unfortunately, there were only a couple of drops left in the small bottle. Using gloves, mask and goggles, he put a drop on a slide and slid it under a microscope.

What presented was an inert substance with an intriguing mosaic design. Not similar to anything he had seen before. He thought it was a fragment of a fungus, possibly a mushroom. He wished he had more to experiment with. He took a drop and put it into the water of a lab rat, one that had a bulging tumor on its neck. He then took the last drop and tapped it on his tongue. The lingering taste was bitter but not terribly unpleasant with a woody aroma.

That night, Walker was up most of the night with abdominal cramps and diarrhea. When he finally fell into a deep sleep in the early morning, he had vivid dreams verging on nightmares. Always the scientist, he had to wonder if this had anything to do with the drops. He dressed and went to the lab. He checked on the rat. It was dead. The poor thing had vomit and diarrhea all over his cage. He gowned up, put on his gloves, goggles and mask and picked up the rat to examine it. When he turned it over, he gasped. The tumor on the neck of the rat was gone.

Chapter 2

Anne Carmichael

She traipsed across the campus, lugging her laptop and a load of books and notebooks, heart pounding, breath coming in shortened gasps. God, she was getting out of shape. Only a year ago, she had competed in a triathlon and had done fairly well. Then, it seemed that she had just stopped and sat on her butt for the last ten months. Well, sat in the library in front of a computer or in the coffee shop for hours on end, poring over journal articles. Unfortunately, too much time was spent on subjects other than the one at hand: studying for her medical boards.

For Anne, life felt like hell right now. She was 38 years old – a little late to be studying medicine - still a daughter trying to please her parents and, add in her recent break up with her long-term boyfriend. Her call, since he had made it abundantly clear that the path he was on did not include a permanent, more formal tie with her, and definitely did not include making babies.

God, she felt so cliché! Why had she ignored these signs for the last five years? And really, did she even want to be married and have babies? The truth was, she guessed, she wanted to at least have the option; she wanted the guy in her life to at least offer a modicum of interest in a venture of that sort. She reflected on the last time they had had 'the discussion,' with a twist in her gut of what? Embarrassment?

"Really, Anne," Christian had started. "Come on, you, me? Parents? This world is fucking crazy enough as it is. Do you really believe in that 'happily ever after' shit? I've got too much I want to do yet, and admit it, so do you. We hardly have time for each other, let alone a kid. Are you going to stay home with it? I'm sure as hell not. I've got my residency coming up and if I'm lucky, I'll be fast-tracking the neuro-psych specialty right after. And here you are studying for your boards…at a piddly slow ass pace, I might add; and sweetheart, you're not getting any younger," he kindly threw in. At which point in the conversation, she tuned him out.

The truth was, he was right. He was four years younger than her and she was beginning to suspect that a lot of his late nights might have more to do with the group of fellow doctors he was studying with than the actual studies. The horrible thing was, and the thing she suspected he understood about her (and not in a complimentary way) was that she was dragging her feet in regards to studying for the boards, because, in reality, her heart wasn't in it. Her heart and interests really lay elsewhere.

Anne already had a degree in ethno-botany. She had been thrilled to get admitted to the UW medical anthropology and ethno-botany program, much to the dismay of her parents, who all along expected her to follow in her father's footsteps and become a medical doctor. She stuck it out though, shutting out the constant chatter and negativity from her mother about her chosen field. Her father had just been silent on the subject, but Anne knew he was disappointed.

Anne loved the program, especially ethno-botany. She enjoyed the field trips and lab work. She'd had an internship at a large pharmaceutical company and thought the world was her oyster. But once she graduated with her master's degree, the jobs had seemed to dry up. Her only course appeared to be to go on for a Ph.D. and then try to find a job teaching.

And then her father had his first bout with cancer. And she switched course and got admitted into medical school. Why? To please her dad, her best friend? She had been pretty impulsive about it….and now she was second guessing herself.

The musical ring tone of her cell phone abruptly brought her out of her reverie, providing a much needed break from the constant back and forth chatter of her restless mind. Noting the caller, she was hesitant to answer.

"Hi Mom."

"Annie, I thought you were coming over for tea this morning."

Oh shit. "On my way, Mom. Be there in five!" Why couldn't she think fast enough to come up with a quick response, that she was busy with something, that she was studying – her mother always liked to hear that – but with her mother, Anne was always stripped to the core of childhood responses – she couldn't say or do anything that her mother didn't instantly read all the underlying truths into. And in this unsettling time in her life, the chaos and drama circling her parents was just too much for her.

God, she really wanted to disappear, go away, travel for a year, do, be anything but what she was doing and being right now: an only child of aging parents, who decided at this late stage in life that they wanted to divorce; her father going through a second round of treatment for prostate cancer, her mother getting cosmetic surgery and tattoos, and both of them clinging to her and wanting more and more of her.

Actually, if she could just step back enough, detach a little, she might be able to see the humor in this life situation - except the part of her father's battle with cancer. Even that tugged at her – she was frustrated as hell that he wouldn't listen to her about the different options for treatment; she had done a lot of research into alternative options and even into all the different types of western traditional medical treatments that he could choose from. And her internship at the large pharmaceutical company left her with conflicting ideas about the myriad of drugs that were being produced. Did they benefit the patients truly or more realistically, the bottom line of the drug companies? Now that was a cynical perspective.

But her father was stubborn – he came from a long line of stubborn males – and once he knew he had prostate cancer, he went to the first specialist his primary doc had recommended and without even a moment's hesitation or ownership into the process, he scheduled the implantation of radiation seeds into his prostate. No thought to the side effects and the future probability of the cancer returning.

Once seeds were implanted into the gland, there were little options to treatment other than hormone blocking if the cancer returned - which, Anne knew, was in the 30% probability. She had just wanted him to slow down, take some time to look into all the options. Maybe change his diet, drink less, and pull back a bit from his stressful medical practice. God, here he was, a well-respected cardiologist, who was 40 pounds overweight, never exercised, worked long hours, and drank too much. He was a love, though - kind and funny.

Ugh! This was when being an only child was a drag. Wouldn't it be great to have an older brother or sister, wise and caring to handle the mess of her parents? Wouldn't it be nice to have a shoulder to lean on, instead of being that only shoulder to her parents? Oh god, I'm feeling so sorry for myself right now!

She and her father had always been a team, a couple of pals with signals and looks, winks and silent messages needed to chart the tumultuous course of life with Caroline, Anne's mother, and Frank's wife – soon to be ex. Her reverie of thoughts was interrupted by her mother.

"What's wrong, Annie? You seem lost in thought and I'm sure you haven't heard a word I've said."

Anne glanced up at her mother. They were sitting at the small breakfast table having a cup of tea. Anne had become mesmerized by the swirling pattern she was making as she was stirring her honey into the tea.

"Um, nothing, mom. Just thinking," she averted her gaze from her mother's piercing eyes. But she knew her mother wouldn't let it go. She never had.

"Annie....? You know I worry about you, always have."

Exasperated, Anne asked, "Why, mom...why have you always worried about me?" stretching out the word always. "Talk about being worried. What about dad? Why don't you worry about dad? He's sick, you know. He's going through treatment. He's not taking care of himself. Why now, mom? Why did you have to leave now of all times?"

Caroline looked at her daughter with dismay. "What do you mean, Annie?"

"His cancer has come back, mom. He's on hormone blocking therapy. Didn't you know?" She looked at her mother with bewilderment. Her dad hadn't told her mother. God, how sad, she thought and with a bit of anger - why did she have to be the one to carry this burden; be her father's confidant?

Caroline reached across the table, taking her daughter's hand. "I'm sorry Annie. I know this is all too much for you. I'll call him today. See if there's anything I can do. You know, Annie, your father has always been so private, kept so much from me." She looked over at Anne's eyes which were filling up with tears. She squeezed her hand. "It's all going to be okay, Annie. Don't you worry about your dad and me."

Anne left her mother's house and caught the bus headed back toward the campus. She felt a little less burdened and she realized that life is short and unpredictable, and she really needed to lighten up a bit -- though it had always been hard for her to keep the sadness at bay. She had a propensity for spending too much time worrying and floating in her river of impending doom.

She knew she needed a distraction and for the most part, she'd always managed to arrange healthy ones, such as training for a race or triathlon.

She felt this pressure building up inside, knowing that she was on the verge of another precipice, and wondered how close she could go to the edge without falling over, or even jumping over. She pushed her gloomy thoughts aside and remembered that she had a cocktail party to attend that evening. She wasn't sure she wanted to go, but knew she needed something to fill her time when she got into a mood like this.

Michael Turner

Michael gazed into the mirror at his image. Yes, the hair was just right, carefully coiffed then tousled a bit for that relaxed – I really didn't spend a lot of time on this – look, which, of course wasn't true. The golden tinged waves on his thick hair attracted men and women alike. He was a very handsome man, and he knew it. Tall, lean, broad shouldered and toned. Women lit up when he entered a room, men produced a silent groan under their breath. He picked his attire for the day carefully. It was going to be a long day of meetings and he wanted to appear calm, cool, and collected for the whole time.

He had been with the company for almost 15 years, pretty much since he interned there fresh out of graduate school. He started out as a junior sales rep, moving up the ladder, accumulating awards and status as a first rate salesperson, committing to memory all the details of each drug he was assigned – you would have thought he was an R & D specialist, knowing the interactions, contraindications, chemical components, and most importantly, the expected purpose of the drug, including the rates of effectiveness. He had a degree in bio-chemistry, after all and an MBA to top it off.

Growing up in a medical family, both his parents and a grandfather were doctors – his father an oncologist, his mother an OBGYN, his older sister was a pediatrician, and his younger brother was a dentist. He thought that he was probably a bit of a disappointment to the family, though they were all very careful to have him think otherwise. Well, he was 40 now, and really it was a little late in the game to be overly worried about what the family thought.

He had made a nice living, travelled around the world on business, and though he felt a little threatened by the younger up and coming junior members of the firm pushing up against him with their bright eyed and bushy tailed enthusiasm, some of them doing quite well in sales, he knew that he was still at the top of his game; but he also knew that some smart dance steps were required in order to keep his bosses looking his way.

His hopes for today's outcome would be the well-coveted assignment of the Southern Hemisphere. His most recent assignment had been Europe, prior to that Asia. Earlier in his career, he was the lead for the Southwest US, followed by Canada. He was interested in the Southern Hemisphere, which covered Mexico, Central and South America.

He endured a long day of meetings with nothing concrete decided upon. Jack Edwards, his boss had hinted about good news, but had not as of yet delivered the news one way or the other. Michael was expected to attend this evening's cocktail party, which was in celebration of a possible merger between his firm Biogenesis, a large international pharmaceutical company and the Meridian Labs, a smaller Canadian firm.

He wasn't quite sure why the merger was a good idea. From his little bit of research, he knew that the Canadians had made a lot of headway into developing some new drugs that had shown promise in tagging and clumping certain cancer cells and tracking their pathways through the lymph system. There was a rumor that one of the drugs was based on a formulary from an indigenous plant in some South American country – not yet divulged. That part did intrigue him. Maybe the merger would be to his benefit. The smaller company certainly could use the financial support of the larger firm and access to a well-developed work force, including a world renowned research team.

As Michael milled around the cocktail party, which was being held in his boss's lovely home overlooking Lake Washington, he toyed with the idea of either slipping out quietly, or having another drink. He knew the second drink was not a good idea. He never could hold his liquor very well, and had experienced some embarrassing moments in the past.

This was not the time or place to be a fool. Though two very attractive women had approached him in the last hour, he found that he wasn't really in the mood to play the game. Over the last few years, he had tired of the shallowness that seemed to occupy the superficial chit chat of strangers meeting in situations such as this. Ever since Debra, he hadn't really been able to connect in any meaningful way with another woman.

As he neared the front door, ready to make his excuses, the door opened and a vaguely familiar face appeared. The woman had long, wavy, sun streaked, auburn hair. He was only a foot or so away, and watched as she handed her coat and bag over to a greeter, and as she turned and looked directly into his eyes, he was taken by the clear light blue eyes and the lilting up lips that tried to hold a smile in check.

"Hello, I think I know you," she said, with a directness he was unaccustomed to.

"Hi. Yeah, you look familiar to me, too." The crowd became intrusive by the door, so he touched her elbow and guided her away and out onto the deck. "I'm Michael. You are?"

"Anne. Anne Carmichael. Hi, Michael. So, I think I've got it. You work for Biogenesis, right?" After Michael nodded, Anne continued. Last year, I interned for almost nine months in the Everett Labs. Could we have bumped into each other there?"

"That's possible. But, I'm a product rep…didn't spend much time at the Everett labs. But, wait…did you attend the Walker Lectures? I remember that there were a number of lab interns present…"

"Yes, I did. Oh well, hello again, I think!" Anne said with a twinkle in those remarkable eyes. "Were you trying to escape just as I was coming in?"

"Guilty as charged."

"Tell me, this isn't that bad, is it?" Anne asked as she looked around the house and the crowd of people. "I really didn't want to come, but needed a distraction from a difficult day."

Michael continued to be drawn to the directness that emanated from the beautiful woman in front of him. He stopped and looked at her more closely. Yes, she was beautiful, but it did not seem to be something she used in any way. She had no make-up on that he could tell. Her hair was simply flowing and he found he wanted to touch it. She was dressed in a soft beige sweater dress and boots. No jewelry, no earrings, no rings on her fingers. Just clear skin, slightly freckled.

"Hello in there…." she whispered lightly. "Anyone home?"

"Why, yes…I do believe someone's home. Someone just came home, as a matter of fact," Michael responded with warmth.

The rest of the evening was a pleasant blur for Michael. He did have that second drink, and then later, a third. But he had spaced them sufficiently, and upon reflection the next morning, he was pretty sure he hadn't made a fool of himself. He enjoyed his time with Anne. She took his mind off the turmoil that usually occupied too much real estate in his brain, and she made a point at the end of the evening to thank him for taking her mind off the gloominess that had preoccupied her that day.

They had stayed out on the deck and talked and talked. Michael opened up about his yearning to do more in his work, his itch to be involved in a new discovery, new healing modalities. He didn't go into detail about the loss of Debra. But, it was clear that Anne didn't miss the significance of a difficult life event.

A few days later, Michael Turner was asked to come in and meet with Dr. Zachary Walker, the director of the R and D division. He wasn't Michael's direct boss, so he was a bit puzzled by the request. He left his building and walked across the company's park-like campus to another building that housed a portion of the Biogenesis labs and its main lab offices. There was a larger, more extensive lab based in Everett, though the general public was pretty unaware of its presence.

Research labs were generally kept under camouflage and non-descript in order to protect them from animal lovers who protested the mistreatment of lab animals. Michael always wondered how anyone could worry about some mice and rats, or even monkeys, when it was possible that life-saving drugs were being developed. He knew that he'd wished a drug had been developed that might have saved Debra.

Dr. Zachary Walker was a legend in the field. He was a man in his late seventies and had been at the helm of the industry designing cancer treatment drugs that to this day could be credited with extending the lives of thousands of people. Treatments that were targeted against even the most challenging cancers, such as ovarian and pancreatic – those silent killers that were usually discovered when it was too late. Of course treatment with these drugs cost the patients and insurance companies thousands of dollars, and there were many that went without the treatment due to insufficient insurance coverage or personal finances.

Michael had heard the company gossip that Dr. Walker was married to his job. No one knew much about his personal life, and most suspected that he didn't have one. No matter how late one left work, the lights were still on in Dr. Walker's office and most believed that he was also burning the night oil down in the labs. He employed the best lab scientists in the field and had a loyal crew that stayed for years. Each year, he would scour the universities seeking the newest and brightest graduates and invite one or two to intern at his labs. Most jumped at the opportunity. And if they passed the muster, Dr. Walker would invite one of them to stay on.

Michael had to ring the bell and speak into the inter-com to identify himself before being allowed into the lobby of the lab offices. The receptionist came to the door and unlocked it, held it open for Michael and then asked him to sign in and gave him a badge to wear. She called Dr. Walker on the phone and reported that Michael was there. She then smiled warmly and directed him through the double doors behind her desk and told him to turn right and go down the hallway to the last office on the right. He did as he was directed.

Once he reached the last office, noticing along the way that there were no numbers, names or any other identifying markers on any of the doors he had passed, he knocked and waited. A few seconds passed, and finally the door was opened. He then found himself face to face with the renowned Dr. Walker. Well, he shouldn't say face-to-face, the doctor towered over him with a ram rod straight posture, a head full of white hair, piercing gray eyes, and a face fairly devoid of wrinkles that belied his age. The doctor was a good 6 feet 4 inches, and it made Michael feel short, even though he stood a little over 6 feet tall.

"Michael, come in, come in. Sit." Dr. Walker motioned with his arm towards two chairs situated in front of a large desk. Michael took one of the chairs and Walker took the chair behind the desk. Michael noticed that the desk was clean of any papers. A laptop computer was the only item on the desk except for a phone and a desk lamp. Behind the desk were wall-to-wall book shelves filled with hundreds of books and stacks of journals – all scientific in nature, and all neatly arranged.

There were no pictures on the walls or on the shelves and the only other items in the large office were a leather couch on the adjacent wall with an end table and lamp. There was another door ajar in the office that probably led to a private bathroom. A blanket was folded over the back of the couch, giving credence to the belief that the good doctor probably spent more nights in his office than not.

"Michael, you've been with the company quite a few years."

Michael heard a statement not a question, but he nodded politely. "Yes sir."

"Jack over in Sales told me that you've got the itch to go south. Haven't been there myself, but I am aware that it's the next frontier for new products – well probably not so new…actually - the alternative crowd have been crowing about miraculous cures for years. The Canadian firm we're courting has made some real headway in finding and experimenting with the indigenous plant life there. Nothing striking yet, though there had been rumors here and there."

Rumors of what, Michael wondered. He had never paid much attention to the claims of cancer fighting plants made by the natural supplements companies. He knew they were in it for the buck just like the pharmaceuticals were. He had often wondered if the large drug companies were interested in cures or rather, and more likely he thought, treatments. Treatments and cures were really two different things in his mind. Treatments might stave off something for a few years – and if it hit the five year mark, they were considered "cures."

Quite often, though, just after the five year mark, the cancer once again reared its ugly head, and this time, it would take an even more aggressive treatment – more costly financially and to the body – to put the cancer away again, albeit temporarily. He really did believe, though, that there were true, caring scientists that were working diligently for that cure. The new direction was in looking at genetic mishaps. Something at the genetic level that went awry. Could we actually go in and "turn off" a switch at the basic DNA level to avoid cancer in the future? If so, what did this really mean for pharmaceutical companies that were in the business of developing drugs to kill tumors? He surmised that experimental drugs could bc developed that could inhibit a gene expression. He was confident that there would always be a role for big pharmaceuticals.

"You know," the older man continued. "I may be able to put in a good word for you, if you're truly interested in a new assignment. I always yearned for time in the field, myself, but could never pull myself away from the labs. How badly do you want to go?"

"Well, I feel that it's a good time in my career to make a change. And it's one part of the world that intrigues me. There are still some remote areas it would be fun to explore. Plus, I know there are some pharmaceutical companies being developed. It would be great to get our own foot in the door. I guess I have a mixed agenda here. Bit of exploration and a bit of expansion." Michael wondered if he had said too much. But he didn't feel like he had much to lose here. This wasn't his boss. They were just having a conversation, weren't they? Really, why did the Doctor call him in? He was a bit mystified by this whole thing.

Over the next two weeks, Michael had met Anne a couple of times for coffee. She didn't seem to be available for dinner or other evening events, but she did readily accept the impromptu invite for a quick cup of coffee. Even during the day, without the haze of an alcohol tinted perspective, he found her delightfully clear and calm, though, every once in a while, something sad would flit across her eyes, causing her brows to furrow. But it was gone before he could comment or ask what might be bothering her.

She grilled him in a friendly way about his work and his thoughts or beliefs about the western medical model. He learned that she was studying for her medical boards, but that she also had a degree in ethno-botany and medical anthropology. She clammed up though when he tried to tease apart that dichotomy.

"When are you taking the Boards?" he asked the third time they met for coffee one very early morning. Early mornings seemed to be her favorite time to meet.

"I'm signed up for next month, but I don't know, I may postpone. My father is sick and I'm quite distracted by that." And then she turned the conversation back to him, which she was very deft at. "Have you heard anything from your company about that assignment you're interested in?"

"Not yet. There are some others quite interested also. But I do have an advantage – I'm single, no dependents – and could actually relocate."

"Why are you so interested?" she queried.

"Honestly, I think it's because I feel that I'm sort of at a lull in my career. I'd like to get a foot up. And if I'm successful in getting some of our products into the South and Central American markets, it might open up some opportunities for me. My company is like a good old boys' club, very tight at the upper management level. Really hard to get moved into that level. Why do I want that? I'm not sure."

And in a rare moment of inner honesty, he continued, "I'm not sure whom I'm trying to impress. Maybe I'm just a little bored and looking for the next real adventure. Brazil, Argentina, Costa Rica, all sound exotic and appealing. Or maybe I'm just running away." Michael colored a little, he rarely rambled on like this. But, Anne just looked at him intently and with curiosity, completely devoid of judgment.

"Hm, I really relate. I'd love to skip this whole medical doctor thing and go into the jungles and spend a year studying with indigenous shamans. I'd like to learn about their beliefs in healing and their use of native plants. Some of my best times were field trips taken during my medical anthropology courses. I once spent two weeks in the Amazon jungle, and even though I came back with a mysterious rash, it was one of the most exhilarating experiences of my life."

Anne paused a second, looking wistfully into her cup of coffee. She raised her eyes and met Michael's, "Boy if you do get an assignment down there, I hope we stay in touch. You never know, I may just show up on your doorstep." With a warm smile, she gathered up her books and bag, stood up and leaning over him, brushed his cheek with tender lips, her hair falling into his face, softly caressing him. And with that, she was gone with a quick, "Gotta run, see ya!"

A week later, Michael received another beckon, this time from his immediate boss, Jack Edwards. Jack and Michael went back to college days. They had bumped into each other often over the years, sometimes working for competitors and sometimes working for the same company. Five years ago, Jack had been recruited from another company to head up the division Michael worked in.

It had been an adjustment working for a frat brother, but once the lines were drawn and positions acknowledged, Michael actually found Jack to be a sensible and fair manager. Jack had had a leg up in life. He had married into a family of wealth. He and his lovely wife, Meredith, were well known Seattle socialites and often graced the pages of the Seattle Magazine in the Who's Who sections, attending this charity function or that opera opening.

"Hey, buddy, it looks like you're seriously being considered for a new assignment. Central and South America. Still interested?"

"I sure am!" Michael noticed that Jack looked strained and wondered what was bothering the wonder boy. He seemed to have the perfect life, as far as Michael was concerned.

"Well, for reasons I don't quite understand, it seems that Dr. Walker and his direct supporters have put in a good word for you. You never did tell me how your meeting went with him."

You never asked, Michael thought to himself. "Hey, can we talk as friends?" Jack nodded. "Quite frankly, I was a little confused, myself, about the meeting. It was very general; we didn't talk about anything specific. Though, Dr. Walker seemed to know of my interest to get a post in the southern hemisphere. I presumed you had mentioned that to him."

"Well, I didn't tell him directly. I was at a luncheon with some benefactors, some really wealthy investors in the company. I'm not usually invited to these events. Dr. Walker was there, but he was sitting at a different table. The conversation at my table was about how we could get our hands on some of the new discoveries that were being touted out of the jungles of Central and South America. My ears perked up at that, remembering your interest in the area. I mentioned that a member of my sales team was interested in working down there.

The woman next to me, a major stakeholder, Gretta somebody, turned to me and asked who on my team that might be. I mentioned your name. After that, the conversation turned to the possibility of acquiring a firm that researched and marketed naturopathic supplements. Everybody chuckled, and someone said something like, so this is where we're headed? If we can't beat them, join them?"

Chapter 3

Puerto Viejo, Costa Rica

Sally Meza grabbed her small backpack filled with a few essentials for the next two or three days. She walked through her small studio apartment into the adjoining book store, checking that everything was as secure as it could be out here in the fairly remote neighborhood of the little beach village of Playa Coclés, located on Costa Rica's Caribbean Coast, a little south of Puerto Viejo. She put extra food and water out for 'puss,' and then walked out the door, locking it and putting up the 'Closed today' sign on the front door of the shop. Her neighbors, Lina and Carlos, had promised to keep their eyes on the place and set out extra food for the cat, when needed.

She was supposed to meet Leslie at their favorite little café in Puerto Viejo at seven a.m. There they would stuff themselves on Mama Rosalina's out of this world Portuguese sausage, wild mushroom, egg and rice scramble. This delectable meal would be accompanied by fresh squeezed orange juice and a cup of thick Costa Rican coffee heavily laden with whole milk and raw sugar.

Sally enjoyed her new-found friend, Leslie Goetz. Like her, Leslie was what is known as an 'ex-pat'—an ex-patriot to be more precise. She had come from the great and vast mid-west of the United States about eight years earlier. She was in her early forties, but looked like a throw-back to a flower-child from the 1960s—long blond hair invariably worn in one thick braid down the middle of her back, large brown eyes with crinkles around them, a wide, high forehead and a strong chin. She was tall, lean, and muscular.

Leslie was completely immersed in alternative medicines and healing and was licensed as a Naturopathic Doctor in Costa Rica as well as back home in the States. She had a small office in Bribri, a town southeast of Puerto Viejo and had a thriving practice there. She came to Puerto Viejo twice a month, where she was also building a small following. She loved the little coastal village, the slow, sleepy mood of the place, which was transformed during the summer weekends, when tourists from all over the world came to party, play, hike, surf and shop in the numerous little beach stands.

"Hey, Chica!" Sally tossed at her friend as she pulled up a stool to the small table where Leslie was already chowing down on an aromatic dish of sausage and eggs. Leslie leaned over and gave Sally a warm embrace, ruffling Sally's short, thick, tousled hair affectionately.

"I like the short hair, much more befitting." Sally's previous hair style had been a runaway tornado of curls, which she had tried to control with ponytails, which invariably stood straight up like rooster tails. Short, indeed, was better and more attractive as evidenced by the inevitable compliments whenever an acquaintance saw her since her 'make-over' by her friend, Najali, the beautiful exotic yoga teacher she had become close to in the last year.

Leslie and Sally had become friends over the last six months after Sally had interviewed Leslie about her practice and her use of indigenous plant materials as part of her repertoire of herbs and teas she prepared for her clientele. Leslie resisted talking about it too much, preferring to stay under the radar because some of the plants she used were untested, and potentially could result in some legal complications for her. Sally was very interested and convinced Leslie that it was for the good of humanity to tell her story.

As it was, Leslie was vague about identifying all the plants and would not name locations, and ultimately refused to say much more as she became very nervous when after Sally's story had run in the San Jose English language paper, the newspaper editor had approached Sally for more information about her sources, as he was getting many requests from the States and even some European countries for more information. Leslie made it clear then -- no more articles. She had conceded, though to let Sally come along on this trip into the jungle.

Leslie liked Sally's energy, her bull-dogged determination, and her friendly and warm commitment to whatever she was intrigued by at the moment. Sally had all the necessary personality traits of a good reporter. A particular trait that she had that might be considered a hindrance by most professional journalists was Sally's propensity to involve herself personally in the story as it unraveled. This certainly occurred in the Nina Navarra case of a year ago.

The two women took Sally's beat-up old red jeep, a cherished possession that she inherited along with the book store that she leased, and began their journey towards the Talamanca Mountains, their goal being a trek deep into the wild to meet up with a guide from one of the indigenous tribes of the region. Their first stop would be Bribri which was only about 30 to 45 minutes away. Leslie had a few things to pick up at her office; plus Sally was interested in seeing the neighboring town.

The small town was approximately 60 kilometers south of Puerto Limon, and unlike Puerto Viejo which was a coastal village, Bribri was an inland border town on the north bank of the 200-meter wide Rio Sixaola, a fast flowing river separating Costa Rica and Panama. It served as a doorway to a remote, lightly inhabited part of its southern neighbor. If one were driving to Bribri the more conventional way from Limon and not from Puerto Viejo, one would take Highway 36 winding inland through the foothills of the Talamanca Mountains and descend into Bribri.

Instead, the two women chose the more direct route from Puerto Viejo which was via a narrow dirt road through the jungle, rarely travelled, but one Leslie had used over the last few years as she journeyed back and forth between Bribri and Puerto Viejo a couple times a month. She enjoyed its peace and tranquility and rarity of vehicular traffic.

On occasion, though, there were some pretty scary rides when one of many tropical storms exploded with downpours of rain and wind slapping the trees and foliage around her. At times like that, the road would turn into a slimy, muddy river. Today, though, promised to be clear, hot, and sunny, and the tree canopy overhead provided a much appreciated shade from the piercing sun.

Sally was taken by surprise with the different terrain as they left the winding dirt road and the jungle and entered into a flat valley containing numerous banana plantations surrounding Bribri. She loved how the valley sloped upwards towards the tiers of the Talamanca Mountains. The sight was glorious and Sally was enjoying herself immensely.

As they entered the town, the dirt road became a bumpy paved one. There was a bustling of activity, people on foot, bicyclists and dusty cars. This was less of a tourist town and more of a regional center of business. Here were the regional OIJ offices, a large jail, and other businesses and industry for the eastside of the country. It was still a small town and it was only by circumstance that Leslie had made this the main locale of her small business.

While studying naturopathy at a university in Seattle, she had come on a long field trip to Costa Rica to learn about the healing rites of the indigenous tribes of the area. She had almost switched her major to ethno-botany, the subject had so fascinated her; but she had a strong innate desire to have a hands-on practice with her patients, so she stayed with the naturopathy courses.

On her study trip she had gone with a small guided group way up into a remote region of the mountains and had the rare experience of being able to stay with one of the smaller tribes of the Cabecar Indians, one that still retains many of its traditional customs and beliefs. Though she had only stayed a few weeks, it was a time in her life that transformed her and set her on the unique course she had taken.

Sally pulled the jeep up in front of a small building as directed by Leslie. Leslie showed her the office and clinic then took her up some back stairs to show Sally her small studio apartment located over the clinic. It was light and airy with lots of windows and ceiling fans. A cat greeted the women and Leslie scooped up the bundle of fur and started cooing in its ears. She fed the cat and gathered a backpack and sleeping bag that were already packed and sitting by the door. Back downstairs, Leslie looked around the clinic, checking that all was secure for the two days they expected to be gone.

As they were stepping out the front door, Leslie remarked under her breath, "Oh shit!" She pushed Sally back into the office and went over the window to look out at the street.

"What's wrong?" Sally asked.

"Look across the street. See that black Toyota?"

Sally looked and saw a dusty, black 4 wheel Toyota SUV. It appeared empty. It was kitty-corner to them, so they could see the back of the car. "Yeah?"

"I swear I've seen that same car around here a lot recently. But the weird thing is that I'm sure it was the same one that I saw in Puerto Viejo yesterday parked across from my office there."

"Did you check the license?"

"No, I didn't think to. But now I will. It could be nothing. It's certainly a typical rental for tourists. But we don't really get too many tourists here in Bribri. It's just...oh well, it's probably just my runaway imagination. I don't know, I'm a little worried. I should not have let you interview me. Maybe I'm just paranoid, but you have no idea what some big pharmaceutical would do to get its hands on some of the stuff I've got access to – either to shut it down or to exploit it. I don't want to put my contacts at risk."

"Gosh, I'm sorry. I shouldn't have been so pushy."

"Not your fault. I just need to remember to listen to my intuition." Leslie set her stuff down and went to the reception counter to grab a piece of paper and a pen. Glancing back out at the Toyota, she jotted down what she could see of the license - only the first three letters and a number. The rest was covered in road dust. She stuck the piece of paper in her back jean pocket.

Sally, being a reporter after all, committed the partial license to memory: JCR 4.

After their short stop in Bribri, they headed out on another dirt road that led west through the gorge of the Rio Sixaola. Sally was excited to get to do a bit of back-roading in her jeep and looked forward to putting it to the test. They took down the top and let the wind blow through their hair, appreciating the vistas as they began their journey up the slopes of the Talamanca Mountains. Sally glanced over at her friend and noticed that she seemed deep in thought, with her brows deeply furrowed. She felt a little guilty if indeed her report was causing any trouble for Leslie.

This was the first time Leslie had invited anyone along on this field trip. And, if she was truthful with herself, she was regretting it somewhat. She liked having a friend as she was by nature a loner; this was a newish kind of experience for her, not having been the kind of girl who had close girlfriends growing up. She was such a book worm in her youth. She had been very careful and secretive about her trips into the mountains, and she was hoping that she wasn't making a mistake by bringing Sally along. God, maybe she was just being paranoid! She glanced over at Sally and thought, damn it, I deserve a friend!

What she hadn't said was that this wasn't the first or second time she had seen the Toyota SUV. A couple of times in the last few days, she had noticed the same vehicle parked across the street from her Bribri office, not thinking too much of that - but it did set the hairs on the back of her neck tingling when she saw the car parked across from her little office in Puerto Viejo. She couldn't be sure it was the same one. And each time she had seen it, no one was sitting in it. Her office in Puerto Viejo was not on the main street or even one or two off. It was three streets back in a more residential area, not one that normally attracted much of the tourist foot traffic.

The women drove higher and higher up into the mountains on a winding road that switch-backed across the slopes, finally losing sight of the valley below and disappearing into tall trees and jungle foliage. The air became cooler and after a couple of hours, they pulled off the road for a break. Sally got out and stretched her back and breathed in the sweet clean air. They snacked on some fruit and nuts and felt comfortable enough in each other's presence that conversation was not required. Sally noticed that Leslie seemed more relaxed.

"You know, Leslie, I'm sorry if I've caused you any trouble with writing that article."

"Hey, it's okay. I'm torn really. I have to tell you a secret. Some of this stuff that I've been using has really helped a couple of my patients. I mean, really helped. I should be able to share it with the world. I think what good it would do. But I'm not a Polly-Anna, I also know how this could end up causing more harm than good if it got into the wrong hands – so I guess I'm a bit careful. I don't want to hurt the people up here. And maybe it's not my herbs that have helped people...maybe it's just coincidence." She paused and took in the vista. Then with a smile at Sally, she said "Well, we better get going. I don't want to keep my guide waiting."

After another hour or so and on even more narrow and winding roads, Leslie directed Sally to pull the jeep over into a clearing. Sally was a bit puzzled, as it seemed like an isolated place.

"Come on, this way." Leslie beckoned.

They walked on a well-worn path through the jungle, and after about an hour of traipsing on the narrow trail, the foliage began to thin and sounds became more identifiable. Sally heard the laughter of children and the rhythmic clucking of chickens.

They walked into a banana tree fringed clearing with latte colored palm frond huts skirting the clearing. Sally counted about ten huts. She then became aware of a number of children who had become quiet and were staring curiously at the visitors.

One of them, a young girl about eight years old jumped up and ran to Leslie and in a sing song voice she chattered her hellos and excitement. Leslie bent down and gave the girl a big hug. She looked up to Sally and said, "This is Lucia. She and I are special friends. Her parents actually think I saved her life. I wouldn't go that far, but she was so sick a few winters back and they bravely brought her into Bribri to see me. The village Shaman still provides most of the health care for their people. Lucia had a high fever and a bad cough, a pneumonia, which is rare for these villagers, and I'm sure the worst of it had passed by the time they had brought her in to see me....but they still credit me for her cure."

Just then, a young man of about thirty years old dressed in jeans and a tee shirt, stepped into the clearing. Sally then became aware of a number of other people peering out of the huts or from between the huts and the jungle.

"Hola, Miguel," Leslie called out to the young man.

"Hola, doctora," he replied. And a small exchange in Spanish ensued between Leslie and the young man. It was too fast for Sally to pick up much of it. But she heard Leslie apologize for their tardiness. By the end of the conversation, others ventured into the clearing and some hugs were exchanged between some of them and Leslie. Sally could tell that the 'doctora' was a well loved and respected visitor. Some of the people stood around Sally with friendly smiles and curiosity on their faces. Leslie smiled and laughed with some of the adults and then gestured to Sally and Miguel that they should be moving on.

"Grab your stuff, Sally. We need to get going if we're going to make it there before dark. It's darn easy to get lost up here. Even Miguel, here, doesn't like to wander around this mountain at night."

More hugs and cheerful 'goodbyes' were exchanged with some of the villagers. Then Sally, Leslie and Miguel picked up their gear and headed out into the jungle on a foot path that took them even further up into the mountain. It was a tough climb on a wet, slippery path that alternately dipped and climbed and twisted this way and that.

Sally lost complete track of direction and began to feel the burn in her thighs after about an hour into the trek. Leslie looked back at Sally and then called ahead to Miguel to ask for a short break. The three drank some water and ate some more nuts and fruit. Sally was dying for a thick, juicy burger....even some fries and a shake. Not likely any time soon, she thought to herself. Then, only after a few minutes, Miguel got up and started off.

Leslie shrugged at Sally and said "Come on girl...we've still got a couple more hours to go."

Sally groaned inwardly and thought...god, what was I thinking? She hefted her backpack up and followed the disappearing back of her friend. A couple of hours later, the path evened out and widened. It was dusk, and the air became thicker with a mist and the sound of falling water that became louder and louder transforming into a deafening roar as they walked around another bend in the path.

Sally gasped at the sight in front of her, a beautiful large waterfall. She craned her neck up to determine the height, but it was camouflaged by the jungle foliage and trees. The path ended at the waterfall, or at least it appeared to. Sally blinked to keep the wetness out of her eyes and gasped as she saw the back of Leslie disappear into the mist of the waterfall. As she got closer to the roaring cascading water, she noticed a path that went along a rocky ledge right behind the falls. Oh no, no, no, she thought, but then, Leslie reappeared and grabbed Sally's hand and pulled her onto the path.

They walked into a cave that deepened behind the falls. It was wet and so misty that it was nearly impossible to see three feet in front of them. Sally was soaked to the skin and scurried to keep up with Leslie. A couple of minutes later, they exited the cave and were on the other side of the falls. Sally's heart was beating wildly, but she couldn't remember ever feeling this exhilarated in her life.

Up ahead, Leslie beckoned, "Come on Sally, you've got to keep up. We're almost there."

They continued to trek higher, climbing winding trails that ran alongside the river. About an hour later, Miguel stopped in a small clearing and waited for the women to catch up. Sally was so exhausted that all she wanted to do was pull out her sleeping bag and crawl into it and sleep for an hour or two. She looked around the small clearing and could not see any path leading off it. Oh great, she thought, we're lost.

Then she heard a rustling behind her and the foliage parted and out stepped an old woman. To Sally's eyes this creature appeared ancient. She had deep crevices in her face, but her eyes were large and youthful. Her face lit up with a huge smile as she came over to Leslie and clapped her hands together in glee. A sing song voice came out of the ancient creature speaking words that lilted and flew and were completely unrecognizable to Sally. She watched as Leslie took the woman's hands into hers and laughed and chattered back.

The ancient lady stood about four feet tall and she had thick, white hair that hung in two braids down her back to her waist. She was barefoot and dressed in a long colorful skirt and a shawl wrapped around her upper body. She had a cloth bag slung over her shoulders. While Sally was observing the interactions between Leslie and the old woman, she noticed Miguel clearing out twigs and rocks from the clearing. He then pulled a tarp out of his backpack and laid it on the ground. So, it looked like Sally's wish for a nap was going to become a reality.

Leslie looked over at Sally and said, "This is it – the end of the road. We'll be camping here for the night." She then brought the old woman over to Sally and introduced her. "Sally, I'd like you to meet Grandmother." The old lady looked up at Sally with a large smile and spoke some sing song words.

Sally responded with a mumbled "Nice to meet you, Grandmother." The old woman peered up at Sally with a twinkle in her eyes and then reached up to pat Sally's hair. She stepped back and giggled at Sally, while chattering something to Leslie. Miguel laughed. Leslie smiled and explained to Sally what was going on.

"Grandmother wants to know what happened to your hair. And if you are a boy or a girl? But she thinks you're a girl from the evidence of your bosom."

Sally looked over at the laughing Grandmother and Miguel and laughed back. "Sometimes, I wonder myself," she responded to Leslie. "So, this is it? What happens now?" Sally asked as she looked around the clearing. She had hoped to see more indigenous tribal life.

"We'll spend the night. Grandmother will come back in the morning with some herbs for me. She will, with the help of Miguel, give me more instructions on the use of the medicines. Someday, when she trusts me enough, she may take me back with her into the jungle to meet the shaman who collects and prepares the different herbs and teas. I've only heard small pieces of the story. But it is not Grandmother who gets this stuff, and it's not the village shaman. As far as I can tell, it is a shaman that lives alone in the mountain and only has occasional contact with the tribe.

Only when someone is really sick and the local shaman of a neighboring tribe has not been able to help, will the people ask to see the forest shaman – that's what they call her. I think it's a woman, because once, I heard Grandmother refer to the shaman in the feminine. But she's very secretive and protective of this shaman. I know I just have to be patient."

"How did you find Grandmother in the first place?" Sally asked.

Leslie nodded towards Miguel, "Miguel. He is what I call a first generation cross-over. You may not realize this, but he is university educated and he has chosen to live in both worlds. He is my source of education and contact. Crazy as this sounds, we met on a bus out of San Jose on one of my first trips here. I've known him for over a decade." Sally noted the tender gaze in Miguel's eyes as he looked up at Leslie.

In the impending dusk the group sat down together on the tarp. Grandmother emptied her bag, bringing out food to share. Wrapped in large banana leaves was a steaming mixture of food that Sally couldn't identify, though it was aromatic and her stomach signaled its interest with a large growl. She brought out her camping dishes and scooped a bit of the gruel into a bowl. Grandmother also took out another container, a flask of sorts and poured the group some warm tea, which had a strong, somewhat bitter, but minty flavor. Sally didn't know what she was eating or drinking but that didn't hold her back from devouring the food and drink in front of her.

She listened to the other three chat amongst themselves. Sometimes, she could pick out a Spanish sounding word, but most of the time, she couldn't make heads or tails of the conversation.

There was gentle chatter and light laughter. As she finished her meal, a deep sleepiness invaded her body. She got up and unraveled her sleeping bag, nodded to the others, crawled in, and within seconds, she was sound asleep.

"Wake up sleepy head. Gotta get going."

Sally woke to warmth and sun and a light breeze caressing her face. She peered up to the figure standing over her. Leslie was smiling down at her. "Come on sleepy girl."

Sally looked at the campsite. Miguel and Leslie had all their stuff packed into their backpacks and looked as if they were ready to leave. "What about Grandmother?" Sally asked.

"She's come and gone. But she did leave something for you."

Leslie handed over a small packet of something. Sally undid the packet and found some fine herbs or plants ground up.

"It's the tea. What she served us last night. She thought you could use more of it. Said you needed more rest," Leslie said with a big smile.

"I missed her? Darn. I really wanted to see her again. You mean I slept through everything this morning? Why didn't you wake me?"

"Grandmother needed to teach me what these herbs are and how to use them. It's best that you slept through this. Not that she doesn't trust you, but it's just taken so long for her to trust me. The fewer people that know this the better."

Man, Sally thought, I slept through it all. I trekked all the way up this mountain, and I slept through all the important stuff.

Grandmother was full of energy and walked with a light step. She was aware that she was old, but old was good in this tribal culture. The elders were held in revered esteem by the villagers. As long as all in the village were well fed and secure, the elderly were not seen as a strain by the others.

Grandmother had left the white doctor, Leslie, Miguel, and the funny lady with the sticking up hair, at dawn. The funny lady had wildness about her and a spark of energy that buzzed about like a wayward mosquito, having no real sense of direction or purpose. She did seem harmless, though – not like the mosquito which could bite and irritate. But then, she didn't really know the funny lady. Most likely, she could bite and irritate, too.

Grandmother chuckled to herself. These people from the city and other foreign places were so intriguing. She had grown to love and trust Leslie – the white doctor. She knew that Leslie was a good and caring healer. That is why, after several years, she had finally felt comfortable enough to share with her the special herbs and mixtures created by the young shaman. Only Leslie, though, and as far as she was concerned that was enough. Most important of all, was protecting the young shaman from those others. Grandmother knew instinctively that the harm would overshadow the good if the others learned about the young shaman.

When Grandmother thought of the young shaman, her whole body would be infused with warmth and a deep love. Zila was unique. Grandmother was a self-appointed protector of the girl. She had, indeed, raised the orphaned child. She remembered the day so many years ago when the tall, white man walked into the village clearing. This was when the village was nearly impossible to reach. There were not walking paths to it, as there are now. It was completely camouflaged and hidden by the jungle and mountainous terrain.

In her memory, no one had ever seen a white person, or any other people from down in the valley. This particular village was so isolated, that the only others they interacted with were the members of two other villages of mountain tribal people, located about a day's walk in two different directions. They traded with these two other groups and intermarried. Each group only consisted of about 100 members.

Grandmother was a woman of around 20 years old at the time the white man showed up. She thought she was about 90 years old now; and thought if the white man was still alive he would be even older than her. She still remembered him. He was thin, tall, had longish light colored hair, and startling blue eyes. The villagers were a peaceful people and circled around the man as he stood in the middle of the clearing.

The stranger looked around at the people with delight. He dropped the pack he was carrying on his back and smiled brightly at the people, saying some unintelligible words in a warm and deep voice. The people gathered around him, some coming up and poking at him, touching his hair, beard, arms, chattering away. He stood a good foot taller than even the tallest man in the village. The stranger indicated that he wished to stay, pantomiming the desire to eat and sleep.

Grandmother thought about the next few years that followed. He had revealed that he was a doctor – which the village shaman was very interested in. He had told them his name was Matthew and that he had travelled from a very distant place called England. And that he had been travelling for months to find a place just like this. The people were polite but remained slightly unsure and distrustful of the white doctor. Grandmother had always been intrigued by him and had befriended him, even while he was somewhat shunned by the others.

He became enchanted by a beautiful young woman and eventually from that union a daughter was born. The village shaman or Zutkia, as it is called in their language, begrudgingly worked with Matthew and shared his intimate knowledge of nature and of the traditions and customs of the people and the healing potions and rituals he used and practiced.

The daughter of Matthew looked startlingly like her mother, not a trace of European traits evident, except for her slightly rounder eyes, and slightly lighter skin and hair color. Grandmother reflected back on this time and with a wave of sadness pondered the early death of Matthew.

Just after three or so years with the tribe, he died, most likely, he had been bitten by some poisonous insect that the rest of the villagers were immune to and no amount of shamanism or even the doctor's own medical knowledge could save him. He died rather quickly. And though, there were some stories passed down, most did not remember him and this particular piece of village history was conveniently forgotten, probably in part due to the absence of European traits in subsequent generations.

Sixty some years later, Zila was born. Grandmother had been there to help with the birthing process. When Zila was born, she looked like any of the other village babies, brown skin, dark hair, and dark eyes. Sadly, her young mother died during the difficult child birth, and the young father turned his back on the baby and left the village to return to his parents' village; he could not bear to stay in the same village as the infant girl. Grandmother took the child in and raised her. Within months, everyone began to notice the differences about the child.

As the young girl grew and her looks became more and more distinctly different, the villagers began to shy away from her. Zila hardly knew what she looked like, though she could tell that her long, straight and light colored hair and fair skin were different from everyone else's wavy dark brown hair and darker skin, and she was much taller. By the time she reached puberty, she stood as tall as the tallest man in her village. She realized that she looked different from the others, but it saddened her that some laughed at her; others cursed and pointed at her yes.

Zila grew to love the solitude of the jungle and felt at peace in the wild foliage. She remembered clearly her early childhood when she would venture out into the jungle with Grandmother. They would spend days away from the tribe exploring, and since Grandmother had always had a close association with the village shaman, an elder like her and of similar age, Zila had grown up as a quiet observer of the shaman's work.

She often went along with him into the jungle to help gather plants, seeds, mushrooms, bark, insects and other materials and then watch as he concocted his medicinal brews. It was unusual for the shaman to allow anyone to observe his techniques, but it was as if he realized that he was in the presence of something other, someone unique. Zila was quiet and unobtrusive but keenly inquisitive and the shaman found that he desired to share his practices with her.

On her own, Zila began gathering different plants and found rare mushrooms that she was sure the shaman had not seen before. She began creating some of her own mixtures, salves, and teas. Once, she applied a salve on a large bump that had appeared on Grandmother's arm and within a day, the bump had completely subsided.

As the village shaman aged, the villagers turned more and more to Zila for her ministrations, even as she began to spend more and more time away, living alone. When they needed her, though, she could be located by Grandmother. Somehow, the two had always been able to communicate in spite of distance or space between them. It could have been something as subtle as a low whistle, or even a small congregation of birds, or the breeze blowing a certain way. The two always knew how to find each other.

Over time, the elder shaman aged and weakened. He looked to Zila to carry on in his place. She was in her late teens or maybe early twenties, by this time. The people did not count their years. She had continued to explore the jungle and gather new and different ingredients.

One day, while on one of her explorations, she came upon a tiny bright red mushroom that didn't look like anything she had seen before. She was in a very isolated terrain about a three day walk from the village. Careful not to touch it, she took a cloth out of her backpack and a small bag, and gathered a handful of the tiny mushrooms.

She sensed an urgency to return to her village. Upon her return, she became aware of the sadness amongst the people and learned that the shaman was very ill. Entering his hut, she smelled the sickness and knew death was imminent. She prepared a sedative broth for him and stayed through the night.

During the night, she experimented with the new mushrooms – never touching them directly for fear they could be deadly. She ground some up into a powder, and made a paste, and took a tiny taste. She then fell asleep, only to be awakened a short time later with abdominal cramping, nausea and loose stools. She broke out in a sweat and felt feverish; she became somewhat delirious and fell back into a deep sleep.

Once again she woke, heaving, vomiting and experiencing a violent episode of diarrhea. This all passed rather quickly. She monitored her breathing and heart rate and by morning she felt normal again. She realized the mushrooms would be beneficial if one needed to purge. In the shamanic culture, purging was considered positive and a beneficial aspect of healing.

She attended to the shaman during the day. Occasionally, she noticed him observing her with an alert gaze. Then he gestured to the bowl of mushrooms. She brought them over for him to look at and showed him the powder. He asked her to make a tea with some of the powder mixed in. She described the experience that she had had through the night, and he nodded and again asked her to make him the tea.

Zila did so and gave the shaman a few sips. He smiled up at her and then fell into a deep sleep. Because the powder had been more diluted with the tea, the shaman did not have the same violent reactions that Zila had experienced. He did groan in his sleep and tossed and turned, but stayed asleep for the rest of the day.

The next day, he seemed healthier. His skin was pink again and the yellow had left his eyes. His breath was no longer sour. He asked again for the tea. And then for many days, he was his old self. Zila only had a few of the little red mushrooms left. The shaman stopped asking for the tea. A few weeks passed where he seemed more robust. Then, he slowly became weak again. Zila readied another brew of the mushroom tea, but the shaman, smiled at her and declined. He thanked her for her care, held her hand and looked deeply into her eyes.

"You are like your great, great grandfather, Zila. He lives through you. You have become a great healer. Guard your medicine and yourself carefully." He then shut his eyes and drifted off to sleep. Zila fell asleep with his hand in hers. When she awoke in the early dawn, the hand in hers was still and cold. Grandmother was sitting in the hut and smiled at Zila and thanked her for helping her friend leave his earthly body in a peaceful way.

Zila then became the village Zutkia and was often called upon to heal members of her village. Word had gotten out to the other nearby villages; and more and more people came seeking her out for healing. But Zila and Grandmother felt intuitively the need for secrecy, so Zila moved even further into the treacherous mountainous wilderness. Days and even weeks might go by without a soul seeing Zila. And then as if she sensed their need, she would appear on the outskirts of a village compound and wait to be beckoned into one of their dwellings to care for an injured or ill person.

After receiving Zila's ministrations, some would speak of having experienced remarkable visions, some beautiful, others frightening—but most spoke of a positive life-changing experience of renewal and well-being. As much as the people were grateful to Zila for her healings, they were also suspicious and wary.

The traditional medicine man of the nearby tribes, the Zutkia, was somewhat jealous of the girl and passed on his fear and distrust to the villagers. But when the people were desperate for a healing, and the Zutkia's efforts failed, they always sought the girl out. And, in most cases, her magic worked.

Zila rarely spoke. More often she hummed a light, clear musical sound. She did this when she laid her hands on people. She smiled a soft, serene smile. She cooed and comforted with her caresses. She made a dark, bitter tea out of the tiny ground up pieces of the stem of the miniscule red mushroom and fed it by teaspoons to the ill person. She stayed with the person for three days, never sleeping, just singing, coaxing, wiping the brow, holding the bowl to catch the convulsive vomit or diarrhea, cleaning and bathing the body.

She would allow only one other person into the dwelling during this time. She preferred this person to be the eldest female relative of the sick person. Most people were mesmerized as they looked into her unusual eyes. Zila would hold the gazes of the elder female and the patient until both felt as if they had entered a hypnotic state. No one ever could clearly report the events inside the healing dwelling. All would leave it transformed, including Zila herself.

Chapter 4

Bribri, Costa Rica

Leslie Goetz was sitting at her desk, back in the Bribri office, intent on the computer screen in front of her. Her little black cat was curled up in a ball on her lap, purring away. Leslie always enjoyed the bundle of warm fur emanating unconditional love and knew she most likely received more benefit from this human-animal connection than any vitamin or supplement could provide. She pulled up her list of appointments for the day. Just two and one of them was a new patient that she hadn't met yet – an M. Brown.

Since it was a Saturday and a quiet clinic day, she was alone in the office. She had a part time staff person who worked a few hours during the week running her office, scheduling appointments and managing the sale of the supplements that Leslie offered. She heard the bell of the front door as it opened and realized that her first appointment had arrived. She gently extricated herself from her cat and stepped out of the office. A slender, petite woman stood at the door.

"Hello, are you Dr. Goetz?" the young woman asked.

"Yes, come in. Are you my 10 o'clock appointment?"

"Yes, my name is Mercy."

"Mercy?" Leslie responded. The woman smiled and nodded affirmative, not offering a last name. Must be M. Brown, she thought.

"Let me get you some forms to fill out. It should just take a minute."

Leslie turned and went behind the counter and put together a clip board with a piece of paper on it and handed it over to the woman. She glanced at Mercy while she was filling out the forms. Perfectly straight, blond - nearly white hair that reached to her mid back draped over the side of the woman's face. Her limbs were delicate; her face had a luminous, flawless quality, her eyes a tawny brown. She was dressed in flowing white pants and a halter top, revealing a tanned and toned abdomen.

Leslie looked away just as Mercy looked up and caught Leslie studying her. It was hard to tell her age, but she guessed Mercy to be about 30 years old. When she finished filling out the forms, she handed them over to Leslie. Leslie stood up and beckoned for Mercy to follow her into her office.

"What can I do for you?"

In a slightly accented voice that Leslie couldn't place, Mercy responded, "I'm actually looking for some supplements that might balance my energy. I've been feeling very sluggish the last few weeks."

"Well, the best thing for me to do is to run a few tests on you. I would like to draw some blood. It could be your thyroid or a lack of vitamin D. But it's hard for me to diagnose without checking your blood counts and doing a physical exam."

Mercy's eyes clouded over for just a second, but as if she caught herself, she offered a bright smile to Leslie. "You know, I'm only here for a couple of days. It's probably not long enough to do the tests and get the results. The young woman at the Honey Moon Café told me to come to see you. She said you had a wonderful supplement that you got from the jungle, ground up mushrooms or something that works wonders. Can I just buy a bottle of that?"

Leslie became alarmed by this statement. She wracked her brain trying to figure out who at the café would have talked about this. This worried her very much. Yes, she had developed her own apothecary of natural herbs and teas, but she had been very careful not to talk to anyone about the powders, only Sally, and really not in too much detail.

Her teas and herbs that she used and sold in her practice were another thing. Some she collected and prepared herself from local flowers and her own home-grown herbs. The rest she got from a friend who was an herbalist who had a large herb farm near Arenal Volcano.

As she stared at Mercy trying to read something in the woman's eyes, she began to feel a chill around her heart and she was beginning to regret bringing Sally along last week, as much as she had enjoyed the friendly companionship, she worried that it might have been a mistake to open up to her so much. When she went up to the mountains, she rarely told anyone where she was actually going. Her acquaintances in Bribri generally thought she was just going to her other office in Puerto Viejo; and the same was thought when she was away from Puerto Viejo – those acquaintances just presumed she was back in Bribri.

She only went up to the mountain a few times a year. She'd had to make the trek last week because her supply was almost gone. She had administered the powder sparingly and to only two different patients. One lived in San Jose, the other in Limon. Unfortunately, Grandmother had not brought any of the precious red powder with her on that trip. She told her she was pretty sure the Shaman would have some for her in a few days. Leslie had felt bad that she had made the trek up and not gotten what she needed. Though Grandmother had supplied her with some rare teas the Shaman had made that helped with inflammation and joint problems.

"Gosh, Mercy, I'm not sure what you're referring to. I do have some teas that I have made from local herbs and flowers....but nothing other than that. I certainly wouldn't offer ground up mushrooms or anything that hasn't been sufficiently tested. I can offer you some vitamins – and some energy teas. But that's about it without doing some testing."

Instead of responding, Mercy glanced around the office as if looking for something; she then brought her gaze back to Leslie. Briefly she held Leslie's eyes with a hardened glint in her own. She then softened her features and smiled. "It's okay, Doctor. Sure, I'd love some of your energy tea. We'll skip the blood test and exam. Maybe next time I'm here, I can schedule some time with you."

"Oh, do you come here often?"

"Uh, no...this is my first trip. My husband and I are considering buying some property somewhere around here. Or maybe one of the coastal towns, possibly Puerto Viejo or Cahuita. We like the feel of the place."

"Where are you from? Europe? I've been trying to place your accent."

Instead of answering, Mercy looked at her watch. "Oops, gotta run. Suppose to meet my husband. Got an appointment with a real estate agent. Hey, thanks for your time. How much for the tea?"

Both women stood up and walked out to the front office. Leslie handed a small bag of tea to Mercy and wrote up a bill. Mercy pulled some cash out of her bag and handed it over. She smiled a long smile at Leslie then stepped out of the office. Leslie walked over to the window and watched Mercy walk down the street and then turn the corner.

Leslie left the office and walked the same route as the other woman. As she turned the corner she saw Mercy half way down the block get into a black Toyota SUV. She quickly ducked into the little shop on the corner. The car pulled up to the corner and stopped. She peered out the doorway of the shop and saw Mercy sitting in the passenger seat and a man with longish blond hair in the driver's seat. They both glanced into the doorway of the shop as Leslie stepped back more into the interior, her heart beating wildly.

"Shit, shit, shit!" she murmured under her breath.

Tomas held on with all his might; his arms and shoulders aching with the effort. The roar of the wind against the small sail was deafening. The black clouds looming over head and the first hard drops of rain fueled his desire to return to shore.

He leaned his body into the wind holding on tight as he maneuvered one more jive away from the shore—and then a swift return jive in the other direction to get the board headed towards the shore. Knees crouched, arms out straight, his board slapping across the waves with the wind pressing on his back, he hung his head back and screamed at the top of his lungs. Rain and water washed over his face and mingled with the tears freely flowing.

As he approached the shore, he straightened his body, pulled back on the boom and turned his board into the wind to slow down his speed, and then when just a few feet away from the shore, he stepped off the board into the shallow water and pulled his board, sail, boom and mast up the beach.

Standing alone on the beach—the few other wind surfers that had been there earlier in the day had the good sense to get out of the water and head back to civilization before the storm broke—he looked across the lake at Arenal Volcano, one of a handful of active volcanoes in the Americas. It was a beautiful example of nature's raw power and supremacy over humankind. The rain was coming down in earnest now—a typical seasonal deluge. True it was June, but Costa Rica's milder and warmer months usually occupied February through April.

As much as he resisted the thought, he knew it was time to pack up his stuff and head back to San Jose. Things, events, and responsibilities were tugging at him; he had not been able to completely clear his mind of thoughts and memories. Coming up to Lake Arenal for a few days had helped, but he still had to go back. He had a new life to engage and he still had some left over things to handle. So much had happened in the last few months.

Sara, his mother, had finally died after many months of slowly fading away. Each day a little more of the light in her eyes dimmed. She slept more and more, barely opening her eyes to acknowledge his daily visit. Would he have even made the daily visits were it not for Evangeline, his mother's caretaker and his childhood nanny? At the end of each visit, Evangeline would follow him to the door and say, "We'll be seeing you tomorrow, Tomie." Not a question – a statement. Tomas knew he was driven more to please Eva, than the mother that held herself always at a distance from her only child.

Sara had been a petite, blond, blue-eyed strikingly pretty young woman. She had studied abroad at a university in England. Her proud, third-generation Costa Rican family had high hopes for their beautiful, well-educated daughter, which included a short list of approved, appropriate suitors. Instead, they were appalled at Sara's choice in husband material.

Though the Vasquez name was well respected, Sara's parents weren't sure what their daughter's suitor's roots were, and they were a bit suspicious of his short, dark, and swarthy looks, in spite of his name, his education, and his accomplishments. Alberto Vasquez, though small in stature, was large in vision and achievements, inheriting his family's dedication to public service.

Sara had poured quite a bit of her own funds into Alberto's political campaigns, but once they were married, her parents cut her off financially. They wanted little to do with Sara and her husband, but they went to great lengths to be involved in their little grandson's life once he came along. Unfortunately, as her parents' hearts softened, Sara's hardened and she began to interfere with her son's visits to his grandparents' estate.

Looking into Tomas' deep brown eyes, she was reminded of her roots and her parents' snobbery and disdain for her choices in life. And though she was glad to have the boy out of her hair on a regular basis, she was also torn between inflicting a measure of power over her parents and the concern about who her son would become if left under their sphere of influence.

As Tomas reflected upon his mother, he thought about the choices one makes in life, and wondered, as he often did, in reality what control does a person really have over their destiny. He knew he had made many mistakes in his life, some that still haunted him to this day. He also knew that there were some things he had no control over – decisions people had made before his time that still impacted his life today.

Tomas loaded up his gear into the back of his small Toyota pick-up. There was a lull in the drenching rain, and with that lull and the quieting wind, a flash of clarity replaced the normal chaos of his mind. Yes, he thought to himself, he had made the right decision leaving the OIJ to start his own company. He was glad to not be tied to the political undercurrents of his old bureaucratic job.

The suite of offices he had leased in a new building was working out just fine. And he was beginning to feel like maybe, just maybe, he could put the past behind him. Tomas felt a lightness of being, a sense of new direction and purpose. And for the first time in months, he was anxious to get back to the city -- his business was taking off and he had a lot to do.

Seattle, WA

He had splurged on a first class seat which had proven to be a luxury that he decided he couldn't do without in the future. A window seat and a couple of glasses of good Washington State wine had made this leg of the trip on Alaska Airlines quite enjoyable. The pilot had just announced that they were preparing for landing at the Seattle-Tacoma International airport.

Tomas looked out the window and was startled by the looming presence of the massive, white-capped mountain on the right side of the aircraft. He knew he was looking at the 14,000 feet high Mt. Rainier that held reign over the Puget Sound skyline with its imposing presence. He knew that it was a volcano, one of a chain of volcanoes in the Pacific Ring of Fire, and that it was considered one of the most dangerous with potential for great destruction. If it blew, it would wipe out many towns and even parts of Seattle with a huge lahar - or mud flow. The mountain appeared quiet, regal; one did not sense a looming disaster.

He contrasted it with Mt. Arenal, at just 5,000 feet high, which was Costa Rica's most active volcano and considered one of the ten most active volcanoes in the world. Arenal offered almost every night a spectacle of lights with its explosive eruptions. In 1968 a powerful eruption took place and destroyed a portion of the mountain and took out the little town of Tabacon, burying it and killing 78 people.

He glanced over the passengers across the aisle and looked out the left side of the plane. He could see numerous islands, lots of sparkling blue water, and lush greenery. The sky was a deep blue, belying the claim of perpetual gray skies. He took in the gorgeous environment below – the mountain ranges, sea, lakes and forests and appreciated its beauty.

Iris had insisted upon picking him up at the airport. He was feeling a little...oh, he didn't know...foolish? A little shy? He barely knew the woman, and yet, when he thought of her, he saw her slight but strong body, her casual short hair that framed her attractive face and compelling eyes full of intelligence....and fear. He felt drawn to her; he had to admit it to himself.

It had been almost a year since Iris Dibiase's visit to Costa Rica, and during that visit, the woman he had observed had the strength of steel and determination that only the deep love a mother can claim to find her only child no matter what obstacles were placed before her.

Tomas was looking forward to a few days of relaxation in Seattle. His last few months had been a whirlwind of activities – getting his new office set up, creating a business plan, setting up a marketing scheme, and the icing on the cake had been his success at wooing Jeremiah Valencia, his younger colleague, away from the OIJ.

Tomas had worried that Jeremiah had lost respect for Tomas, when Tomas had been the subject of an internal investigation and had to respond to charges of corruption in relation to the arrest of the leader of the gang that had kidnapped Nina Navarra, Iris Dibiase's daughter. It had become known that Tomas had had earlier dealings with the gang leader, known simply as *El Jefe*, or by his first name – Chaz.

Years earlier, Tomas had made a promise that he would look after his younger cousin, Robbie, the son of his father's only brother, who had died at an early age. Robbie had always had a wild streak and never wanted to play life by the rules. After his father's death, Tomas had tried to honor his wishes and had tried to stay in touch with Robbie. But Robbie was a hard one to keep up with. He seemed to have an endless stream of cash without a job to corroborate his life-style. He was gone months at a time, ostensibly on long surfing trips.

In the midst of an investigation into a gang of drug and arms runners, Tomas became aware of his cousin's involvement, and ultimately looked the other way. This came back to haunt him, and though he was eventually cleared of misdeed, it had colored his sense of self-esteem and pride, and feeling somewhat shamed he decided to leave the OIJ and open his own private investigation firm.

The good news was that he had already been successful in attracting international clients. His specialty had to do with helping people locate missing persons. His work the previous year in Puerto Viejo had given him a thirst for this type of work. He knew that the outcomes would more likely than not be sad, but it at least gave people closure when dealing with the loss of a loved one.

Iris Dibiase's daughter, Nina, had been found, and that outcome gave Tomas the needed impetus to make this his purpose for his company. Money was not an issue for him, due to family money and a frugal life style, so he had been able to bankroll the first few months of operations, and then he had been richly rewarded by one of his first clients for the safe return of a wayward daughter.

Costa Rica is a young person's paradise. Many come fresh out of college, parental funding and graduation presents in monetary form stashed in their back pocket or their one backpack, which usually was also filled with bathing suits, tee shirts, shorts and sun dresses. They come to experience an interlude of freedom from social norms and rules.

Young people, primarily from well-to-do families, traveling alone or with small groups, thirsty for wanderlust, and enjoying long lazy days on beautiful beaches, and noisy, rum soaked and weed infused nights. Many flock to the Caribbean coast to hot and sticky beach towns like Cahuita, Puerto Viejo, and as far south as Manzanillo, a lonesome hamlet at the end of the road.

The young also come in droves to the Pacific Coast where there are numerous surf camps and small towns catering to tourists from all over the world. A west coast favorite is Tamarindo on the Nicoya Peninsula, a resort area that offers a choice of activities from prime wildlife viewing, beaches with rolling waves that provide excellent surfing action, and a choice of hotels, inns, and camps, spanning shoe-string budgets to high-end sophistication.

There had been growth in the last decade on both sides of the country catering to this influx of carefree tourists, which unfortunately had contributed to an increase of robberies against tourists, and even the occasional assault, or kidnapping of the same carefree young tourist who had become careless.

A young woman alone, or separated from her companions, could easily become prey to gangs looking to extort in exchange for the return of a loved child. Or, something not even so sinister – as a walk in the jungle or along the beach – a wrong turn up an isolated country road; one could easily get lost for hours and sometimes days. Tomas knew the country well -- knew its many spidery back roads that died off in the jungle, or ended at the door of an abandoned shack.

He also knew how dangerous the beaches were on both sides of the country. Many of the missing persons disappeared at beaches, which presented a challenge to search parties. The beaches are beautiful and pristine, but they are also remote; and the infrastructure in Costa Rica is all but non-existent. There are no four lane highways, and generally no emergency services that are readily available. There is limited law enforcement resources and difficulty with local governments.

Tomas' recent case was in Mail Pais, a remote beach for surfers. And although there was an investigating law enforcement office only fifteen miles away, it took searchers over an hour to get to the beach area to search for the missing young woman, due to the condition of the road and the density of the jungle adjacent to the beaches. Tomas was creating a specialty in searching these types of areas, gaining experience combined with his dedication and determination.

Iris Dibiase

The sun shone brightly into her window, though it was still early--this being June in the Pacific Northwest and the month with the longest days of sunlight. Iris stretched her legs, glanced at the clock, and as consciousness became more present, she felt anticipation take over. What, she wondered, what was it?

And then, she awoke fully and remembered that this was the day she was to pick up Tomas Vasquez at the airport. Oh my god, she thought, she needed to get up and get going. She had gotten in late the previous evening, returning from a weekend trip to Portland to visit her daughter, Nina and her little precious granddaughter, Siri. Nina had kidded her mother about the impending visit with the agent from Costa Rica.

"Um, Mom," with a twinkle in her eye, "you better watch out. You never know what could happen when you meet up with that handsome Latin hombre from Costa Rica...."

"Nina!" Iris responded, as her cheeks colored. "I...I..."

"Oh Mom, just relax! I'm glad you're getting out and doing something besides worrying about me and Siri! We're okay!" For a second, a cloud passed over Nina's face and a memory flashed between the two women. The event the year before was one that would be stored in the deep recesses of both their psyches: a daughter kidnapped and tortured, a mother facing the greatest fear of her life.

Nina brought her hand up to her mother's face, gently cupping her cheek, and tucking a strand of hair behind one ear. The two gazed at each other for a long few seconds, moisture gathering in the corners of their eyes. "Mama....I'm okay," Nina said quietly. "Now go....have fun. And call me the second he leaves. I want to hear all about it."

"Okay, sweetheart. You got it.... I can do this!"

"Mom?"

"Yes, love?"

"Say hi to Detective Vasquez for me. And....please, thank him again."

Iris packed a small bag just in case she decided to spend the night in Seattle. She convinced herself that this had nothing to do with meeting up with Tomas -- though the thought of seeing him after all this time caused a slight increase in her heartbeat. Her time with him in Costa Rica had strictly been all business. He was the *OIJ* agent that had taken the lead on the search for Nina when she had gone missing while visiting the small Caribbean coastal town of Puerto Viejo over a year ago.

He had seen Iris at her most vulnerable state: a mother smothered by fear and desperation. And yet, his presence had been comforting and encouraging. And in the end, he had been there to retrieve her daughter and bring her back to her. Iris had regretted that she hadn't been able to spend a little more time with the agent after the situation had been resolved.

But with all the chaos, tears, emotion, along with David, her ex-husband, and Daniel, Nina's husband, showing up in Costa Rica to wrap their arms around the found Nina, Tomas Vasquez had quietly slipped away – not wanting to interfere with the family reunion. And in the ensuing days, Iris had been so preoccupied with Nina's recovery, and helping her walk through the bureaucracy of the country's law enforcement and the US Embassy requirements in handling the case, and being so emotionally drained, herself, she didn't think to seek out the agent to engage in some closure.

Iris loved the chance to visit Seattle, and she thought she'd see if there was a room at the Inn at the Market. She loved the picturesque inn just at the top of the world famous Pike Place Market, and she usually stayed there when she stayed over in Seattle. She loved the little French bakery kitty-corner to the Inn, and her mouth already began to water as she thought of the dark brewed Seattle cappuccino and the rare treat of a chocolate croissant, slightly warmed. As she thought more about this, she decided to settle on the idea, and went on-line to make a room reservation. Thankfully, a room was available, at this late date – rare for a June day.

That being done, she grabbed her bag, closed up her house, got into her little Mini-Cooper and drove off the island. It was about an hour drive to the Seattle-Tacoma International airport, but she gave herself a good hour and a half – just so she wouldn't have to rush – one never knew how the traffic would be. Being a beautiful, clear June day, Iris was treated to the wonder of the view of the Olympic Mountains off to the west, and the majestic Mt. Rainier (which she called 'Mama' Rainier) off to her right.

The drive was easy and with time to spare, she pulled into the passenger pick up zone at the airport. She strained to look at the people standing on the curb – all sorts of people – some clumped in small groups – others standing alone. As she drove slowly along, trying to appease the traffic cop who was signaling to everyone to keep moving, she tried to pick out and recognize a single male – someone that fit the description of the image imprinted upon her brain.

Over the last year, she had seen his face – in her memories, in her dreams, remembering his single but comforting embrace as he picked up her naked emotionally pain-wracked body from the floor of the shower in the little hotel she was staying at in Puerto Viejo. He had wrapped her in a big towel and held her close, whispering, "It's going to be okay." And, it had been.

Ah, there he is, she thought. Maybe dressed a little too formally for the casual outdoorsy Pacific Northwest trend – although he would fit in with the downtown cosmopolitan dress of the Seattle business person. He had on dark slacks, a white shirt, and a dark sports jacket. He had one small piece of luggage in his hand. She pulled the little silver Mini up to the curb in front of him, put on the brake and opened her door to stand outside the car.

She looked over the top of her small car and called his name. He glanced over at her and their eyes met; within a heart beat his face broke into a wide warm smile. She walked over to the curb and was brusquely pulled into a quick hug by Tomas.

"Agent Vasquez," Iris greeted upon being released from the warm hug.

"Iris – please – it's Tomas," he replied.

"You're here," she responded needlessly.

"Yes, I would say so," he said with another crinkly smile.

She opened the car door, pulled forth the front passenger seat, and Tomas pushed his bag into the small car. "Cute little car," he said as he arranged himself in the front seat.

"Yes, one of my little treats to me. How was your flight? Long?"

"Not too bad. Had a brief layover in Miami, then direct to here. Can't complain at all."

Tomas left off mentioning that he had flown first-class. He was feeling a little embarrassed by the splurge. But he knew he'd had a much more agreeable trip sitting up in front in the larger seats with the nicer service, food, and not to mention the drinks. He was feeling pretty relaxed at the moment.

He glanced over at Iris as she concentrated on maneuvering the little car out of the busy airport terminal. She looked more relaxed than when he had last seen her – to be expected of course. Her hair was a little shorter, but still worn in the casual cut, tucked behind her ears. Her skin was clear with few lines, her brow was furrowed as she navigated the on-ramp to the 5 freeway north, and her large brown eyes were intent upon their assignment. She kept glancing up into the rear view and the side mirrors. She was a careful but not shy driver.

After the incident in Costa Rica the previous year, they had not been in touch with each other for about six months. Sally Meza, the reporter who had inexplicably inserted herself into that traumatic situation had remained in Costa Rica, setting up shop in a little town just a mile or so south of Puerto Viejo. She was originally from the Seattle area, and in spite of the troublesome trend of events occurring in the beautiful Caribbean country, Sally had fallen in love with the tropical warmth and relaxed life style of the beachside community and had chosen to make it her home.

She and Iris had remained in touch by email. Sally, in turn, had stayed in close touch with Tomas Vasquez often meeting for coffee or a drink on her numerous trips into San Jose. They had teased apart the strands of the Puerto Viejo incident, and in the process had become good friends.

It was with Sally's encouragement that Iris and Tomas connected by email. And so, a casual conversation developed between the two, the heavily laden aspect of their connection was left unspoken. Iris and Tomas chatted every few weeks about their jobs, politics, the state of international affairs, but carefully avoided anything too personal or reflective about the events in Puerto Viejo – other than Iris reporting how well she thought Nina was doing, how strong she was.

She left unspoken what she felt in her heart -- that at her core, Nina was harboring a vulnerability and a bruising that was alien to the once head-strong, independent being. These days, Nina stayed close to home, wrapping herself in the mundane daily activities of caring for Siri and Daniel.

"You're at the Edgewater Inn, right?" Iris queried.

"Yes. That's where my client suggested. He's put together a meeting with a law firm that serves clients internationally. He thinks it would be a good networking opportunity for me. Could be good for my business."

"The Edgewater is lovely, as the name suggests, it's right on the water. On a clear day, you'll have a beautiful view of the Olympics across the water and you'll see the quintessential expression of the Pacific Northwest: Elliott Bay, sailboats, large ferries transporting thousands of vehicles and passengers across the waters to the islands and peninsulas across the bay."

Iris felt a little bit like a Chamber of Commerce representative. But the truth was that she truly believed there was no other place on the planet as pretty as her Pacific Northwest.

"How far is it from your place?" Tomas asked. He had not missed the little overnight bag sitting on the back seat.

"Oh, at a time when there's no traffic, I can be off my island and to the airport in under an hour, and then it's just another twenty minutes or so into downtown Seattle. Usually, though, if I'm coming up to the city for a day of wandering, I drive up to Bremerton, park my car there, and walk on the Bremerton Ferry to Seattle. It's a lovely hour ride and presents the Seattle skyline at her prettiest, docking at the Ferry Terminal. Then I walk all over town, visit the library, have lunch at my favorite Mediterranean restaurant, trek up to Pike's market, then head back to the Ferry for the ride home. It's a delightful way to spend the day and usually what I do with friends who come to visit," Iris finished, feeling a little breathless and like she was babbling. Breathe, a voice inside her head whispered.

"Sounds nice," Tomas replied.

The freeway and traffic got a little clogged as they drove into Seattle, but Iris deftly managed the lane changes and off-ramp, and within minutes, she had pulled up in front of the hotel.

"Would you like to settle in? I have some errands to run and could come back in an hour or so? Are you hungry? When do you have to meet up with your client?" Babbling again, she thought.

"I am hungry. And I don't have an appointment until tomorrow late morning. I'll meet you here in the bar or restaurant in about an hour. How's that sound?" he responded.

"Perfect! See you soon," Iris smiled.

Tomas stood and watched as she maneuvered the car back out into the lane of traffic. He stepped into the lobby, checked in and an hour later was sitting in the bar at a small table for two set up against the window with a view to write home about. It was beautiful here. He could understand Iris' enthusiasm for the area. And then there she was, pulling out a chair and settling in across from him. She gave him a deep full smile and reached across the table and laid her hand on his.

"I'm really happy to see you, Tomas. I have to admit, I'm a bit nervous and I don't really know why. What we went through last year will forever be etched upon my heart. And I know I couldn't have survived the ordeal without you there. I thank you every single day of my life." As she spoke, her eyes filled with tears, but the smile stayed big and full of promise.

Tomas leaned forward in his chair, turning his hand over and grasping Iris' hand in his. He held it there firmly, feeling the warmth generated from that small, feminine hand spread up his arm and directly into his heart. He smiled back at Iris and lifted her hand to his lips and gently kissed the back of her fingers.

Iris had learned belatedly in life that she shouldn't define who others were. Her ideas of who her mother was, who her ex-husband was, and even her daughter invariably turned out not to be accurate. They were either more, or less, or distinctly different than the illusion she had created of each of these pivotal people in her life. The illusions were always shattered. Her ex-husband was not at all the person she had created out of her desires or expectations. Her daughter was chameleon like - always looking elsewhere for another way to be; and her mother....well her mother couldn't be a mother at all – having stepped away from that role early in Iris' life.

She looked across the table at Tomas and then down at the hand that held hers gently, warmly, and she knew that she would do her best not to define this man. She would make every effort to see him just as he was.

Bribri, Costa Rica

Dr. Leslie Goetz was really bothered by the visit with the young blond woman, Mercy--especially when she connected her with the black SUV that she'd seen a few times around her offices. What did the young woman really want?

Her greatest fear, and therefore her most logical assumption, was that somehow, somebody had found out about her trips into the mountains. It was very important to her to keep her promise to Grandmother and not reveal anything about the special ingredients that Grandmother provided her.

Did this have anything to do with Sally Meza? She hoped not. She didn't think Sally would intentionally reveal anything, but one never knew what people were really up to. Leslie was suspicious by nature and also not very trusting of others, and now she had to face the real possibility that her friend had somehow exposed some of Leslie's activities. What for, she wondered? Money, journalism? A good story? What?

She found the piece of paper with the Toyota's license number and tucked it under a paperweight on her desk. She was leaving shortly to go over to Puerto Viejo. When she returned to Bribri, she would walk over to the police and see if they could offer any advice. For the moment, she needed to put it out of her mind.

Coincidently, one of her two patients that she provided the medicine to was scheduled to meet with her at her Puerto Viejo office today. Simone Jenkins had called and told Leslie that she was out of the tincture. She and her family would be in Puerto Viejo for the weekend, was there anyway Leslie could see her on Saturday? She hadn't seen Simone in about a month. The tincture she provided was prescribed to last a month. She was curious to see her and had set up an appointment.

Leslie got to Puerto Viejo early with time to spare, and impulsively, she called Sally and the two met for breakfast. She shared nothing about her concerns over the blonde visitor and her suspicions and she carefully observed Sally to detect any hidden agendas.

Sally did bring up the trip into the mountains the week before, but only in a way of thanking her for such an incredible experience, even if she had slept through the morning meeting with Grandmother. Sally said nothing about herbs or special ingredients. Then she was off talking about a friend, who was an agent in the OIJ, or used to be, and now was in Seattle visiting a mutual friend.

Sally filled Leslie in about the events of last year in Puerto Viejo, going into detail about the kidnapping of a young woman, Nina Navarra, her mother, who had come to Costa Rica to find her daughter, and Tomas Vasquez' role in the lurid story.

She also mentioned that she thought there was some possible 'unfinished' business between the OIJ agent and Iris Dibiase, the mother of the young woman. Incidentally, Sally relayed, she had played a pretty big role in finding the girl. Leslie recalled a bit about the story, remembering some of the news about it.

Sally walked back with Leslie to her office and they got there just a few minutes before the expected appointment with Simone. As Leslie was unlocking and pushing open the door, a car pulled up to the curb and someone called out from inside the car.

"Dr. Leslie! Hi!" It was Simone. Leslie looked into car seeing Simone in the front passenger seat and her husband in the driver's seat and two squirmy kids in the back seat.

"Hi Simone! Come on in." Simone got out of the car and spoke to her husband.

"Honey, go get the kids a snack. There's a great little bakery down the street. I shouldn't be long."

"You sure you don't want me to come in with you?"

"No, no, I'll be fine." She looked over at Leslie with a questioning look.

Leslie nodded at Simone's husband. "She'll be fine here with me."

Leslie was practically dumbfounded as she observed Simone. This was not the same woman she had seen last month. This woman was a picture of health. She had put on some weight. Her face was all smiles, not scrunched up in the pain that constantly inhabited her visage. She had a bounce to her step and her skin was rosy. Her eyes were clear and her hair shone. It seemed miraculous.

Leslie became aware that Sally was still standing there and turned to her and introduced her to Simone, then gave her friend a big hug and told her they'd catch up again before she went back to Bribri.

She spent a good hour with Simone, querying her about her health and what appeared to be a remarkable remission. Simone had been off the chemo drugs for over a month. Leslie reviewed the other medications and supplements that Simone was continuing to take. Mostly vitamins, iron, immune boosters and the tincture.

Simone had run out of the tincture and was anxious to get a refill. She admitted that she felt a little superstitious about not wanting to stop the tincture, and that was why she didn't want to wait until her appointment set for the following week in Bribri. She had already missed two doses – last night's and this morning's.

"You should have had just enough to carry you over until our appointment next week." Leslie remarked. "It's critical that you take exactly the dosing I prescribed."

"I know. Believe me, I followed your instructions exactly. But, somehow, in my packing or carelessness, I misplaced my bottle on Friday. We looked all over the house and I couldn't find it. That's why I was anxious to see you today. I'm feeling stronger every day, and even if it's in my head...I don't want to take a chance if it's the tincture that is helping me so much."

A chill passed up Leslie's spine, barely noticeable, but definitely present. The tincture... What had happened to Simone's bottle? She only had enough on hand to fill Simone's prescription and as she went into her lab to prepare it, she tried to keep the alarm at bay. No matter what, she would have to go up the mountain to get some more of the powder from Grandmother, and soon.

She also knew she needed to check on her patient in Limon to see how he was doing. She was fearful, on the one hand, that he might be doing better also, and on the other, she was hopeful. What if the medicine was really working on these seriously sick patients?

Chapter 5

The Talamancas

What had she been thinking? Coming up here on the mountain alone? She hadn't been able to track down Miguel. Evidently, he was in Nicaragua, according to his young sister, who also couldn't remember how long he might be gone.

Foolishly, she decided to set out on her own, thinking she could get to the first village and have someone find Grandmother for her. But now she was panicked. She thought she was being followed; and that just couldn't happen.

She'd left early in the morning on Sunday from Puerto Viejo instead of going back to Bribri as planned. She hadn't even said goodbye to Sally. She thought she could get up the mountain, find Grandmother, spend one night and be back in Bribri mid-day Monday.

She almost called her neighbor in Bribri, Toni, to let her know she would be back on Monday, and ask her to check on her cat. But she knew she had left adequate food and water out, and in the hurry to get going, she forgot to make the call. By the time she thought about it, she was out of cell phone range. Her part-time office manager was away for the week, so no need to let her know.

What if she got lost up here, or worse yet, what if she was being tracked up here? Everything would be lost or destroyed. She'd left her car where she normally left it – a secluded pull-out on the dirt road. Locked it and grabbed her backpack.

When she got to the little village, it was eerily empty, except for two old crones who smiled up at her in recognition. The two old women spoke their ancient village dialect with a smattering of Spanish, so Leslie learned that Grandmother and most of the villagers had headed up the river to set up a summer camp and fish. They told her that the camp was past the big waterfall.

Leslie almost gave up at that point. But the two old women pointed to the trail out of the village – the same one she had taken a few times before with Miguel when they had met with Grandmother. Maybe she could find this other village. But as the hours passed, she became more discouraged and began to think about turning around before it got too late in the day. Then she began to sense that someone else was out there.

She would hear unusual rustling and even footsteps that would stop when she stopped. Sometimes, they seemed close by. It could just be some of the village people tracking her. They did sometimes; generally if felt protective. No, this felt different. God, what if she was leading someone right to Grandmother? And in turn to the shaman who provided the herbs?

She stopped and waited. Trying not to breathe or move. Five minutes went by. Nothing. Just the cacophony of jungle noises: birds yakking and insects buzzing. Rustling....there it was. More rustling that suddenly stopped. Her armpits dripped with sweat. Her heart was pounding. She waited five more minutes. Nothing.

She started walking slowly and quietly. If she could get to the waterfall and disappear behind it, she thought she'd be safe. She heard the roar of the fall as she came closer blocking out all sound.

She picked up her pace and then glanced back over her shoulder and her heart stopped. There were two people coming towards her. They stopped dead in their tracks about thirty feet away. They made eye contact. It was the woman with the white-blond hair. Mercy? And her companion – the man Leslie had seen in the driver's seat of the SUV that Mercy had gotten into. He was a handsome man with a chiseled face and hard body. His blond hair was pulled back in a ponytail, and he looked anything but friendly. Christ!

"What are you doing here?! Why are you following me?" she demanded, as she backed slowly away. Mercy and her companion stood still without saying anything.

Finally Mercy spoke. "You need to show us where you get the medicine from."

"What are you talking about? What medicine?"

"You know what we mean. Don't play with us," the man responded. He, too, had an accent that was hard to place and a very cold expression on his handsome face.

"No, no, I don't know what you want! Leave me alone!" Leslie continued to step backwards towards the falls. She was hoping she could get close enough that she could slip behind the falls without them seeing where she went. It was a long shot; but there was so much foliage and only the trained eye could see that there was a space or pathway behind the falls.

"The medicine! The drops that you give to Simone Jenkins! You know what we are talking about!" the man barked at her. Mercy put a hand on his arm.

"Shh, Xavier, you're scaring her. Dr. Goetz, we don't want to alarm you, and we'll leave you alone if you just take us to where or who you get the medicine from. The people we work for are very interested in this product. You could make a lot of money from it and help a lot of very sick people."

"How do you know about this?"

Leslie knew that in a million years she wouldn't give them what they were looking for; she wouldn't dare betray Grandmother or the young shaman who created the powder. She also sensed that these people could be ruthless. She was terrified and didn't know which way to turn or how to play this out.

"We know all about Simone's miraculous cure and we've gotten some of the medicine and sent it to a lab. We need to get to the source now. If you help us, we promise you won't regret it."

Leslie's heart thumped in her chest. Simone's missing bottle! But still too many unanswered questions. How did they find out about Simone? And then a little light went on in her head. Maybe Simone's medical doctor was the connection? God, she was pleased with Simone's state of remission, but she wished she could turn back the clock. She continued to take small steps backward hoping to slip into the foliage.

At the same time the couple moved towards her closing the gap between them. The man, Xavier, pulled something out of his backpack. Leslie drew in her breath as she saw what he held in his hand – a hunting knife. He then picked up the pace and came within a few feet of her and reached out to grab her arm.

They were within feet of the falls. The roar of the water was deafening. She could see Xavier yell something at her. She turned and pushed her way into the foliage and then slipped on a wet rock, falling over a ledge, slipping, sliding, down wet, mossy rocks, hundreds of feet. Somewhere on the fall down, she banged her head and lost consciousness.

"Where is she?! What happened to her?!" Mercy screamed at Xavier.

Xavier looked back at Mercy. "I think she fell. Come here, take my pack and get the rope out. It's very slippery here. I need to tie myself to something here. I think there's a cliff through these trees." They worked together wrapping the rope around Xavier's waist and tying it to a trunk of a tree.

He took small steps through the bushes until he came to a ledge that was mossy, wet and slippery. He slid to his stomach and looked over the ledge. It was a long drop and at least a few hundred feet before it was enveloped by the jungle foliage. He couldn't see a body and he couldn't see how anyone could survive the fall.

Seattle, WA

Tomas had changed his plans and stayed three extra days. Iris played tour guide and shared all her favorite places with him. They traipsed all over Seattle, took long walks in her favorite parks and botanical gardens, visited the beautiful campus of the University of Washington with its fabulous and timeless architecture; enjoyed the tourist attractions of Pioneer Square and the Seattle waterfront, and she even rented a small sail boat, and the two of them spent a lazy afternoon on Lake Washington.

Finally, yesterday, she had driven him home to her house on Fox Island, where they walked and talked for hours. She fixed him a salmon and salad dinner, and over a good Washington wine, they reveled in a new friendship and the intimacy that had developed so easily in such a short time.

Iris had not felt such peace and contentment for as long as she could remember. Even the distress and the trauma from the previous year began to dissipate. She had spoken to her daughter, Nina, and her granddaughter, Siri, earlier, and their cheerful chatter helped soften her heart.

Sitting across from Tomas on her deck, satiated with good food and wine, and a tender feeling of true companionship, she took in the twinkle in his eyes and the warmth of his smile, and sighed. She thought about him leaving tomorrow and wondered how they might continue this relationship from such a long distance. Different countries, different cultures, and even different time zones. And would he even want to?

When Tomas went on his laptop to retrieve his boarding pass for the next day's flight, he noticed an email that was marked urgent. It was from Sally Meza.

"Hmm…an email from Sally."

"What's up?" Iris asked, noting the worried tone in Tomas' voice.

"A friend of hers has gone missing."

"Missing?" Iris' heart began racing. Sally had been a key player last year, when Nina had gone missing. Memories came rushing back to her. "Who?"

"Has she talked to you about her doctor friend? A naturopathic? Leslie Goetz?"

"Yes, she has. It's her? Sally's talked a lot about her and what good friends they were becoming. What else does she say?"

"She says that Leslie has been missing now for three days, and no one knows where she is. She wants me to help her find her. She wants to know when I'll be back. Oh, and she says hello to you."

"Good grief…that's concerning. Are you going to be able to help her?"

"Well…yes…It is my line of business now. Although, this most likely will be pro-bono," he added under his breath. "Hopefully, she will have returned by the time I get home. If not, it looks like I'll be heading over to the east side once again." A pained look passed between them.

The next day, they were up before dawn in order to get Tomas to the airport in time. The sun was rising over Mt. Rainier. The air was clear and the sky was dotted with pinkish-orange clouds. They were quiet on the drive. Iris was afraid to say anything, not sure she could hold her emotions in. They had not talked about the future. What future could there be? Costa Rica held demons and terrifying nightmares for her.

As they neared the off-ramp for the airport, Tomas finally spoke. "Iris, I know your experience in Costa Rica last year was very frightening for you and your family. I know it will always be a dark memory, but I'm hoping that you might be able to give my country a second chance."

With her heart beating rapidly, Iris glanced over at Tomas. Could she ever go back there? Could she get on a plane and fly down there and not relive each moment of that nightmarish time?

She didn't respond until they had pulled up in front of the drop off zone at the airport. They got out of the car and Iris walked over to the passenger side.

Tomas engulfed her in a tight embrace and whispered into her ear, "Just think about it...please."

With tears in her eyes, she pulled away and looked into his eyes. "I don't know…I don't know…" she responded.

He looked at her and gave her another hug, then turned and walked away.

Michael Turner couldn't believe his good fortune. He was being sent to Costa Rica to scout out the potential to open an office there, and possibly a lab. Along with that, he was instructed to expand the company's territory into Brazil and Argentina. It was a dream come true, but the company had been pretty insistent that he settle into Costa Rica first. Before he left, Dr. Zachary Walker asked to meet with him once more. During the meeting, he made two pointed requests of Michael.

"You are aware of our trial with the oncology drug RX-T38?"

Though, Michael was not directly involved with the marketing of this drug – that usually happened after the drug was officially approved, he did know that Dr. Walker was the lead researcher of the drug and heavily and emotionally invested in the trials. He nodded affirmatively to the doctor.

"Well, as you know, we can only do trials of RX-T38 in less restrictive countries. Costa Rica is one of them. There's a doctor there who has four patients in the trials. I'd like you to visit with him as soon as you can. Give him some friendly support and try to get a sense of how he thinks the drug is doing. He's been up here for a symposium once or twice. A nice guy. He recently contacted me about one of his patients doing really well. I'd appreciate it if you'd follow up with him. Find out how his other patients are doing."

"Also, I've talked to Jack, and he's okay with this. I'm making a case for our company to expand into supplements. Costa Rica might offer us the opportunity to extract some indigenous substances and open a lab there. There's a wealth of materials I'd like to get my hands on."

"Sure, sure," Michael responded.

Something was niggling in the recesses of his mind. Fragments of a conversation. Then it came back to him. Jack had been telling him about the conversation at that banquet with Gretta something or other, a wealthy investor, having something to do with alternative healing modalities. He did know, though, that the big pharmas went to great lengths to shut down or discredit natural supplements and their companies' claims of supposed success stories. He tossed the thought aside.

Dr. Walker handed Michael a piece of paper with Dr. Ferdinand Olivera's name and contact information.

"Stay in touch, Michael. I admit I'm a bit envious. If I were a younger man, it would be me making this trip. I'm sure there's an abundance of native plants deep in the jungles that have yet to be discovered. Here's my email. Let me know how it goes with Dr. Olivera."

Michael pondered why such an interest on this one doctor. Well, that would be the first thing he did when he got there. Look up the good doctor. He couldn't put his finger on it, but there seemed to be some mixed messages being handed out here. Oh well, he wasn't about to look a gift horse in the face; he was going to Costa Rica. He couldn't wait to tell Anne about this.

San Jose, Costa Rica

Dr. Ferdinand Olivera had spent his free moments over the last few days – limited as they were – trying to track down the patient that Simone Jenkins had mentioned, the one who was also seeing the naturopathic doctor she had referred to. First, though, he had put in two calls to Dr. Leslie Goetz, the naturopathic. He had left voice mails both times. He had also emailed her. She still hadn't returned his calls or responded to his email inquiry.

He had called Simone who had given him Leslie Goetz's phone number and email address. She said that she'd had an appointment last Saturday with Leslie in Puerto Viejo, and gotten a little bit more of the special tincture, since she had run out of it. She mentioned that Dr. Goetz had given her the last of the tincture and was planning to get more from her source.

He then spent the entire morning calling around in Limon to some of his colleagues trying to find out if any of their patients were experiencing remissions. Finally, he had some luck. An oncologist by the name of Herman Rivera returned his call.

"Dr. Olivera, I'm Herman Rivera. Dr. Goldstein gave me your name. Said you were looking into particular cases of patients with cancer and their treatments and incidences of remission."

"Yes, hello, Dr. Rivera. Thanks for getting back to me. I have been doing some research. I've a patient here with a serious cancer of the blood, which has recently gone into remission. I've been using an experimental drug from the States, and this patient's condition right now is remarkable. I've got three other patients on the same chemo, but they are doing poorly. Tell me, how are you doing with your cancer patients? What treatment regimens are you using?"

As Olivera was talking on the phone to Dr. Rivera, he googled Dr. Rivera's name and came up with a bio-sketch of the doctor. Dr. Rivera had been trained at the Universidad de Costa Rica which was well respected for its school of medicine. Olivera, himself, had been trained in the States at the San Diego branch of the University of California. He knew that he would have had just as rigorous of an education at the University of Costa Rica, but had taken the opportunity to study abroad.

"Well, I wish I had good news to share. I did have a patient who had a serious cancer that had metastasized to the bones, originally started out as a lymphoma. Recently, he had a remarkable turn-around. I was so pleased. You see, two months ago, we stopped all his oncology treatment. The treatment regime had become unbearable for him. His family felt helpless, and they all begged me to give him a break. He agreed. But I knew he knew that the end was near."

"But you said that he had a remission of sorts?" Olivera asked.

"Well, yes, it seems that he did. He had been off all drugs except for a few supplements that he insisted on continuing. And then I saw him after about a month, expecting the worse. Instead, he was so much better. Still thin and weak, but definitely better. Of course, I just wrote it off to being off the chemo, which had really done a number on his immune system. Then I saw him just a couple of weeks ago, and I was confounded by the improvement in the man. He was stronger, had put on a bit of weight. I ordered some blood tests and asked him to come back this week."

"This is amazing. It is very similar to a situation I have with one of my patients. But, I don't understand, this is such good news, why did you say you wish you had better news to share?"

Rivera responded, "The day before his return appointment, I got a call from his wife. She told me he had been killed in an accident. Hit by a car. Can you believe it? The guy is practically cured from a terminal illness, only to be killed in an accident. By the way, I got his blood test results, and there were no indications of cancer markers in his blood."

Olivera was speechless for a moment. "What a shame," he finally responded. "Tell me, what do you credit his remission to?"

"I honestly don't have a clue," Rivera answered.

"Was he being treated by any other doctors? A naturopathic, by chance?"

"Well, I suppose he could have been. He was taking some supplements and herbs; he had to get them from somewhere. I did get a list of the supplements and herbs he insisted on taking. They all looked pretty harmless to me. You know patients sometimes think they're going to offend us if they seek out alternative therapies."

Olivera asked, "I know I'm going out on a limb here, but would you be willing to give me the name of the patient and his wife? I'd like to explore what other treatments he might have been on, if you don't mind."

"Well, it is confidential, but I think though, to cover myself, it would be best if I asked his wife to call you. She can determine what information she is comfortable sharing."

"Thank you, thank you! I'll let you know if I learn anything helpful that can explain these remissions. Please don't hesitate to call me if you have any more information that you might find helpful to this puzzle."

Later that day, a call came through for Olivera. He had just finished with his last patient, so the timing was good.

"This is Dr. Olivera."

"Hello, Dr. Rivera gave me your name and number. He said you had some questions about my husband."

"Yes, yes! Thank you so much for calling me back. Sra., may I ask what your husband's name is?"

"What is it you want to know? Tell me that, first," she replied.

"Um, let's see. How to begin. You see, I'm an oncologist and I have a patient who has recently gone into remission. She, my patient, was on a trial drug, but none of my other patients on the same treatment have gotten better. As a matter of fact, they are having serious side effects from the treatment and no improvement in the status of their cancer. So, I've was piqued by her improvement and wanted to find out from any of my colleagues if they were having any luck with their patients, and if so, what treatment modalities were being used."

"Oh, I see. You want to know if my husband was doing anything else besides getting the chemotherapy from Dr. Rivera's clinic, right?"

"Well, yes, that's exactly what I'd like to know." Olivera noted the sadness in the woman's voice, causing him to feel a twinge of regret for bothering her.

"Joshua, my husband, was seeing a naturopathic doctor in Puerto Viejo, a Leslie Goetz. I went along with it because I felt that it gave him a bit of control over his own situation. In fact, I think it was helping him."

And there it was. Olivera thought it could be a coincidence, but he didn't really believe in coincidences. "Thank you, this is helpful. Do you recall what type of medicine she was giving him?"

"Yes, she gave him a small bottle of drops that he was instructed to put in a tea three times a day. He followed her instructions religiously. After about two weeks of taking the drops, I noticed his health was improving significantly. It was difficult the first few days, and he almost stopped taking the drops due to the severe vomiting and diarrhea. But he insisted on continuing and I'm glad he did."

Olivera was quite intrigued by this news. He was even more anxious to get in touch with Dr. Goetz and find out more about the medicine she provided. "Sra., may I ask what your husband's last name was?"

"Marrone, Joshua Marrone," she responded hesitantly.

Sra. Marrone, thank you so much for this information. And may I say that I am very sorry for the loss of your husband to such an unfortunate accident."

Dully, she responded, "Thank you. It is ironic that he was getting better to just be killed in such a random way. I guess I'm happy at least that he'd had a few weeks of relative health. He died a happier man. Goodbye, Doctor Olivera. Good luck with your research."

Bribri, Costa Rica

Sally Meza was frantic. It had been four days and still no sign of Leslie. She had driven to the Bribri office, and peered through windows. No sign of life. She needed to get in. If nothing else, she needed to check on Leslie's cat.

Where could her friend be and God, please let Tomas get over here as soon as possible. She asked around the neighboring shops and found the shopkeeper at the one next door to be equally concerned.

A beautiful Caribbean woman with a natural afro and flawless skin voiced her worries. "My friend is never gone this long. Yesterday I went into her office and found her cat upstairs. I fed her and straightened up a bit. No sign of Leslie. Just a blinking light on her phone. I went over again, yesterday morning, to feed Kitty again. Still no sign of Leslie. I left a note on her desk, in case she came back late, to call me."

"You have a key to her place?" Sally asked, relieved that at least Kitty had been cared for.

"Yes, we look after each other's places when either one of us is away. I am worried sick, though. I called over to her Puerto Viejo office and no answer. I called and called. I even emailed her. Nothing!"

God, this was bad. She put in a call to Tomas and left a message telling him that she was in Bribri, and asked him to please, please, call her back as soon as possible. She asked the shopkeeper if she would let her in to look around Leslie's clinic and apartment to see if there were any clues as to her whereabouts.

The woman only hesitated a few seconds, and then nodded. "Yes, let me go with you. I have spent a lot of time with Leslie in her place. Maybe, together we can find something that will help us. She is a very private person, and she does go off a lot, but normally, she's not gone more than two nights, and she usually tells me so that I can check on her cat. To be gone this long...this just isn't like her. By the way, my name is Toni."

"Thanks, Toni. I'm Sally. Sally Meza. Let's go."

Toni grabbed the key and the two women walked next door to Leslie's clinic. Toni opened the door, and as she did, the cat flew out the door. The shades had been pulled, and the office seemed a bit dark.

"Hmm, this is strange," Toni said, as she opened the shades and looked around. "I'm pretty sure these were up yesterday, and...oh my gosh, look at the counter!"

Sally looked over at the reception counter that separated the waiting room from the shelves of herbs, supplements and teas. There were dozens of small dropper bottles placed on the counter, most open with their caps off. Some were on their sides with the contents spilled. Behind the counter on the shelves, boxes of teas, and bottles of jars were strewn around and on the floor. Drawers were pulled open. The small refrigerator door stood open, with all the contents tossed out onto the floor.

"This was not like this yesterday!" exclaimed Toni.

They walked through the reception area into Leslie's office. Her desk drawers were pulled out; the filing cabinet drawers were pulled open and patient files were scattered on the floor.

"I think her laptop is gone," Toni said "although, she could have it with her. This is creepy. It looks like someone was looking for something. I mean, I don't think anyone would want to steal her herbs...she doesn't keep any narcotics. That I know for sure. What would anyone want here?"

Sally stood there in shock. She felt sick to her stomach. This wasn't good, not good at all. Just then her cell phone rang, and noticing the caller identification, she answered.

"Tomas! Oh God, I'm so worried. She's gone, she's really gone. And someone has been in her office and ransacked it!" Sally blurted this all out in a frantic voice.

"Sally, slow down a bit. Where are you right now?"

"I'm standing in Leslie's office in Bribri. A friend of hers is here; she let me in. Somebody went through all her herbs and supplements, files, desk drawers. Her computer is missing! And this just happened in the last twenty-four hours!"

"How do you know that?"

"Toni, her neighbor, was just in here yesterday, and said things looked normal then, other than Leslie being gone and not letting anyone know. She usually has Toni check on her cat when she plans to be gone."

"Is her car there?"

"I didn't notice it out front where she usually parks it. Just a minute, let me ask. Toni, have you seen her car around the office?"

"No, but I didn't even think. Let me take a quick run around the block to see if it's here. I'll be right back," Toni responded, as she quickly left the office.

"Tomas, please, can you come over? Or tell me what to do? I haven't contacted the local police yet. Should I?"

"That's probably a good idea. How long has it been now? Four days?"

"Yes!"

"Yeah, you go on over to the Bribri station. When I get off here, I'll call and give them a heads up. They've got a pretty good staff there. I've worked with them in the past."

The door flew open when Toni came back. "No, her car isn't anywhere on this block; I even checked two blocks over. But she never parks anywhere else but on this street, or the side street next to my shop."

"Tomas, her car isn't anywhere in the vicinity. I saw her last Saturday in Puerto Viejo. And Toni said she hasn't seen her back here since. We met for breakfast. She had driven in early from Bribri for an appointment. I'm scared. A couple of weeks ago, she took me up the Talamanca Mountains to get some herbs. But we had a guide. What if she went up on her own?"

"Okay, well, let me think. I just got back into town this morning. Let me take care of some business here; then I should be able to leave this evening. I'll drive over to Bribri. Will you be there?"

"Yes, I'll stay here. I'll get a motel room. Do you want me to reserve you a room? It will be late when you get here."

"Yeah, that's a good idea. You can text me the details. Okay, I should hit the road in a couple of hours, so I should be in Bribri around midnight. I'll see you first thing in the morning. In the meantime, go on over to the police station and make a report. Or it's possible that they know something. Find out what you can."

"Thank you so much, Tomas. I didn't know where else to turn."

"Of course, Sally. I'm sure this will all work out. See you in the morning."

Tomas hung up the phone, but he wasn't feeling very positive about the situation. Four days was a long time for someone to be missing, especially if the person had gone up into the mountains. He knew a bit about the Talamancas. Most of the slopes were a dense jungle with very few foot trails. He knew there were still some indigenous tribes and a few scattered villages across the massive slopes. Some of them still had minimal contact with the town people.

Organizing a search party would be difficult and expensive. He was counting on the local authorities to take the lead. He had so much to do right now; he needed to get caught up on business, and Jeremiah had informed him that they had some new potential clients....paying clients, which would be nice. He had an office and staff, albeit a small staff, to support. His couple of extra days in Seattle didn't help, but he sure didn't have any regrets.

Thinking about Iris brought a brief smile to his face, followed quickly by a pang of sorrow. How could they carry on a relationship? He was pretty sure she'd never step foot in his country again. And, having lived in the States previously for several years, he had no real desire to return and make that his residence. He was probably better off just getting on with the business of putting her out of his mind. But he knew that would be very tough to do.

Sally asked Toni where the police station was.

"Look, I'll just take you there. It's easier for me to show you. Plus, I can help with reporting Leslie missing. I probably should have gone sooner than this! I'm feeling pretty stupid right now," Toni remarked glumly. "God, she's always been so mysterious about her comings and goings. But, she usually lets me know when she leaves and when to expect her back. This time, she just left without telling me. Probably, she didn't expect to be gone very long. "Come on, we can walk," continued Toni. "It's only about four blocks."

Sally didn't find the small town very attractive. It didn't seem to have that Caribbean charm that Puerto Viejo offered. There also weren't swarms of tourists as there were in the coastal towns. They passed a bank, some shops, a few fresh fruit stands, and an office identified as the Red Cross. Wow, thought Sally to herself, the Red Cross here? Toni guided her across the street from the Red Cross building to the local police station -- a one story brick structure that took up half the block.

"This is also the jail," Toni remarked.

The two women entered the brick building and approached the young uniformed man behind the first counter. It took over two hours to go through the reporting process. They found out that Tomas Vasquez had just called the station to discuss the situation. Another officer walked out from a back room and talked more with Sally and Toni about Leslie's disappearance. He barked some orders to the young man at that counter and a couple of other officers sitting at desks at the rear of the room. Sally felt some relief as it appeared that the police were taking some action and were planning to organize a search process.

He queried Sally and Toni about Leslie's routines. Sally explained that she had last seen Leslie the previous Saturday in Puerto Viejo. She and Toni explained about the two offices and then Sally told him about her trip with Leslie up into the mountains the previous week.

She offered the name of Leslie's guide – Miguel, but didn't know his last name. For reasons, she didn't ponder, she left out the part about meeting up with Grandmother. When asked why the doctor made the trips up to the mountain. Sally found herself fudging on that information also.

"Dr. Goetz has befriended some of the mountain people and visits the closest village occasionally to provide some medical care, when requested."

Leslie had been so protective of her journeys into the mountain region to obtain the herbs from Grandmother, that Sally felt honor bound not to disclose anything about why the naturopathic made those trips. Part of her wondered if it was wise for her to protect that information. Could Leslie's disappearance have anything to do with her fears about being followed?

If Leslie was with Miguel, Sally was sure she'd be safe. Or, did she even go up the mountain? Maybe she was lost somewhere else…or kidnapped…Now she was letting her imagination get the best of her, thinking back to the previous year and the kidnapping of Nina Navarra.

"But, when she goes into Puerto Viejo to her other office, she often uses the back road. Maybe we should check that route. It can be muddy from flash floods. Maybe she crashed and is hurt. I didn't come that way today cause it's a pretty crazy drive. Leslie liked it for the adventure of it."

A concerned expression came over the officer's face. Sally could almost hear the thoughts in his head: Crazy chicas! as he responded, more under his breath, "We really need to close that road down."

And then a bit louder, he called over his shoulder to a couple of the men nearby. "Jose, Marco – take the four-wheel and drive the route to PV the back way. Check for any evidence of recent travel and look carefully for a possible accident or car. And while you're in PV, ask around; see if anyone has any information about Dr. Goetz."

He looked back to Sally and Toni and asked, "What kind of vehicle does she drive?"

Toni responded, "Uh, she has a little green Ford Fiesta. It's old and kind of beat up."

The officer rolled his eyes. "And she drives that on that road?" As Jose and Marco were leaving, the officer spoke to them, "Check around PV and the vicinity for the Ford Fiesta."

He turned back to Sally and Toni. "I think I know the 'Miguel' you speak of. He has family in town here. I will check with them. In the meantime, if either of you hear from Dr. Goetz please let us know right away. Your friend, Sr. Vasquez will be here in the morning and he has offered to assist us. It will be needed; it takes a lot of resources to look for missing persons in these parts, especially up on the mountain."

Sally was relieved that the police were taking an interest. This certainly hadn't been the case last year, when Nina Navarra had gone missing. It took cajoling the OIJ, the investigation being led by Tomas Vasquez, to come in before they finally found the young woman.

And it had almost been too late. Nina had been missing for almost a week. She had been kidnapped for ransom, but it had been a case of mistaken identity. The kidnappers had grabbed the wrong woman. And, the leader of the gang had been a ruthless and cruel perpetrator. It was if he enjoyed inflicting pain and control over others, more than the monetary rewards of his schemes.

The police in Puerto Viejo had looked the other way when it came to dealings with the gang leader. One of the officers had been on the take and was being blackmailed in the process. They only pretended to show an interest in the search for Nina.

It took Tomas Vasquez and his colleague, Jeremiah Valencia, to follow the kidnappers deep into the jungle to a small hut where Nina had been stowed. At the same time, some fast thinking on Iris Dibiase's part and Sally's determination set things in motion that ultimately resulted in setting Nina free.

As expected, Tomas Vasquez arrived in Bribri very late at night. He'd been in the town a few times before and had a pretty good idea where the hotel was that Sally had booked for him. It was a small family-run lodge one street back from the main drag of the town. It was also just a three block walk to the police station. When he went into the hotel office, an envelope with his name and a key inside was propped up on the counter. The envelope also contained a small map of the hotel grounds directing him to his room.

The night air was still and humid, the buzzing of bugs and a fountain provided background sound to an otherwise quiet night. The lodgings were made up of adjoining bungalows – two rooms to each small building. Each room had a porch with a hanging hammock and two chairs and a small table. Small lights guided the pathway.

Tomas wandered through the property, peering at the numbers on each building until he located his room. Lights were out in most of the other rooms, but the light was on in the room adjoining his. Just as he stepped up on the porch, the door was flung open and a disheveled looking woman broke the silence of the night with a loud call out.

"Tomas! Thank God you're here!"

Tomas looked over at Sally Meza. The sight of her brought a smile to his weary face. She'd done something different with her hair, short, but still wild and sticking out in all directions. She had on sweatpants and an overlarge tee-shirt. He stepped off his porch and met her on the steps of hers with a big hug.

She was a charmer, so unassuming and with a heart bigger than an elephant's. At first her insistence on staying in touch with him had made him a bit uncomfortable, but now, he counted her as one of his dearest friends. She cared about people, to the point of putting her own life in jeopardy if circumstances required. And here she was again, caring about someone.

"Sally, tell me, have you learned anything new since our call today?"

Sally filled him in on the visit to the police station and exclaimed once again how glad she was that he had come. As if, he thought to himself, he was here and could save the day. Almost five days missing. The chances were pretty slim for a recovery. But, what the hell, she cared...and expected him to...and therefore, he did.

They made plans to meet for coffee at dawn to determine next steps and then parted for the rest of the short night.

Chapter 6

Seattle, WA

Dr. Zachary Walker met Gretta for lunch that day. She had some news about events in Costa Rica. They started with their usual glasses of Dom Perignon champagne and catching up on each other's lives.

"So, Gretta, tell me. What's going on? What news do you have?"

"Zack, my people in Costa Rica contacted me yesterday with some disturbing news. They had followed the naturopathic doctor up into the mountains, hoping to be led to the source of the medicine that she had been giving to Simone Jenkins. Unfortunately, they lost her."

"What do you mean, they lost her?"

"When they confronted her, she stepped away and fell off a cliff. They spent a couple of hours trying to find her, but couldn't. The jungle is too dense. They don't think she could have survived the fall. And then they had to leave, as it was getting late in the day, and they were concerned about finding their way out and back down the mountain."

"Damn it, Gretta! If we can't find Dr. Goetz, or if she's dead, God forbid, then how are we going to locate the source of the medicine?"

"Wait, there's more. Evidently, Dr. Olivera tracked down another patient of Dr. Goetz's not on your trials who had also experienced a remission of sorts."

"How did they do that?"

"They didn't say, but trust me, they have their ways. They are very adept at bugging phones and hacking into personal computers. At any rate, they located the other patient who lived in Limon. They were following him and even managed to get into his house and found a bottle of the tincture; unfortunately, it was nearly empty. It's on its way here."

"That's great. Even a drop would be something I could work with."

"Yeah, but something unfortunate happened. I hesitate to tell you. The less you know the better."

"What? What is it? Don't hold back on me."

"This patient, I won't tell you his name – surprised them as they were leaving his house. Evidently, he was in another bedroom napping. They aren't usually this careless. They had not checked the whole house, and evidently there's a small bedroom at the opposite end of the house from the master bedroom where they found the medicine."

"Oh god, what happened?"

"Well, they were outside walking down the driveway and getting into their car, when this man walked out the front door. He came running after them with his phone in his hand taking pictures of their car as it sped away. The next day, he was hit by a car in downtown Limon and died at the scene."

"Was it your people?"

"I didn't ask. They didn't say. But trust me, they will have covered their tracks. They told me they had been able to extract some information from his patient files – this time going through an electronic medical record system. They didn't need to break into the doctor's office to get this information. The man had stopped his chemo a couple of months ago. The doctor noted in the chart the labs and general overall improvement of the patient just a couple of weeks ago."

Walker pondered the situation. Jesus, what could they do now? How could they get their hands on the source of the medicine?

"Zack, there's even one more thing."

"What is it? I hope it's something good."

"It could be. The local police in Bribri are now involved in the search for Leslie Goetz. And, evidently, a private investigator, someone that used to be pretty high up in the OIJ, which is similar to the FBI, is getting involved to help search for her. My contacts are keeping their eyes on the situation, and who knows, maybe they'll be led to the missing woman, or to people that know something about her connections with the mountain tribes."

Gretta paused for a moment, and looking intently into her friend's aging face, she asked: "Zachary, tell me, why is this so important to you?"

Walker paused and then took a deep breath and let out an audible sigh. He looked deflated, and Gretta noticed for the first time how old and sallow her friend looked.

"Zachary, are you okay? Are you sick?" she asked in a quiet voice.

"I don't know, I don't know. I haven't been well for weeks now. Most likely just the stress of the job."

"Have you had tests done?"

"Not yet. You know that doctors are the worst patients," he responded with an attempt at humor and a sour smile.

"God damn it, Zack. You are my dearest and oldest friend. You need to take care of yourself."

"You asked why this search for the plant is so important. Gretta, I'll be honest with you – it's about time that I was honest with someone. I haven't been honest with myself in months. The new drug RX-T38 that has been in trials in Europe, Mexico, Costa

Rica, and Brazil, has been an abysmal failure. Not even an iota of promise. Zero.

In fact, people have gotten sicker from it. Some have died. I haven't spoken a word of this to anyone, as I am the lead researcher and have been analyzing the results on my own. It's bound to get out. And then I'm ruined, and the company will have a huge stain on it and there will be significant financial consequences."

"But, Zack, surely you won't be held responsible. These things happen, don't they? Lots of trials don't work out."

"I took this on on my own. I was so sure this was going to be the next big breakthrough in the treatment of cancer. I wanted all the glory for myself. I cut corners, kept people out of the loop. I've been working all hours of the day and night to get this off the ground. I've...."

He hesitated, drew in a deep breath and let it out slowly, "I've siphoned some money, actually quite a lot of money, from another project. My department's management analyst has been trying to meet with me lately. I keep putting her off. I don't know, maybe I'm being paranoid, but I swear she's been looking at me strangely. Even some of my lab assistants on the project I 'borrowed' from seem wary around me.

Christ, Gretta, I'm worn out right now. I need something to turn things around, take away the focus off this experimental trial. On top of that, if anyone from the Canadian firm gets wind of this, I fear they will pull out of the negotiations for the merger. The truth is, we need them more than they need us. They are flush with capital. And they're making inroads into the Southern hemisphere. Yes, they're smaller, but they are lean and very efficient. They'd pull out in a minute if they found out about the dismal failure of my much touted experimental trial."

Gretta reached over and took her friend's hand and squeezed it. "Don't worry Zack, we'll fix this. In the meantime, I'll make a contribution to your lab. You can direct it back into the project you took from." She looked up into his eyes and was startled to see tears spilling out.

"Gretta…."

"Shhh, Zack, this is just a bump in the road. We've pulled together and through difficult times before. I will get to that herb or plant, or whatever the hell it is and we'll turn this around."

She looked into the tired eyes of her friend and wondered if she could pull him out of this. She'd never seen him look so deflated. Again, she wondered if he was ill.

Michael Turner was pleasantly surprised that the company had provided him with a business-class ticket. He relaxed comfortably in his seat, enjoying a mimosa and a delicate omelet, feeling a little guilty as he thought about the rows of cramped travelers behind the dividing curtain.

The last few days were a blur. He'd had to work quickly to sublet his apartment, change his mailing address, handle some business and let his family and close friends know that he would be gone for at least three months. He was hoping to make it more like three years.

Surprisingly, the hard part had been telling Anne about his plans. He couldn't really grasp what he was feeling about her. They hadn't been intimate, other than a few hugs and one or two lingering kisses. He was attracted to her and felt that she was attracted to him, but somehow the heat stayed deep inside as if they didn't want to jinx the relationship. She hadn't given him any indication that she was looking for anything more. She felt like a good friend and he believed she was a good person.

Something weighed on her and he thought that whatever it was, it was interfering with her getting too close to him. Yes, he knew about her parents, about her father's illness, and also her confusion about next steps in her professional life. She was unique. Different than any other woman he had encountered before. Even Debra.

It was still hard to think of Debra. She was quite different from Anne. Debra had been petite, with short, black hair, huge dark eyes, and wide full lips, in a perpetual smile. God, he missed her.

It had been four years since she died, and it still felt like just last week. They were so in love. Had been friends since high school, lovers in college, and married when they both turned 25. They had ten blissful years together, putting off having babies because they were so darn wrapped up in each other. They both had good jobs and travelled a lot.

Just when they began to think about settling down a bit and considering starting a family, he felt a lump in her left breast. They had been in bed together and it was during a languid love-making session that he felt the lump. It was already peanut size and hard. He remembered clearly how his heart started beating wildly. He had a bad premonition that he wanted to shove way down into a black hole.

He pulled her hand up and laid it on her breast. She touched her breast and looked over at him. Tears filled her eyes. The thing they had managed to push out of their everyday consciousness now engulfed them. Debra's mother and her older sister had both had aggressive breast cancers and both had died in the last five years.

Michael and Debra had talked about her risks in the past. They had considered going to a geneticist to test for the breast cancer gene that sometimes runs in families. But, unfortunately, they kept putting it off. Both stayed in a state of denial, not wanting to imagine anything that could alter their idyllic existence. God, how naïve.

"Don't worry, darling," Debra finally said. "It's probably just a cyst. I've had one before. I'll make an appointment first thing Monday morning."

Well, it wasn't a cyst, and they both knew it wouldn't be. And it all happened fast, way too fast. Within a week, Debra had a double mastectomy and lymph nodes removed under both arms. Within two weeks, she was on a course of daily radiation therapy, coupled with intensive chemotherapy. The prognosis was grim.

Six months later, Michael buried his beautiful wife and all their dreams and life with her. In the ensuing four years, he was more or less functioning on auto pilot at work. Surprisingly, he did well at work; it was the only thing that kept him going. Got him up out of bed after sleepless nights and out the door.

San Jose, Costa Rica's capital, is situated in a fertile upland basin in the heart of the country. Michael found the city to be congested and noisy. He had taken a taxi from the airport and was dropped off in the commercial center of the city which was crowded with large hotels, shops, and modern high-rises.

He checked into his hotel, unpacked some of his luggage and flopped down on his bed. The room was air-conditioned, which was good, as he was sticky and hot from his trip and the taxi ride. He thought a nap, followed by a shower would revive him.

Later, feeling somewhat refreshed, he wandered down to the lobby and picked up a city walking map. The hotel was located on a large park-like plaza. The evening dusk was settling in, but there were still many people sitting on the park benches, children playing and chasing pigeons, numerous little carts were in place, selling fresh mango on sticks, flavored with chili powder and fruit smoothies. The air was warm and humid; large bulky clouds threatened a downpour.

He strolled around the plaza, taking in the sites and noting the lush tropical smells overlaid with a sooty odor. The people were an interesting mix of tall, light skinned, blond hair with European physical traits, and squat, dark skinned people with black coarse hair and long braids trailing down the backs of the women and girls. He noted that the European characteristics outnumbered the more indigenous look. He'd read somewhere in his research on Costa Rica, that the early Spanish settlers had done a fairly efficient job of decimating the indigenous people.

He finally settled on a park bench, taking it all in--the aromas, the kaleidoscope presentation of people, the competing music in the background. Glancing around, he noted several outside restaurants, with tables pouring into the walkways. Patrons enjoying an evening drink or cup of coffee and a smoke. It was all exotic to Michael and he was thrilled at this interlude in his life.

Later, he wandered back into the hotel, found the restaurant on the top floor and enjoyed a nice steak with rice and beans and a decent wine, before retiring for the night. The company had made arrangements to lease him a furnished apartment in a high rise, which he thought was nice. He had no idea, otherwise, how to go about finding a place to live.

The firm had also given him the name of a local contact to guide him about the first few days. His contact was with a law firm which specialized in helping people navigate the different avenues of doing business and living in Costa Rica. He had a breakfast appointment to meet with Eva Monroe, the contact, the next day. They were to meet in the hotel lobby.

Michael woke before dawn. The time change put him about three hours off his clock. He decided to check his email and see if anything was going on at work that he needed to attend to.

There was a new email from Anne. She wanted to know how his flight was and his impressions so far of San Jose. He smiled as he responded back, his heart warming. It had been a long time since someone showed a genuine caring about him. It didn't seem as if Anne had any hidden agendas.

By the end of a long and tiring day, a lot had been accomplished. He met the lovely Eva Monroe early in the hotel lobby. She was a statuesque, voluptuous sight, dressed in a tawny gold suit, with a skirt that ended mid-thigh and a tasteful, slightly plunging silk top with a jacket and several long gold chains around her neck.

She greeted Michael warmly with a light hug and brush of a kiss on his cheek. She had a mischievous glint in her green eyes and shoulder length golden blond hair. She put her arm through his and guided him to the door. Bob oh boy, he thought, it would not be too hard to adapt to this intimate Latino warmth and friendliness that seemed a norm.

Outside the hotel, a black sedan pulled up and they got into the back seat. Eva gave instructions to the driver in Spanish, and off they went. The day started with a lavish breakfast at a grand old hotel several minutes away from downtown. Eva gently quizzed him on his readiness to embrace a new culture and gave him many tips on the tico way.

Later, they went to a high rise apartment building that was situated on the edge of a beautiful park. Here, she presented him to his roomy two bedroom apartment that had a view of downtown. The apartment was nicely furnished. One of the bedrooms was converted into an office with all the necessary amenities. Even the kitchen was stocked with dishes and appliances. He looked in the cupboards and found some food items and the refrigerator was full of fresh fruit, juices, beer, eggs, and vegetables.

Eva introduced him to the concierge who gave him his keys and took him on a tour of the building. Michael was duly impressed with the effort of preparation for him. He had never experienced anything so first class in all of his other assignments in other countries. Eva then took him to a bank to get him set up with a bank account, and she gave him directions to food markets and the pharmacy.

Later in the day, they ended up in his hotel lobby enjoying a refreshing drink and appetizers before he went up to get his belongings and then checked out of the hotel. Eva then deposited him back into the black sedan with instructions to the driver to take Michael back to his new dwelling. With another brush of warm lips to his cheek and a quick hug, she said goodbye, giving him her card and telling him to not hesitate to contact her if he needed anything...anything at all, and with a wink, she turned to leave.

The next morning, Michael was up at his new desk and setting up his calendar and tasks that he needed to accomplish. He planned to make some appointments with some other pharmaceutical reps stationed in the country to develop some collegiality and community.

Contrary to what one might expect in relationships between competitors, pharmaceutical reps often sought each other out to learn about the big players in the community, to give each other tips, and to form a club of sorts. Often, they were selling different products anyways, so working together opened doors and provided important connections and allies.

Not only was Michael charged with engaging big health systems and introducing them to new products from his company, but he had the somewhat vague, but in his mind more compelling charge to research the potential to buy or partner with a 'natural' or 'alternative' supplemental or health modality company. He really had no idea how to go about this task. But ever the adventurous sort, he was intrigued by where this effort might lead.

As he was going through his notes, he came upon the slip of paper that Dr. Walker had given him with the name of the doctor here that he was supposed to connect with, Ferdinand Olivera. Walker had wanted Michael to check in with him, as he was the oncologist involved in the RX-T38 trials, Walker's pet project. Ah, the doctor's office was in San Jose. Why not call him now? Get that assignment out of the way.

The phone call was actually quite comical. The receptionist answered in rapid Spanish. Though Michael spoke the language reasonably well, it was always hard to carry on a conversation on the phone when he couldn't read the body language or facial expressions to help translate the message. Finally, the receptionist slowed down and he was able to set an appointment with Dr. Olivera, after explaining who he was and why he wanted time with the doctor. He offered to take Olivera to lunch the next day, and so it was set.

She had been delirious for days. Coming in and out of consciousness. Aware only of a deep and penetrating pain in her shoulder and one ankle, and a voice singing, humming, a face leaning over her, long, soft hair brushing across her senses.

Later, crooning, another voice joining in. A familiar voice. Pain in her head, behind her eyes. Something warm and woodsy being spooned into her mouth. Falling back into a deep sleep, into dreams of falling, falling and then blackness.

Bribri, Costa Rica

Tomas managed a few fitful hours of sleep. He got out of bed at the crack of dawn and decided to take a walk around town. As he stepped out his door, he heard movement on the porch next door.

"You're finally awake, Tomas," Sally remarked.

"Uh, yes," he replied, glancing at his watch. "It's only 6 a.m., Sally." He could see that she had gotten little sleep. "Come along with me. Let's go find some coffee and make a plan."

She stood up and threw a small back pack over her shoulder. She was already dressed to take on the day. Jeans, a sweatshirt, and high-top sneakers. "Yes, let's go!" She exclaimed.

Over coffee and sweet rolls, they outlined their agenda for the day. "First, let's go to the police. I'll introduce myself. We need to impress upon them a sense of urgency. You and I cannot do this alone. For this area and terrain, we'll need a guide and some other trackers."

"Alright. Yes! A plan of action!" Sally responded.

As they walked the two blocks to the police station, Sally filled Tomas in on Leslie's trips up into the Talamancas and her use of indigenous plants to make herbs for her patients, and gave him more detail about her overnight trip with Leslie and her guide, Miguel, and meeting an ancient old lady whom Leslie called 'Grandmother.'

"She gave Leslie some more plants or mushrooms, or something. Leslie was very secretive about it. And stupid me, I was asleep when the Grandmother actually handed over the stuff. I think they put something in my tea to make me sleep."

"Do you think she might have gone up there? Back up to the mountain?"

"Well, I guess that's a possibility. But, maybe she got in a car accident on the back road coming back here from Puerto Viejo last weekend. It's a tricky, one lane, rutted dirt road, with lots of twists and turns.

But, if she did go up to the mountain, I can't imagine that she would go on her own. Miguel always accompanied her. It's a grueling trip, hours of hiking. And it would be easy to get lost if she was by herself. I hate to think what could happen to her if she was on her own. Or why she would even try to make the trip without Miguel. If she fell…or got lost…." Sally glanced off into space, imagining her friend at the bottom of a deep crevice.

She brought her attention back to Tomas. "Anyways, I told the police about Leslie's drive to Puerto Viejo, her other office, and how she usually took the back road. They sent some officers to make the drive and to see if they found anything. They'll probably have something to report about that. Plus, the police know Miguel; at least they said they know his family."

"Good – that's where we'll start."

By the time they arrived at the police station, the streets were filling up with people going about their business. There was a dusty, buzzing feel about the town, and it was already heating up and very humid. Shops were opening, and people were placing merchandise on the sidewalks.

They walked into the Bribri Police Station and up to the counter, where a young Latina woman in a khaki police uniform greeted them with a friendly smile. A couple of officers sitting at desks behind the counter raised their heads to study Tomas.

Tomas exchanged some greetings in Spanish and asked to speak to an Officer Hernandez, the officer he had spoken to on the phone yesterday. One of the men at the desks stood up and walked around the counter to greet Tomas Vasquez and Sally.

"Hola, Senor Vasquez y Senorita," with a nod to Sally. "I'm Sergeant Hernandez. I've been expecting you. Come along with me, we'll go into a conference room to talk."

Hernandez grabbed a folder off his desk and led them down a hallway into a small room. They sat around a small conference table. He exchanged some pleasantries with Tomas, which Sally caught the gist of. And then Hernandez abruptly switched to English which he spoke with an excellent command of the language.

"I'm glad you're here Sr. Vasquez. This case worries me. She's been missing for quite a while, and my contacts from the accessible villages have not come up with anything. Nobody's seen her, at least nobody from the closer villages. I'm aware that there are two or three villages way up in the more inaccessible and remote regions of the mountain. But, generally, they're hard to get in contact with and they move around a lot."

Tomas interrupted, "What about the guide, Miguel? Have you been in touch with him? I understand that he often takes the doctor up the mountain."

"We've talked to his family here in town. Miguel Puido has been away in Nicaragua. They expect him back today or tomorrow. Just yesterday, they phoned him and told him about his missing friend. He said he would get right back. The family knows la doctora and are very fond of her. They are also very worried and said that Miguel is concerned.

I've asked Miguel's family to have him report to me as soon as he returns. We'll see if we can get him to guide us up the mountain further and help us talk to some of the natives. He's trusted up there. When we go, it should be a small group.

The villagers are shy and don't welcome strangers too well. I've also got people looking in Puerto Viejo, the back road from here to there, the beaches and some of the trails leading away from PV into the surrounding jungle. So far, nothing's turned up."

Sergeant Hernandez turned to Sally, "Senorita, can you stay here in town, maybe even spend time in Dr. Goetz's office, field calls and visitors. Possibly something would turn up or someone might know something. We do need to get into her office today first, though, to investigate. You had said it looked like the office had been broken into and that things were scattered about as if someone had been looking for something."

"Yes, I can stay. Maybe I'll just stay at her place, take care of her cat, and watch her business until she's back, if you think that's okay."

Tomas broke in, "Yes, Sally, that's a good idea". And turning to Hernandez, he said, "Let's hope Miguel Puido returns soon. If we decide we need to go up the mountain, we should start up as soon as possible – today, if we can. I don't care what time of day it is. There's no time to waste."

Hernandez nodded in agreement. "I'll put the word out for some of our best trackers. It's possible that she veered off a path or fell down a crevice or a cliff."

"I've also got a couple of my guys on standby to come over today, tonight…whenever we need them," Tomas added.

He glanced up towards the sloping vast flanks of the Talamancas. This was going to be a difficult search and he wasn't feeling positive about the outcome.

San Jose, Costa Rica

Michael Turner took a taxi to Dr. Olivera's office. The doctor had told him that they would walk to a nearby restaurant. He stepped into a small waiting room that was empty except for a woman standing in front of the reception counter speaking to a woman behind the counter. Out of respect, he stepped back and took a seat and picked up a magazine while the two women finished their conversation. The room was quite small, so he couldn't help but overhear.

"Oh Rosa, no worries. I don't mind filling out these papers again. I was so sorry to hear about the office being broken into. Why do you think someone was going through the patient files? What could they want?"

"We can't figure it out. You know the doctor handles only special cancer patients, so there aren't that many files. But a few had been emptied out. Unfortunately, yours was one. I'm only telling you this so you can be aware that someone may have your address and some of your personal information, Sra. Lopez. Please let us know if you have any concerns or unusual phone calls or visits. Better yet, get in touch with this police officer," as she handed over a card.

Michael looked up when he heard this. Sra. Lopez was a middle-aged woman, wan looking, with thin hair and dark circles under eyes. Not a picture of health. The cancer or the cancer treatment, or more likely – both, were certainly taking a toll on the woman. The office had been broken into? For what? Drugs? But then why rifling through patients' files?

Rosa, the woman behind the counter, called out to Michael. "Are you here for lunch with the doctor?"

"Uh, yes, I am – thanks."

She smiled and picked up her phone, speaking Spanish, she informed the doctor that his lunch appointment was here. A few seconds later, a short, lean man stepped into the waiting room. He looked to be in his early sixties. He had graying curly hair cut short, a mustache and a neat goatee.

"Senor Turner, I apologize for the wait. I was just finishing up some notes." He glanced over at Sra. Lopez and gave her a warm smile, while he raised his eyebrows at Rosa. "I hope Rosa's not keeping you from your lunch date with your family."

"Oh no, Doctor. It's fine. She was just filling me in on the break-in." Olivera raised his eyebrows even further as he looked at Rosa with exasperation.

"Rosa, please don't be worrying Sra. Lopez, here. All is well, Sra. Nothing of value was taken."

"But I'm concerned that they've taken personal information. Like where I live. Why? What would they want this for?"

With an even more pronounced glare at Rosa, Dr. Olivera responded honestly, "Well, yes, charts were rifled through, and I'm not sure what they were looking for. Has anything unusual happened that you're concerned about?" Olivera glanced over at Michael with an embarrassed shrug as if to say just give me a minute here.

Sra. Lopez frowned, trying hard to think and finally responded, "No, I can't think of anything."

"Well, let me know if anything comes up. I'm working with the authorities on this, so any information might be helpful. Now go off and enjoy this beautiful day and I'll see you in a month." Then he turned to Michael reaching out for a handshake. "Let's go to lunch."

It wasn't until after they had finished their main course, a delicious dish of roasted chicken, salad, beans, rice, tortillas and fried plantains, that Michael was able to broach the subject of the trials.

He was surprised that the doctor had enjoyed two large glasses of wine and was finishing off the meal with a coffee and liquor mixed with warm milk. Maybe it was the alcohol, but he found Dr. Olivera to be very forthcoming about the successes and failures of the drug trials.

Only one of his patients of the four on the trial was experiencing any remission at all. The other three were not doing well at all. He felt an honest remorse in having offered these patients a glimmer of hope, knowing that short of a miracle, these patients were on borrowed time.

Michael wondered if the woman in the waiting room was one of the patients on the trial; if so, she was not the one that was doing well, from the look of her.

"Doctor, what do you think is different with the one patient that is doing so well? Was her cancer not as serious?"

"Oh, no, Si...." He hesitated, catching his error in almost naming the patient. "This one was quite ill. Dreadfully so. And so young. It was heartbreaking. But miraculously, over the last couple of months, she has made an amazing turn around. Her blood tests are negative, and have been so each of the last three times I checked them."

"Well, maybe the experimental drug is working on her. Maybe she was a good recipient for it. Were all the cancers the same for these four patients?" Michael noted that the patient was a young woman.

"Well, yes, they were all serious blood cancers. Slightly different though. You could be right. Maybe she was the one that it did work for. I'd like to think so. I think so highly of Dr. Walker and his dedication and efforts. But, curiously, I had stopped the trials almost two months ago as the treatment was beginning to be too hard on her. I planned to give her a month off. And then she started getting better. It's a quandary for me...do I put her back on the drugs because they might have been working...or do I give her more of a break?

And then I'm torn. Do I take the other three patients off the chemo, too? Might they have a miraculous recovery? Well, actually, one of them is stopping voluntarily. He said he couldn't handle it any more. He stopped about three weeks ago. When I saw him yesterday, he looked like a skeleton and was in such obvious pain. But he was adamant about not going back on the trials. I haven't had the heart to report this yet to Dr. Walker."

And then Dr. Olivera frowned and took a large swallow of his coffee. "And then there's the break-in at thc office. I didn't want to alarm Sra., uh.. the woman you saw in my office. But the files that were torn apart or are missing – well three of them were patients on the trial. Now, I can't figure that one out. Just coincidence? One file is completely missing..." and he paused before continuing. "The one missing belongs to the patient who is in remission." The doctor paused and frowned, and seemed to be struggling with how much to say to Michael.

But then he continued, "There's another element here, and I may be letting my imagination run away with itself, but my one patient that is doing so well is seeing a naturopathic doctor and taking some supplements she prescribed her. I didn't think there was any connection to her remission, but I pride myself on being open minded and I take a very holistic approach to the care of my patients. I do believe the mind is a powerful healer and I was convinced that this was at the root of her improvement.

But, ever the curious researcher, I checked around with other oncologists in Costa Rica, and found another cancer patient that had experienced a remarkable improvement in his condition. A patient of a doctor in Limon. I would have liked to meet and examine this patient, but sadly he met with an unfortunate accident not too long ago."

Michael was intrigued by this chain of events. Still, just two patients having experienced a turn-around in their cancer was not a significant number.

But then the doctor continued: "So here's where it gets interesting. When I finally tracked down this patient, well actually, not him – his wife, I found out that he was also a patient of the same naturopathic that is treating my patient."

Now this really piqued Michael's interest. He knew the doctor wouldn't divulge any identifying patient information, so as much as he would love to know the particulars of the patient doing so well, he knew he couldn't ask. He also knew that even Dr. Walker did not know the names of the patients involved in the trials, as per protocol. But he did venture a question.

"Do you know the name of the naturopathic? One of the things I'm supposed to do here while in Costa Rica is explore alternative modalities of healing. This doctor might be a good place to start."

Dr. Olivera hesitated as he mulled over the ramifications of giving out this information.

"Since you are here in large part to learn about the trial, and I have such respect for Dr. Walker, I suppose it would do no harm..." and in mid-sentence Dr. Olivera stopped. No, no, in good conscience, he could not give the name of the naturopathic.

Good God, the last thing he would wish upon her would be for a large U.S. corporation to descend upon her practice to get information about her herbs and other medicines. There was a reason she was practicing here in Costa Rica, and it probably had a lot to do with the desire to be independent and free to care for her patients as she saw fit.

"Uh, give me your card. I'm still trying to track her down. I've put in a few calls this past week and left several messages. She hasn't returned my calls. Maybe she's on a trip. But when I do talk to her, I'll ask if she minds that I give you her contact information. I'm sure you understand. She may be hesitant to meet with a rep from a large U.S. pharmaceutical company."

Damn, Michael thought, though he understood the doctor's reticence with imparting information about the naturopathic doctor.

Well one patient was in Limon, and he guessed that Dr. Olivera's patient lived in or near San Jose, where Olivera had his clinic. He knew that Limon was on the Caribbean coast and guessed it was probably a four to five hour drive. Now where would a naturopathic doctor be that both patients would visit? And how could he find out? Well there can't be that many naturopathics in the country. Maybe just a google search or telephone directory would at least give him an idea of how many to check into.

Olivera glanced at his watch and said, "Oh look at the time. I've got to get back for my afternoon clinic. Look, please give Dr. Walker my regards. I'd love to know how his drug trials are working elsewhere. It would help me decide whether or not to continue with my patients. Four patients is definitely not a significant number. So I'm curious how it's going overall with the other patients. Do you know how many he as on the trials?"

"No, I don't, but I'll check. And thanks for your time, doctor. Um, and good luck with your patients. If you do hear back from the naturopathic, and she's willing to see me, I'd be very appreciative." And that was another clue, he thought, the naturopathic is a female. That was how Olivera had referred to the doctor. That would certainly narrow his search.

He would send Dr. Walker an email and report about his conversation with Dr. Olivera about the trials when he got back to his apartment. He didn't think he had much to report, but he had promised to stay in touch.

It was a pretty day in San Jose, so Michael had the taxi drop him off a couple of blocks away from his building. He wandered a bit, before settling on a bench in a typical downtown park-like square where old women fed the pigeons and old gentlemen in suits sat and watched the world pass them by. After a while, the sun became blocked by some dark clouds, the temperature cooled, the breeze picked up and a few sprinkles of rain motivated him to get back to his building.

The doorman greeted him and Michael got into the elevator with a young attractive couple. They nodded hello and pushed the button for the floor that he lived on. Neighbors? The three of them got off the elevator, the woman smiling and wishing him a nice afternoon.

He watched as they went down the hall and stopped at a door about three apartments away, opened the door and stepped in. He was struck by their exotic attractiveness and the almost white, long, straight hair that flowed down the woman's back.

After a quick shower and a beer, Michael sat down in front of his computer to send a message to Dr. Walker. He told him about his meeting with Dr. Olivera and was very frank about the doctor's consideration to stop the trials. Michael also reported about the patient who was in a remarkable remission; so maybe the medications were working on this patient. He did say that he was going to try to track down a naturopathic doctor that the patient was also seeing.

He then made an appointment for the following day to meet with the pharmacy lead at the Hospital CIMA in San Jose. He had been advised that this was a good place to start. This was a new hospital with cutting edge services. It also included a large outpatient medical department with a variety of advanced diagnostic and treatment services and modalities, including chemotherapy and a radiology department. His local contacts had told him that the medical and administrative staff were eager to be seen as a world class hospital and were happy to partner with U.S. and European pharmaceuticals in offering emerging treatment options.

Michael's Spanish was coming in handy. Though most of his contacts were fluent in English, it was paying off when he tried to make connections that he could speak the local language. It didn't hurt either that he had the striking good looks that appeared more European than typical mid-west Americano. When he was done with his phone calls, he noted that Dr. Walker had emailed him back. Man that was quick.

It was an innocent enough response, but something struck Michael as odd. Dr. Walker had thanked him for meeting up with Dr. Olivera so quickly. And then Michael became disturbed by the rest of the message.

"I've decided to stop the trials in Costa Rica. It's such a small trial there, and though it appears that one patient is doing well, at least at this time, I'm not sure it has anything to do with my drugs. You can move onto your other assignments now, though I would appreciate some continued exploration of successful alternative modalities that you may run across while there." And with that, he signed off.

Wow, Michael thought. It didn't seem like Walker to give up. He then thought about the naturopathic that Olivera referred to. And the other patient who was doing well that used the same naturopathic. Well, this naturopathic sounded like a good place to start if he was going to do as Walker had asked.

He was concerned about the scientist, though. He sensed weariness in Walker's email. He got up from his desk and walked over to the sliding door leading out to the balcony. He opened it wide and went out to get some fresh, albeit humid, air. He stripped off his shirt and settled himself on a lounge chair. What was up with Walker?

She was awake more often now. Someone was taking care of her, feeding her, and spooning a tea into her mouth that she knew was soothing her pains. It also enveloped her in a cocoon type of haze, and she would fall right back into a deep sleep within seconds of taking the tea.

Her vision was blurry and she could never quite make out the person who was caring for her. Right now she wanted more tea, craved it in a way. But she knew she needed to get some clarity about her situation.

She opened her eyes, and though things appeared blurry, she was able to make out her surroundings a bit. She was in a small thatched hut, circular and about eight feet in diameter. There was a cloth hanging over the opening, but light was coming through, so it must be day time.

She carefully moved her head from side to side and was relieved that there were no sharp pains, only a dull throbbing in her left temple.

When she tried to move, she realized that her left arm was in a sling and wrapped tightly to her chest. She laid still and did a mental scan of her body. Ahh, a throb in her right ankle. She wiggled her toes and thankfully they responded. She couldn't move her right leg, though, as it seemed to be wrapped tightly with a cast like material. Her left foot and leg were pain free and easily responded to attempts to move them.

She started to doze off again and began to dream. There was the roar of a waterfall and then she was falling, falling, bouncing down slippery rocks, crashing through wet stinging brush and trees, someone was crying close by, and then just before she landed, the fall slowed down, the waterfall roar became a soft shushing sound.

Someone was holding the back of her head, cradling it, and wiping her brow with a cool cloth. She opened her eyes and a cascade of soft silk draped across her vision.

As she cleared her vision, the soft silk became long, soft golden colored hair, framing a beautiful face with striking eyes. This vision smiled at her and then offered her some broth. They locked eyes, until she once again slipped into the cocoon.

Bribri, Costa Rica

Tomas and Sally left the police station. They planned to go over to Leslie Goetz's office and poke around while they waited for Miguel Puido to show up. Sergeant Hernandez said he would be right behind them, as he wanted to see if they could learn anything new from Leslie Goetz's office with Sally there. In the meantime, Tomas contacted two of his trackers and asked them to come over to Bribri as soon as possible. They were expected to arrive by early evening.

Along the way they popped into Toni's store and Sally introduced Tomas. She saw an unmistakable twinkle in Toni's eyes as she appraised the good-looking detective. This got Sally to wondering how things had gone in Seattle between Iris and Tomas. Maybe if he didn't head up the mountain today, she'd have a chance to grill him about Iris over a beer. Though their time together last year was short, Sally missed Iris and wished to see her again. Would she ever be able to convince her to come back to Costa Rica?

Toni gave Sally her key to Leslie's office and Sally told her she'd handle the cat for the next couple of days, as she planned to stay at Leslie's place, having received permission from the police.

Sally unlocked the door to the clinic, but Tomas stopped her from entering. "We need to wait for the police," he said.

Just two minutes later, Sergeant Hernandez and a young officer pulled up in front of the clinic. They got out of an open topped jeep and stepped up to the door. Sally held the door open for the officers and stepped in with them.

"Stay by the door," Hernandez instructed Sally, nodding for Tomas to follow him in. The three men wandered back behind the reception counter and into the back office and exam room. The young officer took pictures as they looked around. Tomas stuck his head back out and waved Sally over.

"Is this how you saw it yesterday?" he asked.

Sally glanced around and responded, "Yes, it looks the same as we found it yesterday."

Sally walked back into Leslie's office and looked at the patient folders strewn about on the desk and the floor. She sat down at Leslie's desk and pulled open the file drawer. Several of the folders had been rifled. Then a name caught her eye. The folder was undisturbed. She pulled it out of the drawer and started looking through it. *Simone Jenkins* – ah now Sally remembered. She had met Simone the last time she had seen Leslie.

Upon closer inspection, she could see that some patient files had been ransacked, but that also Leslie's appointment book and her business cards and other business papers had been scrutinized. Maybe it wasn't just patient information the intruder was after. She walked back into the clinic and looked at the bottles and medicines that were scattered about.

"Tomas," she called out.

Tomas stuck his head in and asked, "What is it, Sally?"

"Well, two things. First, I recognize the name of one of the patients. I met her the day Leslie went missing – Simone Jenkins. Healthy looking young woman.

I remember her thanking Leslie for seeing her on such short notice and on a Saturday. And she said something about needing a refill of her tincture. The other thing is - did you notice that it's not just patient files that were pulled apart? It looks like whoever did this also went through her business papers, her financials and her appointment books. And they also were looking through the medicines. I wonder if any of them were taken."

"Well, it wouldn't hurt to track down this Simone Jenkins and see if she can remember anything from last Saturday's visit that would give us any clues."

"I'm on it! Sally replied. "Her address and phone number are in her folder. I'll call right now."

She went back to Leslie's desk and picked up the phone. While she was dialing, she saw a scrap of paper sticking out from under a large rock paper weight. She pulled it out and looked at the quick scribble of letters and a number: JCR4. It struck a chord of memory for her and then came back in a flash. It was the license number - or part of it - of the black Toyota SUV that had Leslie all worried.

She set the phone back down and called out to Tomas again. He popped into the office, "Yeah? What is it?"

"Well I don't know if it's anything," she started, as she waved the small piece of paper around. "Last week, when I was here with Leslie, she told me that she thought that she was being followed. She had seen a black Toyota SUV a few times here and also near her office in PV. When we were leaving the office, she spotted the car again and jumped back into the office in fright. She told me a little about her fears of people trying to track down some of her herbs that she got from up on the mountain. She thought she was becoming paranoid and even mentioned that she regretted letting me write an article about her. I told her to write down the license number. This is it. I found under this paperweight."

Tomas walked over and took the scrap of paper from Sally's hand. He walked out of the office with Sally following. He handed it to Sgt. Hernandez and asked him if he could run a check on it. The officer looked at Tomas quizzically.

"Could be something. Sally just thought to tell me," with a frown in Sally's direction, "that Leslie was worried that she was being followed. She'd told Sally that she'd seen a black Toyota SUV around her office here and also in Puerto Viejo."

Sally shrugged peevishly, "Well...yeah, I should have mentioned that. It just kinda slipped my mind." She was appalled at her lack of reporter's edge during this episode. "We really need to see Miguel. I'm sure he can help us. I have a really bad feeling and think we need to get up on the mountain as soon as possible."

As if on cue, the door swung open and a slight built, handsome young man burst in. "Have you found her?! Any news? My mother told me that Leslie is missing!"

"Miguel, God, I'm glad you're here! Tomas, this is Miguel – Leslie's friend. He's the guide."

Tomas strode across the room and shook Miguel's hand and introduced himself. Sergeant Hernandez nodded at the young man and introduced himself. The officer and Miguel started a rapid conversation Spanish that Sally had a hard time completely following. Tomas joined in and the conversation went on for a couple of minutes, before they looked over at Sally and reverted to English.

"You told them about our trip up the Talamanca?" Miguel asked with a worried look.

Sally responded somewhat apologetically, "Well, yes I did. I think it's important. I know Leslie was secretive about her trips, but Miguel, I think someone was following her. We need to find out who it was."

"What?! She never told me that. Who? And why?" But as he asked the why, a dawning look came over his face. He turned to the officers. "We need to get up there. Now!"

"Okay, well...." Tomas looked at his watch. "My team should be here in a couple of hours. They're on the road. I'll text them to meet us at the police station. Hernandez, are your guys ready to go?"

Sgt. Hernandez nodded yes and stated, "We need to get some jeeps and gear together. We may be up there a couple of days. I'll meet you over at the station in an hour. Miguel, we need you to take us up where you think she might have been headed. Can you leave soon?"

"!Si, si. Let me get my stuff and I'll be over to the station right away." Before he left he followed Sally into Leslie's office. He lowered his voice and whispered to her, "You didn't say anything about Grandmother, did you? Or the shaman?"

Sally gave Miguel a worried look. "Look, Miguel, you can trust Tomas Vasquez. He's my friend. I only said something about the Grandmother and Leslie making trips up the mountain to get some herbs from her. But, I didn't mention the shaman. I also told him that Leslie was worried about somebody following her lately. Last week, when I was here, she saw a black Toyota SUV parked nearby, and she was sure it was the same one she'd seen a few times in PV near her office."

"She never told me any of this. But I do know that she'd never forgive herself if anyone got wind of the shaman and her medicines. I gotta go. We gotta protect the people, Grandmother and the young shaman. But most importantly, we have to find la doctora." He turned and left the office, telling Tomas he'd meet him shortly at the station.

Tomas stuck his head in the door of the office. "Everything okay in here?" he asked.

Sally took a deep breath. "Look, Tomas, I'm going out on a limb here. Leslie was really worried, paranoid, I thought, about people finding out about some special medicine she had been getting from the Grandmother. She'd said that it had actually cured a couple of people from cancer. Leslie went up to meet with the Grandmother just a few times a year. Always with Miguel.

On our last trip a couple of weeks ago, I gathered somehow that Grandmother had not brought any of this particular medicine with her. Something Leslie said about needing to get back up soon, as she was low on the red powder. Maybe that's what she went back up there for..."

Tomas gave Sally an exasperated look. "Jesus, Sally, what else are you keeping from me?"

"That's all, really. I promise. I'm sorry...I....it's just that Leslie was so secretive about the mountain trips and I know she regretted letting me write an article about her...oh, I guess I forgot to tell you that part, too. God, I wonder if somehow I am responsible for all this..."

"Article? What article? Was it published? When and where?" Tomas asked, talking fast and in an irritated tone.

"Well, three or four weeks ago. In the San Jose Tribune – the English version. But, I really didn't say much about the mountains or the tribes. Just that Leslie used herbs that she gathered to make some medicines and teas. And that some people believed that these teas and such were preventing illnesses.

God, it was just kind of a flowery, woo woo thing. Though, the editor did want more. Said that there was a lot of interest for more details. Had even had requests from readers in Europe and the U.S. But, by that time, Leslie said no more and made it clear that she regretted letting me interview her in the first place."

Tomas looked at Sally with a perplexed look. He was trying to put the pieces together. Was it worthwhile to go up the mountain? The search efforts would be horrendous. It was a big area. But nothing had as of yet turned up on the roads to Puerto Viejo, and nobody had anything to report in the town of PV.

It looked like it was going to be necessary to go into the Talamancas. He was grateful that Miguel Puido had shown up. It appeared that the young guide knew a lot about the mountain and the people that lived there.

"You make the call to that patient and see if you can tie anything together about last Saturday. I'm going over to the police station. Make sure you keep your cell phone charged, and I'll keep you posted as to our progress. At least until we run out of cell phone coverage. As soon as my guys arrive and Hernandez has his team set, we'll head out." He looked at Sally and tried to smile encouragingly, but failed.

Sally read the look of pessimism in Tomas' eyes. She felt her eyes water. "You know Tomas I really appreciate you doing this."

Tomas made another attempt at a smile and turned and left the clinic. Sally let out a deep breath and went back into the office and sat at Leslie's desk. She opened Simone Jenkins' file and picked up the phone and called the number listed in the file. A small child answered after two rings. After much fumbling about on the other end the phone was handed over to the child's mother.

"Hello, this is Simone. What can I do for you?"

"Hi. I'm Sally Meza – a good friend of Dr. Leslie Goetz. You and I met briefly last Saturday morning. Do you remember? It was in front of her office in Puerto Viejo."

"Um, yes.... What's up?"

"Well, I'm wondering if you've heard from Dr. Goetz since you saw her last."

"No, I haven't. Why?"

"Did she say anything about her plans to you? Like, where she might be going this week?"

"No, she didn't. What's going on? Is something wrong?"

"Well, no one has seen Leslie, I mean Dr. Goetz, this last week. The last time I saw her was when I met you outside her office in Puerto Viejo."

"Oh yes, I remember you. Have you checked her Bribri office? I know she only comes into Puerto Viejo a couple of times a month. Actually, I think she came in on last Saturday just for me, since my family and I were planning a little beach holiday for the weekend. I've been so sick lately, and this was the first time in months that I felt good enough to get out of the house. Oh, I'm sorry, I shouldn't be talking about myself. Are you worried about Leslie?"

"Yes, we are. We've called in the police and are considering activating a search party. I'm very worried. I'm concerned that she might have gone up into the mountains on her own."

"Oh God. I hope not. She's talked about the mountains a little bit. She's mentioned that she gets some of her medicines from there. Now that I think about it, she did seem a bit alarmed that I had run out of my tincture. I fully believe that this is what has turned my health around. Anyways, she seemed very concerned that I had misplaced the bottle. It should have lasted me until my next regularly scheduled appointment which would have been last Monday. She started to say something about having to make a trip to get more of the ingredients."

"Well, thank you so much for talking to me. Please let me know if anything else comes to mind."

Sally gave Simone her number and then hung up. God, it seemed more and more likely that Leslie went up to the mountain on her own to try to meet up with Grandmother in order to get the special medicine. She put in a call to Tomas and briefed him on her conversation with Simone Jenkins and her conclusions.

She thought about Simone and how healthy she looked and her mentioning how sick she had been. She wondered if the red powder that Leslie needed from Grandmother was the special ingredient used in Simone's tincture. That would explain Leslie's concern about Simone losing her bottle. She wished she knew more about it.

She called Simone back. "Just one more question, Simone."

"Sure. What is it?"

"How much of the tincture was Dr. Goetz able to give you?"

"Just enough to last me a couple of weeks. She's decreasing the doses a little each week. But I still need more. She said that I should be on it for at least three more months. She said that she would get me more and that I was going to have to come back or send my husband to get it this next weekend."

"Um, if you don't mind me asking. How sick were you?"

"Very sick. I have a rare deadly blood cancer. It's terminal...or it was. I was on chemo for six months. But we agreed, my doctor and I that it was taking too much of a toll on my health and that it didn't look like it was working. I've been off the chemo for the last month. I feel so much better. And I really think I've turned a corner. Crazy as it may sound, I really think Leslie's medicine is what is saving my life."

Whoa, thought Sally. She could now better understand why Leslie would risk her safety and go up the mountain in hopes of getting more of the medicine. If it was this precious and really helping people....Of course, she'd make the trip. Now Sally remembered Leslie saying something about some of her medicines really helping a couple of people.

Sally asked, "Simone, do you know if Dr. Goetz was treating anyone else with the tincture?"

"I do. The way I found out about Dr. Goetz was through my cousin who had a friend in Limon who was seeing her. He also had cancer."

"Do you know his name?"

"No. But I'll call my cousin and have her call you. It would be better if you talked directly to her. She may be hesitant to give out her friend's name."

"Alright, that sounds good. I look forward to hearing from your cousin. Thanks, Simone. You take care."

"I will. And please let me know if you hear from Leslie."

Chapter 7

Seattle, WA

Iris loved coming over to the UW. It was a beautiful campus and she had fantasized early in life about Nina attending. She herself had even thought about going back to school here to do some post graduate studies. Ahh...the time for that has come and gone, she thought. Whenever possible, she took her continuing education credits on site at the UW. She enjoyed taking a week off here and there to take an intensive course in a short block of time.

It was a good plan – though not one she had intentionally set in place – to have this distraction this week. Tomas had just left a day ago, and she already missed him terribly. She felt achingly drawn to the man, joy and love coursing through her body, only to be in the next instant crushingly depleted by the reality of the situation.

He was in Costa Rica and planned to stay there, and here she was, immobilized by events, lacking the requisite courage to put her fears in their place and get on a friggin plane and get down to Costa Rica. Unfortunately, she just couldn't let go of the fact that the place had claimed much of her peace of mind for a terrifying week of her life, and it still lingered.

Well, it didn't take a rocket scientist or more accurately a trained psychotherapist to understand her fears and immobilization. As she walked across the campus to the classroom, she realized she had time to kill and ducked into a Starbucks attached to the student union. God, was Starbucks everywhere? Apparently, so. Still her favorite coffee, though.

She ordered a grande café latte and stood waiting at the pick-up counter, her eyes scanning the room and noticing the occupants of the small coffee shop. Some people were sitting and chatting, and others were sitting alone glued to their laptops. She created stories about each person she observed. A professor, a med student, an older student, a young couple with piercings in brows and noses and holding hands – artists or musicians...or good grief, probably school teachers.

Her eyes fell on the profile of a beautiful woman, not so young, hm...maybe in her 30s, a tad older than Nina. A student? A teacher? The woman glanced up and smiled at Iris. Clear, light blue eyes and long, wavy, sun streaked, auburn hair. Pretty girl. She looked at peace. Iris felt her normal cut of pain in the center of her heart as she reflected upon Nina and her experience last year in Costa Rica.

The young woman was reading a book and Iris could see the cover. Weird...it was a book on Costa Rica. Now how coincidental is that? The woman looked up from the book and gave Iris a big smile. "Are you planning a trip?" Iris asked.

"Maybe....just contemplating the possibility. I have a friend there, right now. He's invited me down. I'm trying to figure out whether or not I should do this. Have you ever been?"

Iris hesitated for a second, before answering. "I have."

"What did you think? Did you like it?"

Just then, the barista called out Iris' name. Iris grabbed her coffee. "Well..." she began, then paused to quiet the inner turmoil. "Um, yes, it's a lovely country. You should go." Then she gave the woman a smile and left the shop.

How weird. She almost turned around to go back into the coffee shop to tell the woman not to go. Under no circumstances should she go. That it was a dangerous, scary place. That she had almost lost her daughter there.... But she didn't turn around.

Millions of people visit the country and don't have terrible things happen. Only her. Only her. Just her daughter. God, she needed to get a grip.

Anne glanced at the woman's back as she left the coffee shop. Hm, she thought. Was it a sign? Should she go to Costa Rica? She finished her coffee and closed her book. She'd love to go and traipse around the country, go into the jungles, see the fauna and flora, maybe meet up with some indigenous people and study their healing practices. She'd heard that there were still some remote tribes and some shamanic practices still in existence.

And, really, she admitted to herself. She'd like to see Michael. She was envious of him and his new assignment--though she'd never want to work for a pharmaceutical company. After her summer internship with Biogenesis, she'd become pretty disillusioned with large drug companies. She was so much more interested in true healing modalities and felt that these companies were driven by the bottom line more than finding cures.

Well, nothing was really holding her back now. She had just that morning met with her advisor and told him that she was going to postpone taking her medical boards. He brushed her off, barely listening as she explained that her heart just wasn't into this path at this time, and that she needed a few months to think about it.

"Fine, fine," he said. And pushed some papers over for her to read and sign. Within ten minutes, she was in and out of his office feeling elated, though somewhat slighted.

Anne left the coffee shop and meandered across the campus. She felt somewhat at a loss. She had a part time job as a lecturer in ethno-botany, but the school was on a break between sessions, and now that she didn't need to spend hours studying for the medical boards, the old feeling of floundering began to grow in her gut. Plus, Michael hadn't responded to her last email, where she had hinted about coming down for a visit. A familiar sense of anxiety began to develop. She knew she needed to put a lid on this, or she'd be dealing with the cascading flow of panic soon to follow.

Things were actually mellowing out a bit with her parents. The hormone blocking therapy was giving her dad some breathing time, as his testosterone was being obliterated and consequently slowing down or possibly halting the growth of cancer. Her mother had reached out to him and was being supportive and spending time with him. Both her mother and father were going out of their way to alleviate Anne from her concerns about them. They had even backed off pressuring her about her career plans.

It was also interesting to Anne to observe the changes in her father as a result of the hormonal shifts in his body. He was much more sentimental, quick to hug and much sweeter. Are we nothing more than chemistry, she wondered. She had floated the idea of going to down to Costa Rica, and her parents had all but put her on the plane. Go, they said. Life is too short. Wow, what a switcheroo.

When she got back to her apartment, her quiet, clean, sparse apartment, she opened all the windows, had a long cool glass of water and sat down to her computer. She was hoping there was a response from Michael.

Oh God, what did she want from Michael? They hadn't even slept together yet. But she did like him and she knew he was interested. She was too old for this. Too old to be confused. Too old to be lacking direction. Too old to be alone. Crap.

Ah, there was an email. A long one. It was nice....and very inviting. Come on down, he said. He'd love to have her. They could do some exploring together. He even offered to send her the ticket to fly down. Wow. Anne started to get excited and began to plan when she could go and for how long.

Bribri, Costa Rica

Sally spent the morning cleaning up Leslie's office and clinic. Tomas' two guys had shown up, one of them being Jeremiah Valencia who Sally had met the previous year. A tall, well built, strikingly handsome black man with a crisp but slightly lyrical island accent. He was a gracious person and had taken the time to stop by the office to say hello to Sally, causing events from the previous year to flood over her once again. She gave him a crushing hug and thanked him for being there.

Sgt. Hernandez had organized a search team of four trackers including Miguel Puido, and the team joined up with Tomas and his crew and had left about an hour earlier. Toni had come by bringing lunch and hot coffee and had hung out for a while, giving Sally a hand with the mess. Sally was lost in deep thought and memories when the front door swung open, startling her back to the present moment.

Whoa. A really good looking dude who looked completely out of place in this one-pony town stepped into the office. Sally drew in her breath, wondering at her crazy attractions. She had been in love with women mostly, but a handsome man could also stir her libido. And she had to be honest with herself. She had a crush on Tomas and his main man, Jeremiah. She smiled big.

"Hi there! Can I help you?"

"Hello. I'd like to see the doctor. Are you Doctor…." His question trailed off as he looked down at a piece of paper. "Are you Leslie Goetz?" he asked as he read the name. "I'm sorry, but I don't have an appointment. Just doing a bit a research."

"Oh, no. I'm not. She's not in." Sally's journalistic antennae popped up. Research? She groaned inwardly. Was her article responsible? "And you are?"

"Oh, sorry. Michael Turner. I'm doing a bit of research on holistic healing modalities. Um, just talking to naturopathics in the area."

He hardly looked like a researcher, she thought. More like a male model that should be on the cover of Esquire magazine. Who wears a white suit shirt in a dusty town like Bribri? Granted, his sleeves were rolled up revealing tan, muscular forearms and the top two buttons were unbuttoned showing promise of touchable skin.

"Um, no, Dr. Goetz is out of town for a few days. I suppose I could take your name and number and have her contact you when she returns." Most unlikely, Sally thought.

The gorgeous man hesitated while glancing around the clinic. He walked over to a shelf displaying an assortment of herbs, tinctures, and teas. He picked up one, turning it over in his hand to read the ingredients and instructions. He looked up at Sally with curiosity.

"Where does Dr. Goetz get her medicines? Does she have a supplier?"

"I'm not really the person to ask. I'm just a friend kind of house sitting here," Sally replied. Her heart was racing a bit. Could this have anything to do with Leslie's disappearance?

"Oh, so she's away for a trip?"

"Um, well, yes."

"And when do you expect her back?"

Sally let out a deep breath. Never one to beat around the bush, she asked, somewhat harshly, "Hey, just what the heck do you want to see her for? Just what kind of research are you doing? Does this have to do with my article?"

Turner shot a piercing quizzical look at Sally. "What article?"

"The one in the San Jose paper. On indigenous plants and their healing potentials? I had interviewed Leslie...." Crap, I've said way too much.

"Hmmm, noooo. When was this?"

"Oh come on, now. What is it you're really doing here? You don't just walk into some random office in a teeny tiny town, dressed like someone from Paris, and say you're doing some 'research.' Give me a break. Who are you and what have you done with Leslie?!"

"What have I done? What are you talking about?"

Just then the office phone rang. Sally walked over to the counter and picked up the phone.

"Hello, this is Dr. Goetz's office."

"Yes, hello. This is Simone again. Dr. Goetz's patient."

"Yes, Simone. What's up?"

"Well, I did find out the name of the other patient in Limon. My cousin told me and said it didn't matter much anyways, as the guy met with an unfortunate accident not too long ago."

The hairs on the back of Sally's neck bristled. She turned her back away from the man in the office, aware that he was inching a bit closer.

Simone continued: "His name is Joshua Marrone. Evidently he had also experienced a remission like me. He had been taking medicine that Dr. Goetz prepared for him. Who knows, it may have helped. But you'd have to ask Leslie what she was giving him. Oh, and my cousin said that he had stopped his chemo a while ago. Things were looking pretty grim, until he had this sort of miraculous turn around. But, then he got hit by a car and died. Really sad situation. Oh, and you might like to know that I told my doctor about Dr. Goetz."

"Really? What did he think of you seeing a naturopathic?" Sally thought that most traditional doctors would scoff at the alternative approaches.

"Well, actually, he was very receptive. He told me that he liked it when his patients took charge of their illnesses. He was curious though and wanted to know what she was giving me. I'm due to go back in a couple of weeks for another blood test. But I feel so well, I don't want to jinx it by having the test done. But my husband says it's just information and it will only inform our next steps. The chemo was so brutal, neither of us want to go down that path again…God forbid."

Simone's voice trailed off and Sally heard a catch in it. Poor thing. Sally didn't believe in miracles and was sure that the break from the tortuous illness and chemo were just temporary. Oh well, wasn't everything temporary? Just a bit more temporary for the beautiful, slender and healthy looking young woman Sally recalled from the week before.

"Gosh, I'm sorry, Simone. I can't imagine how hard this has been for you and your family."

"It's okay. Right now I feel great. And it's a feeling that I'm thankful for. For however long it lasts," Simone added quietly. "Hey, please let me know if you find out anything about Leslie. She's been such a wonderful doctor for me."

"Of course, I'll call you the minute I hear anything. By the way, I wonder if you would mind telling me your doctor's name. Just in case the police want to talk to him."

"Sure, as a matter of fact, I just talked to him a little while ago and told him Leslie was missing. He seemed very concerned. He had been trying to reach her himself. Dr. Olivera -- Ferdinand

Olivera, that is. He has an office in a small suburb of San Jose. Here's his number."

Sally repeated the name and number as she jotted them down on a piece of paper. "Thanks, Simone. I'll get back to you if I find anything out," and she hung up. She realized that Michael Turner was standing there looking over her shoulder at her note. She tried to cover it with her hand.

"I've met him," he indicated with a nod to the note.

"You have?" Sally asked warily.

"Yeah. Look, let's start over here. I really am doing 'research' of a sort. But I don't know anything about your friend being missing."

Sally looked at him suspiciously.

"No, really," he stated in response to her stare. "I just came to Costa Rica a couple of days ago. I'm here representing a large pharmaceutical company. Oh, don't look at me like that..." he stated in response to Sally's look of disgust.

"Well, this is just what Leslie was worried about!"

"What are you talking about?"

And then Sally spilled her guts. Well just about it all, except she left out the part about the trip into the mountains and the Grandmother.

"Leslie has been giving a couple of her patients some special medicine, a tincture, she called it. She gave it to some very sick people." She glanced toward the phone and continued, "That was one of the patients just now. Simone. She's had a miraculous recovery, evidently. I met her last Saturday, just before Leslie went missing on Sunday or Monday. I thought she might know something."

Michael looked concerned and asked, "And did she say Dr. Olivera was her doctor, her oncologist?"

"Yes, he is. And she got the name of another patient that had been getting better who also was a patient's of Leslie. But not of Dr. Olivera's."

"When I visited Dr. Olivera, he mentioned a naturopathic, but would not give me Dr. Goetz's name. Patient privilege. But he also told me that his office had been broken into and ransacked." He looked around the office and said, "Sort of like this, I'm guessing."

"Simone's doctor's office had been broken into? This is weird. And now her naturopathic's office? Maybe this has something to do with Simone. I mean, she seems to be the connecting factor between this here and Dr. Olivera."

And then Sally looked up inquisitively at Michael Turner. "And what are you up to, I wonder? Here you are here in this office and you say you met with Dr. Olivera. Why did you meet with him?" Sally stared penetratingly at the man. What really was going on here? Did she start this whole thing with her stupid article? Oh god, if anything happened to Leslie because of that, she'd never forgive herself.

"Look, I came here on an assignment from my company. I'm really not the ogre you're trying to make me out to be."

"Really? Well then explain why you're here in this office in this little shit hole of a town looking for my good friend?"

Michael looked at her with a speculatively. "Tell me what's going on here. Why did you ask me what I did with your friend?"

Sally looked at the man, wondering what she could say to him. Was he part of some big conspiracy? "How do I know that you're not one of them?" she asked bitterly.

"One of whom? I don't know what you're talking about. I just got here a few days ago. I came by myself. Really. Look you can call my company, if you want."

Sally looked at Michael, wondering how much she could trust him. He seemed sincere, but she wondered if she was just being taken in by his charm and good looks. With a big sigh, she finally responded.

"Leslie thought she was being followed. Just last week, before we went up...before we went out together, she saw a car that she had seen before in front of her other office in PV. She jumped back in the office, scaring the piss out of me. Told me then that she was worried people were following her." She looked suspiciously at Michael. "Are your people following her? Are you trying to get your hands on her medicine?"

"No, no, I don't know anything about this. Really."

"Well, then, tell me why you went to see Simone's doctor, Dr. Olivera? Any why are you here to see her naturopathic? Tell me that if you will!"

Michael stepped back, pulled up a chair and sat down. He seemed to be pondering the situation.

He looked up at her and said, "My company's research doctor asked me to check in with Dr. Olivera. Dr. Olivera is doing patient trials for a new oncology drug that is being developed by my company. When I saw Dr. Olivera, he told me about one of his patients on the trials who was doing really well. But then he said that he had actually stopped the chemo on this patient a couple of months prior. This could be Simone?"

That's when he mentioned that she was seeing a naturopathic. And he went so far as to say that there was another patient seeing the same naturopathic who had been doing better also." Michael glanced towards Sally's note – "Could be that Joshua Marrone. Also, my company is interested in partnering or buying a natural supplements company. Hence, my interest in all of this," he finished.

"Oh great. Just what Leslie was worried about. A big pharmaceutical coming in here and taking over her business and supplements."

Michael looked pained, "Well I guess that's what it looks like. But I don't think they would do anything sinister."

"Well, it just seems pretty coincidental to me. Leslie's worried and thinks she's being followed. Then she disappears. And now here you are...."

And then more to herself, Sally continued. "I wonder where Simone ties into all of this. She's seeing Leslie and this Dr. Olivera. And you say that his office was also broken into...I need to wrap my head around this. Then there's this other dude who was Leslie's patient that is now dead." She looked up at Michael, puzzling the pieces she was trying to assemble.

"You mentioned the police to Simone. Are they involved?"

Sally pondered how much to say. If he was somehow involved, was it wise to warn him that the police were involved? He certainly didn't seem very guarded.

"Yeah, as a matter of fact, they are out searching for her. They've formed a search party and left early this morning." She observed a flicker of concern cross his eyes. He furrowed his brow and glanced at his watch.

"I need to get going. I've got an appointment this evening back in San Jose. I need to get on the road." He got up and moved toward the door, glancing around the clinic as if looking for something. As he put his hand on the door, Sally called out.

"Wait! You can't just leave!"

"I really know nothing about this," Michael said quietly but firmly.

Sally didn't believe that for one minute. "At least give me your number. I may need to get in touch with you."

He hesitated and it looked as if he was just going to walk out, ignoring Sally's request. Then he pulled a card out of his pocket and walked back over to Sally.

"My card. It's got my company name and US address and number. This email will work, and let me write my cell on the back." He then placed the card on the desk and left the office.

Sally's gut was churning. She couldn't quite put her finger on the connections here. But her suspicions were on high alert. Was Michael Turner involved? Somehow he was connected, she was sure. She needed to follow up on the guy and also let Tomas know about him. Though that may not be possible until Tomas came back down the mountain. He definitely was out of cell phone range at this point.

She picked up Michael Turner's card. Biogenesis. She went back to the computer and googled the company.

It was a lot of driving in one day, from San Jose to and back from Bribri. He had spent most of the drive back preoccupied with questions. What had happened to the naturopathic doctor? Who had broken into Dr. Olivera's office? And what about the naturopathic's office? Same people?

Well, the authorities seemed to be concerned, concerned enough to organize a search party for the missing doctor. And what about the other patient of Dr. Goetz's. Joshua Marrone. How did he tie into all of this?

Michael was stiff and tired by the time he parked in the parking structure under his apartment building. Also hungry. He hadn't eaten since breakfast, and he wasn't sure he felt like going out. Maybe he'd just scramble some eggs. That and a glass of chilled white wine ought to do the trick.

As he pulled into his assigned parking space, another car pulled into a spot close by. A dusty black Toyota SUV. Nobody got out. He could faintly make out two people sitting inside, but as he walked by they turned to each other in an embrace, so he could not see their faces. Though he was able to make out that the woman had long very blond hair which was draped over and partially concealing their faces. Oh, probably that couple that lived down the hall from him.

He said hello to the Concierge in the in the Lobby and got in the elevator up to his floor, half anticipating the couple to make it up in time to ride up with him. But no one joined him on his ride up. It was a quiet building, and he hadn't bumped into many other occupants since he moved in.

He walked into this apartment, noting its chill. Had he left the air conditioner blasting when he left? He went over to the wall and turned it off. Then he went and opened the sliding glass door to his balcony to let in the fresh, albeit humid, air. He was getting used to the country's humidity. The air was thick and floral, but unfortunately, also mixed with some obvious pollution.

As he stood looking out over the city, something niggled at him. Someone had been in his apartment. He glanced back at his kitchen counter where he kept his I-pad tablet. It had been moved. He hadn't yet arranged for a cleaning service, but he supposed someone from the building could have been in.

Michael was a very precise and organized person. His wife had complained that he had a bit of OCD. He smiled briefly as he thought about her teasing him about his well-organized closet and sock drawer. And then the well-known ache followed quickly as he remembered her stacks of books and magazines haphazardly displayed throughout the house. And random bits of rocks and shells and vases of colorful flowers in different nooks and crannies.

With her gone, he had reverted to his painfully sparse and exact placement of all things tied to his existence. Nothing out of place. Ever. Though he did try to have a big vase of fresh flowers always present in the center of the coffee table; it helped him feel her presence. Hadn't gotten to that yet. First thing tomorrow, he determined.

He went over to the phone and rang the concierge. "Si, Senor Turner?" the young man answered.

"Hola, Alberto. Hey, I was wondering if anyone had been in my apartment today while I was gone."

"I don't think anything was scheduled. But let me check." The phone was silent for a few seconds and then Alberto spoke. "Nothing scheduled. But we wouldn't have anyone going in without notifying you in advance. By the way, did you want to schedule a weekly cleaning service? We have an excellent crew here."

"Sure, that's a good idea. Do let me know their schedule, though." Michael then thanked the concierge and hung up. Maybe he just imagined it. It had been awfully early when he left that morning. He went over to the tablet and examined it. It was off. Strange. Usually he had it on and set up to play music from a Pandora station. He turned it on and put in his passcode, and it went to his main menu. He was unable to determine if any recent activity had happened on it.

He then went into this office. At first glance, everything seemed in its proper place. But then he noticed a small discrepancy from the normal order of things. Someone had sat in his desk chair. It was pulled out a bit from desk. Enough so that a person could slip in and out of it. Michael always pushed his chair into the desk at the end of his work day there. He hadn't used it this morning.

He had his laptop on the desk and he went over to examine it. He opened it up and turned it on. Using his passcode, he went to his emails. He wasn't sophisticated enough to figure out how to check recent activity. Then he thought that he was being paranoid. Why would anyone be in his apartment? It didn't look like anything of value had been taken.

Oh well, he had been in a bit of a hurry that morning...probably just not paying as much attention to all his usual routines. Wouldn't that be a switch? Maybe Costa Rica was getting under his skin a bit causing him to relax more.

Chapter 8

Seattle, WA

Gretta was extremely worried about Zachary. He hadn't shown up for the shareholders' annual luncheon where he was scheduled to speak about new products being developed. This was very unlike him. He was very adept at providing stimulating and exciting new data that would remind major benefactors that their money was in the right place and at the right time.

She felt the heat rise in her chest and neck as she observed the whispers at her table when someone else besides Zachary stepped up to the podium to apologize for Dr. Walker's absence and explain the change in the program. One of Zachary's prized new lab researchers, a young attractive woman did a very adequate job of filling in.

After the luncheon, Gretta called Zachary. After several rings, he finally picked up. "Hello?" Zachary asked in a raspy quiet voice.

"Zack, it's Gretta. Are you okay? I was worried about you when you didn't show up today?"

"Show up? Where?" he asked.

"Zack! What's going on? Today was the annual shareholders' luncheon. You were the keynote speaker? Did you forget?" Gretta asked in a loud exasperated tone.

"Oh my god, Gretta...I'm so sorry. This week just got away from me. I've not been feeling well. But....."

Gretta cut in. "God damn it, Zack. What the hell is going on with you? You need to tell me after all I've done for you!"

"Alright, alright I will. But it would be better in person. Can you come over?"

"Where are you? At home?"

"Yes, I haven't been into the office for a few days. Come on over. The front door's open."

Gretta looked at the phone as the line went dead and wondered what to expect when she went to see Zachary Walker. She called her driver and asked to be picked up immediately.

Twenty minutes later, the car pulled up in front of an old three-story turn of the century brownstone on Queen Anne Hill. She hadn't been to Zachary's house for over a year. She ran up the stairs and pushed open the front door. She entered to a musty smelling environment.

"Zack? I'm here."

"Back here, Gretta. In the sunroom."

She walked through a messy kitchen, the sink full of dirty dishes with old dried food still on them, and through a short passage way to a sunny screened in porch. The smell here was fresh. Zachary was sitting in a big white wicker rocker with the newspaper spread out in front of him on a glass coffee table. All the windows were open and a nice breeze flowed in the room.

Gretta looked out the windows across the lawn to the ever gorgeous view of Elliott Bay and the Olympic Mountains cresting in the background. She looked back at Zack and caught her breath. He looked like he'd lost two sizes since she'd last had lunch with him.

"Zack? What's going on? You look....?"

"I know, don't say it. I look horrible. But, believe it or not, I'm feeling much better," he said with an attempt at a smile.

"Zack, please. Are you sick? Is it cancer? You can tell me. I'm here to help."

"Well, it's not official, but yes I finally went to see a friend, an oncologist, last week, and it's pretty likely that I have pancreatic cancer."

"Oh, Zack."

"Shush. Just listen. I'm going to be okay. I know it."

Gretta was a bit alarmed by the wild look in her friend's eyes. Had the stress gotten to him? Put him over the edge? This was not her cool, calm and always competent friend that she adored.

"I got that bottle of the medicine, the empty bottle that you had sent to me. The stuff from the naturopathic in Costa Rica. Well it wasn't entirely empty. I mixed a few drops of some herbal tea with the residue in the bottle and then took it. That was two days ago.

I experienced some minor abdominal cramping but none of the serious purging from the first time I used it. I fell into a deep sleep. I've been asleep solid for the last two days. And, Christ, Gretta, when I woke up just before you called me I woke up feeling refreshed and so much better. This stuff is the real deal, I'm telling you, it's magical. We've got to get our hands on this."

"Zack, come on now. You can't be sure when you've only had a miniscule amount of this."

A frown flickered across Walker's face. "Yeah, yeah, you're right. But I've got a strong sense about this, and we need to get more so I can do the proper testing of it. Have you had any luck tracking it down?"

Gretta wasn't sure how she felt. Things weren't going all that well in Costa Rica. No sign of the missing naturopathic doctor and more and more attention being brought to the situation. She knew now that a search party was on. And that they were searching a remote mountainous area called the Talamancas.

She'd done some research and knew that the area was home to some indigenous tribes that were protected and considered a national treasure. Outsiders were discouraged from going up into the area. On top of that it was dense jungle and nearly impossible to traverse.

The couple she had hired to find the medicine were illusive and not always predictable. She knew this when she hired them. She did know that they took great pride in getting their assignments done. Sometimes going to extreme lengths to accomplish the job.

She was scheduled to hear from them this evening. She planned to grill them on what forward movement had been made and if there really was any hope of tracking down this 'magical' formula. She looked over at her friend and did note a glimmer of old life in his eyes and a faint blush to his sallow cheeks. Maybe just thinking that there was a cure was all it would take to get her friend to hold on for a while. She did love the man.

She looked around the room, glancing into the kitchen. "Zack, I'm going to get my staff over here to clean up a bit and I'm sending over a personal assistant, a nurse, to get you back in shape. You need to eat better and move around a bit." She held up her hand to him as she could see he was beginning to protest. "No, Zack, this is the way it's going to be if you want me to continue helping you."

"Alright, alright. Yeah, I could use a little help. Hey, can you check and see if the other patient, the woman, can you see if she was given any more of the stuff? Maybe we can get our hands on that to tie me over until we find the source. What do you think?" He asked hopefully.

"I'll check. I'm scheduled to talk with my people down there tonight. I'll ask them."

"Any news about the missing doctor? She's probably our key to tracking this stuff down."

"I haven't heard anything. I'll let you know as soon as I hear."

"You said she got lost up on a mountain, didn't you? Your people followed her up there, right?"

"Yes, it's a protected natural reserve. Some indigenous tribes still live there."

"Well, I guess that means we can't just buy the mountain."

"Uh, no, Zack, I don't think we can do that," Gretta chuckled to herself.

Although that might not be such a bad idea. If they could just locate the plant, maybe it also grew elsewhere, for instance on land adjacent to the Talamancas, land they could purchase. Now she was dreaming.

But it wasn't unheard of, large pharmaceutical companies buying up swaths of land in the Amazon jungle and other remote territories in order to claim ownership of plants. Sometimes they did this in order to squelch the production of alternative medicines. Drug companies did not always want a cure to a disease; they wanted drugs that might treat a disease, drugs that continued to be in demand because the disease still existed. Not the same thing as a vaccine that potentially could wipe out a disease.

She looked at Zack with a prodding smile and instructed him. "Now, get up and get showered. I expect you back in the lab this week. And you better call the President of the Board and apologize. Don't make too big deal out of being sick though; you don't want to lose their confidence. Think of some good excuse why you missed today's event."

San Jose, Costa Rica

Xavier and Mercy had several things on their to-do list. They had reported to their client the movements of the man down the hall, Michael Turner, and his visit to Bribri. Gretta told them that they needed to figure out a way to use him to their advantage. She knew he was very interested in succeeding and probably could be enticed to see things from a perspective beneficial to the company. She told them to keep their eyes on him and if needed nudge him in the right direction.

She also asked them to check on Simone Jenkins, if possible to see if she had any of the medicine that they could get their hands on. If so, send it on to her as soon as possible. Also, more effort needed to be made to find the source of the medicine. Someone besides the missing doctor was involved. Did they have anyone in the area that they could involve? Anyone that could join the search teams? Time was running out and she was paying them a handsome sum of money. They needed to get on it.

They told her they were headed back to Bribri that night; they had made contact with someone that was willing to help them for a fee. They would stop on the way and see if they could get into Simone Jenkins house once more. Gretta knew it was fruitless to tell them to be careful. They would do what they had to do to get the job done.

Anne was coming. Michael wasn't quite sure how he felt about that. If he was honest he had to admit that he was a bit lonely and somewhat overwhelmed by being in a strange country, albeit one as beautiful and friendly as Costa Rica. She made it clear that she had made arrangements to stay with a family in a suburb of San Jose, and was going to use this time to hone up on her Spanish language skills. She had signed up for a month.

So, this was good. She would be nearby. They could continue to explore their relationship. So far it was unlike any other he had experienced with a woman. Usually, his relationships (if you could call them that) over the last few years were initiated with a quick flurry of sexual attraction which often led straight to the bedroom, followed by a few follow-up dates, more sex, then Michael finally losing his ardor and beginning the usually painful process of distancing himself. Most of the woman looked at him with hurt in their eyes as he made his case for ending the affair.

Anne said in her email that she hoped she wasn't intruding on him. She was taking time off to think about what she really wanted to do and was putting the whole medical doctor thing on hold, probably permanently she added parenthetically. She reminded him that her most exhilarating experiences had been when she was out in the Amazon jungle during her ethno-botany field trips.

Anyways, she added, she'd love to see him, and she'd picked Costa Rica because he was there. She hoped that was okay and not too scary for him. Boy, the girl was direct, yet illusive. He wrote her back and said he was thrilled. Where was this going? She was so different from anyone he had ever met before. A remarkable contrast to Debra, and yet she was beautiful in a clear, so unadorned way.

He had been in Puerto Limon for the day following up on business calls to the hospital and labs. Anne was arriving today, so he needed to wrap things up and drive back over the Pali and go straight to the airport. She didn't expect him to pick her up, so he decided to surprise her.

He did not like the city of Limon. It was big, dirty and crowded and had not adequately recovered from a devastating earthquake in the early 1990's. The area had since gone to seed. And he knew there was a serious drug problem there. But the city did have a new modern hospital and some medical industry developing, so it was worth his time to make some business contacts.

He also spent some time sleuthing around into the mystery of Joshua Marrone – the other patient of Leslie Goetz, the naturopathic. Local newspapers reported that Marrone had been the victim of a hit and run auto versus pedestrian incident. Police were on the lookout for a dark jeep or SUV. Nobody got the license number. Witnesses said it happened just as Marrone stepped off a curb to cross a busy intersection. It seemed as if the driver had sped up, hit the man, then reversed the car a few feet, making a quick U-turn and sped off. Okay, that seemed kind of deliberate to Michael. But no one had come forth with any more information.

Dusk was beginning to drift into the mountains. The trackers, led by Miguel, had stayed together. There were eight of them. The fact that Leslie had indeed come up the mountain on her own was confirmed when they came across her car. Miguel had led them to this spot right away. It was located about a mile away from the first village. They searched the car and could find nothing in it that gave them any further clues. Miguel concluded then that Leslie was attempting to locate the Grandmother on her own, though he didn't say anything about this aloud.

After finding the car, they continued their search, staying on the trail that Miguel was familiar with, the one he had taken many times before and a few times with Leslie that led to the first village. There were no signs of Leslie on the trail. They came to the village, but mostly there were just a handful of older women and small children present. They were told that most of the villagers had headed up to higher grounds for hunting and fishing.

Miguel Puido talked in a rapid dialect that Tomas could not decipher to the elderly women and learned that indeed Leslie had come through the village. They pointed to a trail that she had headed out on.

Tomas asked about the Grandmother. Did anyone have anything to say about her and where she might be? Miguel looked at him warily.

"Look, Miguel, Sally told me about her trip up here with you and Leslie. She thinks Leslie may have come up here to meet with the Grandmother."

A pained look crossed Miguel's face. The Grandmother must be protected at all cost. If someone got to her, it was conceivable they could then be led to the young shaman.

"Grandmother often goes off on her own for days at a time. It would be impossible for Leslie to find her on her own. I can't imagine that she even would try to do that."

"Well, obviously, she did. Her car's here, so at least now we know she's up here somewhere."

Miguel shrugged his shoulders and picked up his gear and waved the trackers on, leading them away from the first village higher up the mountain. They followed an even narrower trail, one that at times was nearly impossible to see. The jungle became darker and darker.

Finally they came to a second village, but it too was only occupied by a few women and children. They also had nothing to report about the missing woman and denied any knowledge about the Grandmother, her whereabouts, and frankly they were coy about even acknowledging her existence. Miguel and Leslie did not have the same close relationship with this second village. These villagers were quite wary of outsiders.

Tomas looked around the darkening jungle and stated the obvious: "It's getting dark and we need to find a place to sit out the night or head back down to the town."

Miguel nodded in agreement: "We need to stay the night. It would be pitch black and too hard to stay on the path back down. But we need to move away from this village. They don't trust us. Come on, I know a place, a clearing about a half mile away. Everyone needs to stay very close together. There are cliffs and the path is very slippery."

He led the team to the clearing and supervised the setting up of camp. They pulled out thermoses of hot coffee and chewed on some jerky and granola bars. Finally, they crawled into sleeping bags. Miguel offered to take the first watch.

Miguel was very worried. He was worried about Leslie and even more worried about the shaman. He couldn't let this crew find the shaman. Where was the Grandmother? Where was Leslie? He feared that she was at the bottom of a cliff covered by the brush, never to be found.

Did Grandmother even know that Leslie was missing? If he could just find the Grandmother, then he'd know what was at stake and he would be able to protect the shaman. That was the most important thing of all.

Tomas lay in his bag wondering about the futility of all of this. He listened to the light breathing of his partner, Jeremiah, and noted when the other man finally dozed off. The other men in the search party, including Sgt. Hernandez had all drifted off.

Finally, he started to fall asleep when a crack of a twig nearby woke him out of his near sleep state. He put his hand on his gun and listened intently for a few minutes. He raised his head and noted all the lumps of sleeping figures around him. No one was stirring. Maybe just his imagination or a breeze rustling the branches. Finally, after a long while, he was able to fall back asleep.

In the early light of dawn, Tomas was awakened by an urgent calling of his name.

"Tomas, wake up!" Jeremiah whispered.

Tomas jerked up to a sitting position and tried unsuccessfully to disentangle himself from his sleeping bag.

"What?!" he asked.

"He's gone!" Jeremiah exclaimed.

By then the rest of the men were stirring. Sitting up in their bags, crawling out, stretching and looking about.

"Who's gone?" But as Tomas looked around the circle of men, he immediately knew who it was. Miguel Puido was gone.

"Miguel, the guide. I thought maybe he'd just had a nature call. But then I realized his gear is gone, too," Jeremiah remarked.

"Well, crap, this is good," Tomas responded sarcastically. He looked around at the group. "How the hell are we supposed to get back down the mountain?" he asked of no one in particular.

Sgt. Hernandez approached Tomas with an attempted look of authority. "Mira, we just need to carefully back track. Once we get to the last village we came across, we can ask for help in getting down the rest of the mountain. Unfortunately, I think we have to call off the search. At least until we find Miguel or another guide. This is treacherous terrain."

As if to cement his last statement, a loud crack of thunder startled the group and the sky opened up in a downpour. "God in hell," Tomas muttered under breath.

It took the men the better part of the day to get back down to the first village. Slipping and sliding, they became soaked; even Sgt. Hernandez started to lose his cool.

"I've always hated this mountain," he grumbled under his breath in Spanish. Two of his men slipped and twisted their ankles, which slowed down their progress even more, the men groaning and complaining the whole time.

Even though Tomas wasn't familiar with this terrain, he had enough experience in tracking, so between him and Jeremiah, and his two trackers, they were able to lead the group down the mountain. The rain was coming down in sheets by the time they found their vehicles. Tomas did hope that Miguel Puido was okay.

He figured the guide could find his way down on his own. There was no sense in all of them hanging around hoping the young man would return. . They loaded in and took a harrowing ride down the rest of the way into the muddy town of Bribri.

Tomas was discouraged by the whole venture into the mountains. He was not looking forward to reporting to Sally the dismal details of the last two days. He split up from Hernandez's group and took his men back to his hotel and checked them into rooms, ordering all to take hot showers, eat, and rest up.

As he opened the door to his room, Sally bounded out of her room next door.

"Tomas!! You're here! Did you find her?!" But Sally already deciphered the answer to that question, just by acknowledging the look on Tomas' face and the weariness apparent in her friend's shoulders.

"No, Sally, we didn't. But we did find her car, so your suspicions that she went up the mountain are correct. Also, the guide Miguel left us in the middle of the night, so we had to find our way back down on our own in the middle of a blasted downpour," he grumbled.

"Oh God, Tomas! I'm so sorry!"

"Not your fault. But I don't get why the guide left us, unless he knows something that he wants to keep from us."

"I think he's probably being protective of the Grandmother. He and Leslie were very secretive about her. Probably didn't want to lead you to her."

"Well that's not very helpful to us or to the missing woman. Sounds like he's got a bit of misplaced priorities going on. I'm going to take a hot shower and go get a bite to eat. I'll come get you in a few minutes if you want to come along and then we can catch each other up."

Fifteen minutes later Tomas yelled into her room. Sally grabbed her backpack and met Tomas and Jeremiah on the pathway in front of her room. Always happy to be in the company of these two, she was eager to catch up on their two days in the mountain. As they walked towards Main Street and to Sally's favorite cafe, they filled her in on the fruitless search and their frustration that the guide had split the scene.

The question on everyone's mind was whether or not to find another guide and go back up the mountain to search some more. Tomas had an appointment with Sgt. Hernandez first thing in the morning. They would make a decision then.

They got to the café and all ordered a hearty late dinner and drank lots of coffee in order to clear the dregs of fuzzy minds. Sally was ruminating over a delicious piece of sausage and wondering if she dare order more when she remembered to tell Tomas about the visit with Michael Turner.

"Hey, someone else was here yesterday looking for Leslie. A dude, I mean a really cute dude, totally out of place, a guy from the US."

Tomas looked up from his plate with interest. "Yeah? Who was he? What did he want?"

"Well, he said he worked for a pharmaceutical company, and he was interested in her herbs and teas. And I thought 'great' here we go, just as Leslie feared."

"Really? How did he come to know about her and her stuff?"

"Well, that's the intriguing part. His company is involved with some drug trials here. And, get this, the one patient – Leslie's patient – the one you had me call – Simone Jenkins…well, she is or was anyways one of the patients on the drug trial….and this dude – a 'Michael Turner' – a hunk by the way, has been in touch with the doctor doing the trials here. A doctor in San Jose – I think his name's Dr. Olivera or something like that. I have it written down back at Leslie's office."

"Alright, Sally, I get that he's a dude and a hunk and really cute," Tomas replied with an exasperated expression. "But it is very curious that he was here and looking for Leslie. How can we get in touch with him?"

Sally pulled Michael Turner's card out of her pocket and handed it to Tomas. Tomas punched in the phone number on his cell and listened a full five rings, fully expecting voice mail, when a live person answered.

"This is Michael Turner."

"Yeah, Mr. Turner, my name is Tomas Vasquez and I'm involved in an investigation of a missing person. It seems you were in this missing person's office early yesterday. I need to talk to you."

"Uh, sure. You mean the naturopathic?"

"Yeah, where are you now?"

"Well, actually, I'm driving back from Limon. I'm headed to the San Jose airport. I'm picking up a friend. Where are you?"

"I'm in Bribri."

"Well, unfortunately, I'm on a tight schedule, otherwise I'd head that way. I could possibly come out there tomorrow. After I get my friend settled. Will you still be there tomorrow?"

"Yeah, but we may be going back out on a search. Depends on the weather and whether or not I can arrange for a guide to go with us. Call me early in the morning; if I don't answer, leave me a message. If I've left with a search party, my cell phone goes out of range pretty quickly, once we head up into the mountains."

"Alright, I'll do that," Michael responded. "Maybe I'll just head on over there early and wait for you," he added.

Tomas was impressed with Turner's willingness, but also not sure if he should be suspicious instead.

When Anne Carmichael got on the plane in Seattle, she was met with an interesting, albeit serendipitous experience. Sitting next to her in the window seat was someone who looked familiar to her, though she couldn't think of how, when or why.

The woman was busy texting in her cell phone – probably a quick good-bye to a family member. The woman finished her texting and shut her cell phone off before finally looking up at Anne and giving her a warm smile. There was an empty seat between them that Anne hoped would stay that way. She didn't like being snuggled up against strangers.

"Have we met before? You look familiar," the woman asked.

Anne smiled and said, "You know, I was wondering the same thing. You look familiar to me, too. Are you ever on the UW campus? I spend a lot of time there."

"Yes! That's it. Last week, in the coffee shop? Right? You were reading a book on Costa Rica."

"Oh yeah. Oh my goodness, this is funny. I do remember you. I wasn't even sure I was going to make this trip then, and now here I am. Wow, this is so coincidental. I remember asking you if I should go and you said yes – to go, that it was beautiful. But you hesitated for just a second. Do you remember that?"

The other woman paused and looked away from Anne for a second. She looked back and smiled, "Hm, it's a long story, maybe after a glass of wine. My name's Iris, by the way. Iris Dibiase."

"Hi, I'm Anne. And I'm off on an adventure."

"I bet you are," Iris responded.

"So, are you going for pleasure or business?" Anne asked.

"Well, I guess that's part of the long story. Let's just say I'm going to surprise someone."

Chapter 9

After a day and a half, Miguel had found no trace of the Grandmother. He did locate many of the villagers who were camping out along a portion of the river way up stream high in the mountains. He knew some of them, and they all claimed no knowledge of Grandmother's whereabouts and knew nothing about the missing doctor.

He was at a loss and not sure what to do. He probably shouldn't have left the search party. Now they were going to be very suspicious of him. He started back down the mountain, wondering if he would be able to meet up with them, but presumably they had given up the search and headed to town, considering the drenching storm.

The mountain was a mess, muddy, and slippery, with intermittent sheets of rain making the hiking miserable. He started to feel pretty guilty about abandoning the group. He slipped and slid down the trails and when he finally got to the campsite and found it empty, he groaned inwardly and continued down to the spot where the jeeps had been parked. They were gone too. Well at least the search party had found their way out.

He backtracked a half hour to the spot where Leslie's car had been left. It was still there. Unfortunately, it was locked. She must have taken the keys with her. He thought about breaking into the car and trying to start the car, but the truth was he didn't have a clue how to hot wire a car.

Now he needed to get to town and begin explaining himself. He started walking out on the main road, hoping to hitch a ride with someone, though he knew that was a long shot. The road was sparsely traveled. Most of the villagers did not have vehicles. It was usually a relative or friend from town that came up this far in a truck or jeep; bringing some supplies or offering a ride to those that occasionally went into to town.

Some of the younger generation ventured into civilization now and then. Most came back, but a few, like Miguel's family stayed in town. Miguel's father had left the villages when he was a young man, but had introduced his son to his indigenous relatives as a way to know who he was and where he fit into the world.

A few hours into the hike down, Miguel finally heard a motor. Only problem was that it was coming up the mountain, and not going down as he had hoped. He stood out in the middle of the narrow dirt road and waited. The motoring sound came closer until he saw a black dusty Toyota SUV slowly emerge around a bend into view.

Miguel lifted a hand in a wave and the SUV pulled to a stop in front of him. There were three people in the vehicle. The back door swung open and one of the trackers from Sgt. Hernandez's team stepped out.

"Hola! Miguel!"

Miguel recognized Estefan, a young relatively new officer on Sgt. Hernandez's team. He knew he had only recently moved to Bribri. He noticed that Estefan had his gun in his hand. The two people in the front seats did not get out. He couldn't really make them out as the windows were very dirty.

"Hola, Estefan. What are you doing up here? I hope I didn't cause a big raucous by leaving the camp."

"Well, yeah you did. Hernandez is pretty upset, and that guy from San Jose, the private detective, man he's pissed. Where did you go? Why did you sneak away?"

At that point, Miguel noticed that the driver had rolled down the window as if he or she was trying to listen to the conversation. Who were the people in the front seat? Sgt. Hernandez? Another of his men?

"Look, I messed up for sure. I thought I could get further on my own. I know my way around the mountain and thought it would be better if it was just me and not a troop of people, crashing and banging through the foliage. The people up here are very skittish. I thought if I could go out on my own I'd have more success in tracking down the doctor."

At that, a man got out of the driver's seat. Medium height. Strong looking. He had his hair tied back in a ponytail. He nodded at Miguel.

"You find the lady?" he asked in Spanish, but with a foreign accent. To Miguel's ear, he guessed Portuguese.

"You mean the doctor?"

"Yeah, the doctor. The one you're all looking for."

Miguel had a seriously funny feeling in his stomach. Who was this guy? He had never seen him before. He wasn't a cop. At least not one he was aware of. Another tracker? Maybe someone connected with the San Jose guy.

"No, I haven't found her. Who are you anyway? Are you with the San Jose team?"

Instead of him answering, Estefan stepped forward and came within a few feet of Miguel.

"Look Puido, I know you are familiar with this area. We need you to take us back up this mountain and find where the lady doctor was getting her medicine from."

The other guy just stood there leaning up against the SUV. Miguel saw movement in the passenger seat then noticed that that window had been rolled down. A woman leaned her head out the window.

"Xavier, you better watch..."

With that Miguel turned and ran into the forest. But within seconds a shot rang out and then the stranger had slammed into him pushing him to the ground. He rolled Miguel over onto his back. Miguel looked up and saw Estefan standing over him with the gun. Xavier grabbed him and pulled him up.

"Get your ass up. You try that again and you're dead."

Estefan tried to remedy the situation. "Miguel, come on, bro. You need to help us out here."

"What the hell is going on? Who are these people?" he asked looking at Xavier and the woman who was now standing by the car.

"Hey, they're just trying to help out. Come on, you're going to take us back up this fuckin mountain," he growled as he grabbed Miguel's arm and spun him around and shoved him back to the clearing. The man with the pony-tail gestured to the car and Estefan opened the back door and pushed Miguel into the back seat. He crawled in beside him and turned to face him. He still held the gun pointed at him.

"Alright, bro, take us up as far as you can in this car. And no pussying around – we aim to find the good doctor and you're leading the way. Comprende?"

Miguel glanced over Estefan's shoulder into the forest. The sun filtered through in geometric forms. His head was pounding and his heart beating ferociously. He saw a glimmer of form distinguish itself from the foliage and sunlight. A slight movement which froze then disappeared into the green.

San Jose, Costa Rica

It was getting dark by the time Michael reached the airport. He glanced at the time and realized he had about an hour to kill before Anne's plane arrived. He parked the car and decided to go sit in the bar, have a drink and get a quick bite to eat. He hadn't eaten all day.

He was perturbed by the call with the investigator. He was able to distract himself by watching the evening news on the television hanging over the bar. Though he didn't get the whole gist of it, his Spanish was improving every day. More terrible stuff going on in Iraq and Syria. Who were these lunatics, anyways? He just didn't get it. And Ebola. Good grief, what more do we need to worry about?

It would be nice if the pharmaceutical companies would put a little effort into developing a vaccine for Ebola. But he knew that was rather unlikely. No profit in something that might only help a few thousand people in Africa.

Finally, the plane landed and he went to wait by the baggage claim area hoping to find Anne there. The deplaning passengers would first have to go through customs, so he knew he had a while before she would show up. He hung around the baggage carousel and noted when it started dumping luggage from the shoot. And then passengers started showing up.

It took a minute to recognize Anne. Primarily because she was not alone. She was walking with another woman and they were engrossed in an animate conversation. He was struck again by Anne's beauty. She was long legged, hair flowing, clear, slightly freckled face laughing with her companion, who was an attractive woman, maybe in her fifties, trim with a nice body, someone who did yoga he thought, confident looking. The two women stopped at the carousel looking at the luggage bouncing down the shoot.

Michael walked up to the pair. Anne looked up and a big smile lit up her face. "Michael! Oh my God, you're here!" She dropped her handbag and threw her arms around him. "I didn't expect you to pick me up! How lovely!" She turned to her companion her arm still wrapped through Michael's, "Iris, this is Michael. Michael, this is Iris. I met her on the plane....although, actually we had met earlier last week on campus. Small world! Wait till you hear her story."

The excruciating pain had subsided. All he felt now was numbness and a bone-chilling coldness. He became aware of a shushing sound in his ears. He forced his eyes open and saw a face leaning over him looking at him intently. Soft hair cascaded down from the face, golden with flickers of light seeping through. He stared into eyes that looked deeply into his, striking eyes, full of love and tenderness.

He couldn't get the image of the Grandmother out of his mind. She faced down the murderous trio with such calmness and courage. Unlike him in the final moments.

The figure above him started humming and gently caressing his brow and face. She rearranged his body gently. He became colder and colder. He felt her compress something on his neck. She then held his face with both hands continuing the soft humming. Miguel closed his eyes and drifted off.

Bribri, Costa Rica

Tomas now had to concern himself with two missing persons. Miguel Puido, the guide, still had not shown up in town. Sgt. Hernandez was getting to the point of washing his hands of the whole thing. He had other things going on that demanded his attention. On top of that, he mentioned in passing that one of his new officers had skipped out on his job. One of the guys that had been on the search party with them.

Hernandez figured that the young man had decided that climbing mountains and looking for a missing woman in the jungle really wasn't what he signed up for. He guessed that Estefan had headed back to Limon where the real excitement was. Wouldn't be the first time he had staff leave the area. It really was a back woods, end of civilization kind of terrain – both geographically as well as culturally. Pissed him off though and he wouldn't be giving a good recommendation if indeed he was even asked for one.

Tomas and his team had spent the morning canvassing the town. Checking to see if anyone had seen the young guide and if there was anyone else who could take them back up the mountain. Puido's family was very concerned, stressing that it was very unlikely that Miguel would deliberately sabotage the search for la doctora.

A younger brother said he could go with the searchers as far as the second village. Miguel had taken him up there a couple of times. He was anxious to join the search team, especially since his brother hadn't returned. Everyone kept saying that this was very unlike Miguel, that he could always be counted on.

Tomas and Jeremiah were weighing the pros and cons of going up that afternoon or waiting until first thing in the morning.

If they went up now, they would only get so far and then have to camp. They finally decided to go ahead and head up to the first village that afternoon and camp nearby and then start the search from that place first thing in the morning, saving several hours.

A lot of Hernandez' team fell off. Hernandez could only offer two of his best trackers. So it was down to Tomas, Jeremiah, two of his men and the two men from Hernandez, and the younger brother of Miguel Puido, Alex. They took two jeeps, some camping gear and more food and water to sustain them for a minimum of three nights. Tomas was determined to find something or someone that could tell him whether the doctor was alive and hopefully also catch up with Miguel.

Hernandez provided the teams with some radio walkie-talkies. He advised Tomas to station one of his men at the first village to function as a messenger between the search party and Hernandez.

They reached the first village just as dusk was setting. There were still only a few of the older women and younger children present. Though not as adept at the dialect that his brother was, Alex was able to talk a bit with the villagers and determined that no one had seen Miguel or the doctor since they had last been at the village.

The search party went off into the jungle about thirty minutes away and set up camp. This time Tomas and Jeremiah took turns keeping watch until the first creep of dawn appeared. Much rustling and jungle noise kept Tomas on edge, but he was able to catch a couple of hours of much needed sleep.

In the morning, they packed up their camping gear, all of them carrying a back pack and headed out with Alex leading the way. His goal was to take them to the next village. By mid-morning, the sun was beating down, the humidity was 100% and all the trackers were dripping wet. They came to a large waterfall which Alex led them through behind a curtain of roaring water.

As they traipsed on, Tomas became aware of something moving just out of the periphery of his vision. He stopped several times and did a full circle scan, feeling as if something was out there and just out of sight. Something was moving along with them.

At one curve in the trail he halted the men behind him. He called ahead to Alex who was about ten feet away and told him to wait a minute. Tomas immediately turned to his right as he sensed something in the bushes. A movement. And then nothing. He walked quietly about five feet into the brush staring at something that didn't quite fit in with the flora. Something laying against a large tree. Something covered with large leaves.

As he stared intently, another movement caught his attention to his right, as he turned his body toward this sound all he could decipher was a breath of soft wind leaving and the sound becoming more and more distant.

He turned his attention back to the shape near the tree. A butterfly had landed on it. Then it flitted away. His breath became caught in his throat as he realized that where the butterfly had perched was a human hand.

He looked at the site carefully before moving towards the hand. He could see that the area was a bit disturbed, a bit trampled. As if someone had been crashing or crawling through the brush. He took off his backpack and set it down away from the disturbed terrain and came closer to inspect the hand.

The hand was connected to an arm. He carefully removed some large leaves and found himself staring into the face of Miguel Puido. A dead Miguel Puido. His body had been laid out to rest. He pulled a wet leaf away from Puido's throat. The leaf looked like it had been placed there carefully. Puido's throat had been sliced. A deep, penetrating slice. He could see that Puido had also been stabbed in the gut.

But, it seemed that someone had cared for Puido. Someone had laid him out gently and had applied some pressure to the neck wound. Possibly someone had found him and tried to help him or stayed with him until he died.

There had been nothing Zila could do but watch the horrific scene unfold. She was well hidden, though only a dozen feet away. It was as if she had blended into the foliage and had cleaved herself into a split of a large fir tree.

Three people, two men and a woman, had drug a young man into a clearing. It was apparent that he had already suffered a vicious beating. She understood enough of the Spanish language to gather that these people were looking for someone or something.

Just when it seemed that the young man could handle no more, she saw the Grandmother step quietly into the clearing.

"I am here. Leave him alone. He knows nothing."

Zila's heart stopped beating for a moment as she watched her beloved Grandmother with her small proud figure standing as tall as she could in calmness and address the group.

One man dropped the injured man to the ground. Though Zila had never come face to face with Miguel, she knew who he was and his ties to the Grandmother and her doctor friend. She watched as Miguel tried to crawl away a few feet, but the other man walked over and put his foot on his back, holding him there.

A young woman with whitish blond hair walked up to Grandmother and spoke in Spanish.

"Look, old woman, we mean you no harm."

Grandmother just stared back with her piercing eyes. "What are you doing to my hijo here?" she asked.

"He only fell; we are trying to help him."

"No, you do not tell the truth."

Zila nearly cried out when the woman took three large strides towards Grandmother and back-handed her across the face. Grandmother stumbled back a few steps but regained her erect posture quickly.

"Vieja! You will listen carefully and do exactly as I say. You will take us to where you get the medicine that the lady doctor was giving to her sick patients. You will do that now, or we will kill your boy here. We will slit his throat in front of you unless you give us what we want now!"

Grandmother looked down at Miguel. He struggled to get up. The man who had his foot on him kicked him in his side harshly. Miguel twisted his head to the side and whispered, "No, Grandmother...do not tell them."

Grandmother looked at Miguel with great love and in a dialect only Zila and Miguel could understand, she said: "Do not worry my child; she is safe as is la doctora."

Grandmother turned back to the young woman. She moved closer to her and said in a soft voice, "You are a foolish young woman."

And then, before anyone could react, Grandmother took a small sharpened poison quill and pushed it directly into her own heart. She smiled at Miguel and gracefully folded into a sitting position, then fell over onto her side.

Miguel gasped. He reached across the ground to grab Grandmother's hand in his. One of the men kicked his hand away, while the one with the blond hair tied into a pony tail, took out his knife and screamed at Miguel.

"You will die right now unless you tell us where the medicine comes from!"

Miguel cried out in a raspy voice, "I do not know! Only she knows!" he cried as he nodded toward Grandmother."

"Xavier! We need to get out of here! It's getting dark. Finish him!"

Horrified, Zila watched from her hidden vantage as the man with the knife slashed it viciously across Miguel's throat and then thrust the knife into his gut. Then the three intruders to her paradise left, leaving Miguel bleeding and dying.

No stranger to death and knowing that Grandmother had already left her body, she waited patiently in her hidden space until she could no longer hear any remnants of the killers. Finally, she crept over to Miguel and ministered to him in his last minutes as his spirit left its earthly body.

She was then able to wrap Grandmother's body in her shawl and lift her small lifeless body onto her back to carry her to her hut high in the mountains. There she would tend to the body and prepare the rituals that would honor the journey of Grandmother's spirit.

She'd been awake most of the day. No one had come into the hut to tend to her. She must have dozed off, because the next time she awoke, she noticed the aroma of something woodsy and aromatic. She turned her head to the small table on her right and saw a covered wooden bowl.

She was able to scoot up on her mat to a sitting position, grateful that the pain in her shoulder had diminished significantly, though her left arm was still bound tightly to her chest. Her right ankle ached severely, but she did not think she had any broken bones there. Probably a bad sprain.

She leaned over the small table and removed the top of the bowl. A warm broth presented itself. There were no utensils, so she lifted the bowl to her lips and sipped the broth.

It was delicious, mushroomy with flavors of the woods. She drained the bowl and laid back down, the effort having taken a bit of a toll on her strength. She ran her free right hand over her naked belly and noted its leanness; she massaged it, feeling the tenderness there.

She dozed off again, and then was awoken abruptly by a low humming nearby. She scooted herself into a sitting position and was able to drag herself over to the opening of the shelter. It was dark, but there was a bright moon light and near a small fire, a young woman with long, flowing hair was hunched over another figure, singing.

As Leslie crept out of the hut, the young woman stopped singing and turned to Leslie. Leslie was captivated by the sight in front of her. The young woman was tending to a body laid out in front of her on a blanket. As her eyes adjusted to the darkness with only the moon light and light from the fire to guide her, she realized with a catch in her throat that the figure laid out on the ground was that of the beloved Grandmother.

"Oh no!" she cried.

Once again Tomas had to cut the search efforts short. They needed to return to town with Miguel's body. The men carefully laid the body into a sleeping bag and then headed back to the jeeps. Tomas also had to tend to Miguel's brother, Alex, who though trying to remain stoic, was visibly shaken.

This whole ordeal was unfolding quite differently than Tomas had expected. Now they had an obvious murder on their hands. This did not bode well for the missing doctor. In his quick assessment of Miguel's body, he concluded that a large hunting knife had been used, which in his mind, pointed to the likely scenario that it was an outsider that had committed the deed.

Alex had explained that the indigenous hunters used bow and arrow and poison darts to take down their prey. They only used knives for skinning and dismembering the bodies of the small animals they hunted. The people were peaceful and a couple of generations had passed since the times the tribes used to fight each other or compete for territory.

As the team moved slowly through the jungle, Alex diverted them from their previous trail, saying he thought he could find an easier and quicker way back to the jeeps. They headed out in the opposite direction from where they had come, and nearby, they came to a clearing.

Jeremiah halted the group and called Tomas over. The area in question was trampled and there was evidence of a struggle. Tomas examined every inch of the area and concluded that this might have been where Miguel had been killed. Jeremiah pointed out that it appeared someone had been dragged to the clearing and that there were a minimum of three other sets of footprints – two larger ones and one smaller set. Two men and a woman?

How had Miguel's body been moved to where they had found it? Propped up against the tree and covered, though not completely? The hand exposed as if to call them over, a wave hello, or possibly goodbye.

Something else caught Tomas' eye. He looked closely at the disturbed ground. There were three strands of long, gray human hairs, caught in a beaded necklace, partially hidden by the dirt.

Alex walked over, saw what held Tomas' attention and started to reach for the necklace.

"Don't touch it," warned Tomas. Tomas picked up a twig and pulled a small plastic bag out of his pocket. Using the stick, he picked up the necklace, noting the long gray hairs entangled within in the beads.

"I believe that belongs to the Grandmother," remarked Alex quietly.

"Why do you think so?" Tomas asked. Have you met the Grandmother?"

"Yes, only once. Last summer. Miguel had brought me along on one of his trips up. I recall that Grandmother had long gray hair and I think she wore this necklace. It is a sign of a particular village and one that only a shaman or healer wears. Though, there are several old people with long hair in braids, if you look closely at the jewelry that they wear, you can identify their village and their status. I think this necklace is from the furthest up village and indicates a high status."

Tomas and Jeremiah studied the area more carefully. They found some spattering of blood and also a path where Miguel's body had been dragged to the tree where they found it, just a dozen feet or so from where it looked like he had been killed.

And if the Grandmother was also here, where was she now? Finding the strands of hair and her necklace but no other trace of her left Tomas with many questions. Was she hurt? He asked the men to walk out in a circle of about 50 to 100 feet to see if they could find any more evidence of the old woman. They did, but could find nothing of her – no trails or paths, no disturbances.

It was if she had just been picked up and carried out, but there was nothing to indicate how this had been accomplished. Maybe she was carried out by the killers. But where were they? How had they gotten this far up the mountain?

They left the spot and continued down the mountain back towards their jeeps. This alternate route brought them to the road quicker and up about an eighth of a mile higher than where they had left the jeeps.

As they walked down the road towards their jeeps, Jeremiah pointed out that there were fresh footprints. Again, it looked like there were three sets. No, actually, Tomas noted a fourth, being pushed our pulled along between two of the sets. Is this where the killers met up with Miguel? Pushing him into the jungle, prodding him along?

And then, how did the old woman get involved?

They walked a few more hundred feet down the road when they came to another pull-out. Fresh tire tracks indicated that another vehicle had recently been parked here. Tracks into and out of the pull-out were obvious. Tomas kneeled down and examined the tracks.

"Four-wheel drive. Most likely a Toyota, maybe a Jeep. In and out. See? Look here."

The rest of the men gathered around and looked at the tracks. One of the men left the group to go relieve himself in the bushes. He went about six feet into the brush before he called out.

"Hey, come here!" he yelled.

Tomas and Jeremiah walked over towards the young man, one of Hernandez's trackers. As they got closer, he halted them with his hands.

"Hold on...there's another body here."

Tomas looked at Jeremiah with a weary, what now look. They waved off the rest of the men and walked carefully over to the area where the young tracker was standing. Hidden in the brush, they could see a leg protruding.

Jeremiah pulled away a large palm frond from the leg to reveal a dead body. It was Hernandez's man, Estefan. Good grief thought Tomas, what the hell?

As with Miguel, Estefan's throat had been slashed and his belly ripped open with the same heavy thrust. Well, it looked like Estefan had chosen the wrong people to hook up with.

Now they had two bodies to carry out.

San Jose, Costa Rica

Michael had convinced Anne and Iris to come home with him. Iris Dibiase had no plans, no reservations for a place to stay. Evidently, this trip had been a spontaneous thing. She seemed quite happy to have someone take over and make plans for her. He told her he had a guest room that she and Anne could share for the night. Anne was a little hesitant with this plan, as her host for her home-stay would be expecting her.

Finally, Anne was able to get through to the hosts and they were quite happy to have an extra day before their guest arrived. Her stay was paid for at any event.

They arrived at the high rise apartment building and pulled into the underground garage. Michael maneuvered his car into his parking spot and the three of them grabbed the luggage and headed towards the elevator. On the way, Michael noticed his neighbors' Toyota SUV a few spaces away in its spot. It was very dirty and muddy. Looked like they had done some jungle back-roading. He really needed to be a bit more friendly. Maybe he could invite them over for dinner while Anne and Iris were around.

They stopped in the Lobby to pick up mail. Coincidentally, the same couple he had just been thinking about were just leaving the Lobby desk. They stopped and exchanged a few pleasantries making promises to get together soon for drinks and dinner.

When they got up to his apartment, Michael showed Anne and Iris around and invited them to settle in. Iris excused herself to shower and freshen up. As she let the cool water wash way the sweat and grime of travel, her mind went back to her last time in Costa Rica, over in Puerto Viejo, at the end of her rope, on the verge of collapsing from the fear of her lost daughter. She remembered the moment of a particular shower, where she was drowning in her grief, and then the strong enveloping arms of Tomas Vasquez, raising her up from the floor and wrapping her in a towel and holding her tight.

Why had she come back? Her heart started beating violently. She had to stop and tell herself to breathe. She hadn't told Tomas she was coming. Should she just turn around and get out of here? Take a taxi back to the airport and take the next flight back to the US? What was she thinking? The smells, the humidity, the lush terrain....all reminders of that time.

As she was dressing in the guestroom, she heard voices drifting in from the living room. More than just Michael and Anne. Another man's voice. She finished dressing and ran a comb through her wet hair. Glancing in the mirror, she decided to skip the make-up routine. Somehow, she remembered, less was better in the humid Costa Rica. Less clothes, less stuff on the face. If only she could drop the other excess stuff around her heart and head...

She entered the living room and saw the same couple they had chatted with in the lobby. A strikingly pretty young woman with long white-blond straight hair dressed in a clingy black strapless sun dress, and a handsome young man with a pony-tail, khakis and a loose blue linen shirt. It looked like they were on their way out for the evening.

"Ahh. Here you are," Michael said. "Come join us. Our neighbors brought over an exquisite bottle of champagne." He said all this as he poured Iris a glass and plopped a juicy looking strawberry into it.

Iris smiled her thanks and took a sip. "Yum. This is good. Hi, I'm Iris." And she extended her hand to the young woman who took it with a warm firm grip.

"Hi Iris. I'm Mercy and this is Xavier." Xavier came up and brushed Iris' cheeks with a kiss. She tried to place their slightly exotic accents. They weren't Americans. There was something very appealing about them, while also something that made the hairs on her neck stand at attention.

"Hey, have you two been back-roading in the jungles or the mountains?" Michael asked.

Iris noted the brief look between Mercy and Xavier. Mercy answered, "Well…why do you ask?"

"Oh, I just noticed your car in the garage. I've been planning to do some exploring myself. Maybe rent a jeep and go up to the volcano."

"Yeah, we did just get back. Did a day trip up into the Monte Verde rain forest yesterday. It was pretty wet and muddy," Xavier responded.

"Well, I'm hoping to talk these two into some exploring with me," Michael said with a nod towards Anne and Iris. Actually, I'm hoping to drag them along with me tomorrow when I head over to the east side. And then maybe add an afternoon exploring the Talamancas."

Iris' heart did a little extra beat. "Where on the east side, exactly?" she asked.

"Well I promised some detective guy over there that I'd come meet him. He's looking for someone who's been missing for a few days. I'm supposed to meet up with him in Bribri."

"That's odd," Iris started, but paused in mid-sentence. She glanced around the room, taking in the look of wariness on the face of Xavier.

"What?" asked Anne. "What's odd?"

"Well, I have a friend….the one I was telling you about, Anne, who has a company that searches for missing people." She glanced over at Mercy and Xavier, hesitant to continue, but couldn't put her finger on why.

"Wait a minute," interrupted Michael. He pulled out his cell phone and looked back at his recent calls. "Is it a guy named Tomas Vasquez?"

"God, this is a small world," Iris exclaimed. "Yes, that's my friend. You're going to meet him tomorrow? Why?"

"Well that sounds mysterious," Mercy said softly, glancing at Xavier.

"Yeah, it's all kind of coincidental," Michael responded. "I was doing some research on naturopathics here and had some information on this one in Bribri. My company is interested in developing an arm of the company in Costa Rica that would focus on indigenous plants that have healing properties. I'd heard that this particular doctor may have had some success with some of her medicines. But evidently she's gone missing."

"At any rate," Michael continued, "I told this Vasquez guy that I would meet him over there in Bribri tomorrow. I had visited that Naturopathic's office a couple of days ago, and the man seemed curious about my interest in her. I offered to go over. Really, it's just an excuse to see more of the country. The wild eastside... I'm hoping you two will go with me," he said with nod to Anne and Iris.

"Hey," Anne added, "You could surprise him. That would be fun," she said with a smile at Iris.

Iris' head was spinning. How could this be? Another missing woman and Tomas being involved in the search. How weird was this? She took a big sip of her champagne and looked up at the people in the room all focusing their attention on her.

"Are you okay, Iris?" Anne asked. "Your face got kind of white, there. Here, come sit down beside me." Anne patted the space beside her on the couch.

Iris looked at the people around her. What was she doing? These were strangers. Here she was staying in someone's home that she had just met a few hours earlier. How random was this? It felt as if there were forces in play that were beyond her control, starting with seeing Anne in a coffee shop at the UW with a book on Costa Rica in her hands and then serendipitously sitting next to her on a plane to Costa Rica within a few days.

She ached to see Tomas. But she was so afraid to see him at the same time. The stress and fear attached to the search for another young woman made her wonder if she had the strength to witness this.

"I'm okay. Sorry. I think I'm just a little light-headed from travelling and not eating much. And I'm drinking this champagne like it's water." She smiled up at the others.

"Oh, yes. You should be careful," Mercy said quietly. "Honey," she said as she took Xavier's hand, "we should let these ladies settle in."

Xavier and Mercy had packed a bag. They were headed back to Bribri that night. After their visit with Michael Turner and his lady friends, they decided they needed to be close to the action in case anything turned up. Staying out of sight in Bribri would be difficult, though, as they did stand out a bit. But fortunately, they were rather adept at disguises.

Instead of taking the SUV, which they thought was probably now drawing too much attention, they rented a little sports car. But first, they had a stop to make.

They drove by Simone Jenkins' house slowly. The young mother was out in the front yard tending to a flower garden. Two little blond headed children were chasing each other around with a hose, squirting water into the air, laughing and screaming at the top of their lungs.

"She does look healthy, doesn't she?" Mercy stated to Xavier.

"Yeah. How do you want to play this?"

"Hm, let me handle this," Mercy responded as she got out of the car and walked across the street.

She approached the playing children. They paused in their activity looking warily at the woman. Just then, Simone looked up. A young pretty woman with spiky short jet black hair was kneeling down by the children.

"Kids, come here," Simone called.

Her daughter, just five years old, smiled shyly at the pretty lady and ran over to her mother. Her son, an old soul at age seven, frowning, said, "We're not supposed to talk to strangers." He gave her a stern look and walked over to his mother.

Standing up, Mercy called out to Simone. "Hello. I didn't mean to alarm your children." She walked over to Simone. "I'm new to the area. My husband and I were driving around looking at the different neighborhoods in this part of town. We're looking to rent a house around here. This looks like such a nice neighborhood."

Simone looked over at the woman and across the street at the convertible sports car parked a few doors down. A man with dark glasses waved at her.

"Hi. Um, I'm not aware of any rentals around here. But you could probably check with any of the real estate offices in town to get some listings." Simone stood there with her arms around both children, holding them close to her body.

"Oh, okay. That's a good idea. We were just trying to get some ideas of areas that we liked."

"Well, I need to get these kids in for a nap. Good luck with your house hunting."

"Thanks! Have a good day," Mercy responded and turned to leave.

Simone watched the woman walk over to the sports car and get in. The couple sat there for a few minutes, before starting the car and driving away slowly.

She took the kids into the house, made them some cheese sandwiches and lemonade. After lunch, she settled them down together onto her big bed. She snuggled in between the two of them and read them a story. The children fell asleep within ten minutes.

Feeling drowsy herself, she laid the book down and started thinking about the woman who had approached her in her yard. People just didn't do that around here. She couldn't put her finger on why she was so suspicious. Maybe it was just her nature. She had always been very protective when it came to her kids.

After a few minutes of pondering this, she dozed off. A while later, something pulled her out of a deep sleep. She looked over at the clock and realized she'd only been asleep for about 20 minutes. She listened carefully for any noise. Not hearing anything but now fully awake and needing to use the bathroom, she carefully extricated herself out from the entanglement of her small children's bodies snuggled up closely to her.

She used the bathroom then walked out to the kitchen. She stopped when she noticed that the back door was slightly ajar. She always locked her doors when home alone with the kids. Or did she forget? She was rather forgetful these last few months.

As she stood in the kitchen searching her mind for the memory of locking the door, she picked up a fragrance. A slightly floral perfume.

She picked up her glass on the counter and walked over to the sink to fill it with water. She stood there at the sink looking out the window, when some movement reflected in the window caused her to freeze. Someone was in the kitchen with her.

She started to turn around and just before an arm shot out to grab her, she glimpsed a man with dark glasses; she crashed up against the counter, and slipped. And as she slid down to the floor, her head struck the counter top and blackness enveloped her.

Chapter 10

Bribri, Costa Rica

Sally had done all she could to clean up Leslie's office and clinic. She had been fielding patients' phone calls and drop in visits. Telling them all to call back in a week or two to reschedule. She was just getting ready to open up her computer and check her own emails when the front door of the clinic opened and Tomas Vasquez walked in. She could tell by the exhausted look on his face that he didn't have good news to report.

He looked at her wearily and shook his head. "I'm sorry Sally. It's not been good. We found the young guide's body," he said quietly.

"Miguel? Oh my God. Leslie will be devastated. What happened?"

"He was murdered."

"What?! Murdered? How?"

"Let's just say, it was not pretty. His was throat was slashed." Tomas said, noting the tears welling up in Sally's eyes. "I'm sorry, Sally."

"So, this is much more involved that we thought. Someone may have gotten to Leslie."

"There's more," Tomas continued. "We also found the body of Hernandez's guy that went missing. He'd been murdered too."

"Tomas, this is crazy! Did you find any signs of Leslie? Or the Grandmother?"

"No, I'm sorry. Hernandez has pulled the rest of his men off the search. He now has two murders to investigate. He thinks the search for your friend is fruitless at this point. Miguel's brother is very angry. The villagers have scattered. They're all way up in the mountain hunting, gathering, and fishing, evidently. Only a few old women and small children are left at the two villages we reached. And they're not telling us anything."

Sally looked at Tomas with deep sorrow in her eyes. "What are we going to do? I just can give up on Leslie. I'm sorry I've drug you into this Tomas. This....this is so much like last year."

"Yeah. But I'm afraid this story may not have a happy ending."

"It already doesn't. Poor Miguel. I don't know what to do. I don't know how long I should stay here on the off chance that Leslie will miraculously walk through that door."

"Well, I probably need to let my guys get back to San Jose. I can't really afford to keep them here much longer. And unless I have a really good tracker, I don't think I can rationalize going back up that mountain."

"This is shitty!" Sally exclaimed. It's probably all my fault!"

"No, Sally...don't go there. We have no idea what this is really about. I'm going to head back to the hotel, and take a hot shower. Afterwards, let's meet up for dinner and come up with next steps."

Tomas turned to leave just as the office phone rang. Sally held up her hand indicating that he should wait.

She answered the phone. "This is Leslie Goetz's office."

A male voice spoke. "Is Dr. Goetz there?"

"No, she's not. Can I take a message?" Sally responded.

"Has she been found yet? My wife had said that she was missing."

"Who is this?" Sally asked.

"Brad. Brad Jenkins. I'm Simone's husband. She's a patient of Leslie's. She told me that Leslie is missing. I need to know if she's returned."

"I'm sorry to say that we haven't found her yet. We don't know where she went. Is Simone doing okay?" Sally asked.

"For the moment, she is. But something weird is going on. Someone broke into our house and attacked her. I think they were after her medicine. The stuff she gets from Dr. Goetz. Her bottle is missing and this isn't the first time it's gone missing."

"Hold on, Brad. I'm putting this call on speaker phone, if you don't mind. I have a friend here who is part of the search party. He needs to hear this."

She put the phone on speaker. "Brad, Tomas Vasquez is listening in. He's helping the local police search for Leslie."

"This is Simone Jenkins' husband on the phone," Sally continued. "He said that someone broke into their house and attacked her."

"Hello Brad. Can you tell me what happened?" Tomas asked.

"Sure. She's still shaken up a bit. But what I got out of her is that she was lying down with our kids when something woke her up. She went into the kitchen to get a drink of water and felt that someone was in there. Somebody was standing behind her and reached for her and she thinks she slipped and cracked her head on the counter. A few minutes later she woke up on the floor. "

"Did you call the police?" Tomas asked.

"Yes. They just left. We couldn't find that anything had been disturbed or taken. But just a few minutes ago she realized that her small dropper bottle of medicine that she gets from Dr. Goetz was missing. I don't think we would have thought too much about that, except that this is the second time this has happened."

"What do you mean? Tell me why you think this."

"Well, the reason we came over last Saturday was to get this refilled. Dr. Goetz was concerned that we had run out. Simone explained that she hadn't run out of the medicine, but that she had misplaced it. Now I'm beginning to wonder if it wasn't taken. Clearly, someone was in our house today."

"Have you or your wife noticed anyone unusual in the area?"

"No, not really. Wait a minute. Simone's listening in. She has something she wants to say. Go ahead honey."

A soft feminine voice came on the line. "It could be nothing. But today, I was out in the yard with the kids and a woman approached us. I'd never seen her before. She was asking me about rentals in the area. I got a funny feeling from her, but I'm not sure why. She was very polite."

"Was she alone?" asked Tomas.

"No, I saw her walk back to a car parked a little ways down the street. There was a man in the driver's seat."

"Can you describe her?"

"Yes. Very pretty. Very short black hair. Stylish. Big sunglasses. Probably in her early 30s. A faint accent. I can't really place it."

"What about the car?" Tomas asked.

"Um, a little sports car. A convertible. But the top was up. Blue. I'm not sure what the make was."

"Did you tell this to the police?"

"Yes, I did. They looked around, checked with some neighbors and said they would get back to me. I'm not sure they really think anything happened. That maybe it was all in my head. They couldn't find any evidence of breaking and entering, and since nothing was missing – at the time I didn't realize my medicine was gone, I think they think I was sleep-walking or something."

"How do you think they got into your house?" Sally asked.

Brad responded: "Simone noticed the kitchen door slightly ajar when she came into get a drink of water. She was sure she had locked it before they went in for their naps, but now she's not sure."

Sally asked: "Simone, how are you? Do you need to see a doctor?"

"I'm okay. A little headache. But I'll put in a call to Dr. Olivera just to be sure. I'm more concerned about getting a refill on my medicine. I know I'm being a bit self-centered here and probably very superstitious, but I've been feeling so much better these last few weeks, the cancer has gone into remission, and quite frankly, I credit Leslie and this medicine for my cure..."

"We're doing all we can to locate Leslie. It looks like she went up to a remote area in the mountains here. As soon as we find her, we'll let you know," Tomas said.

"I hope she's okay. That's the most important thing. That she's okay. She's really a wonderful person. Please let me know right away when you find her. I'm sure I'll be okay."

They ended the conversation with Tomas asking Brad and Simone to contact him if they learned anything from the police.

A weary Tomas and a saddened Sally stood at the same time. Tomas reached out to Sally and she went into his arms.

"I'm just not sure which way to turn right now, Sally."

"I know, Tomas." She pulled back from him and said: "Hey, you need to get that shower and then a good bite to eat. I'll close up here and meet you in about an hour. I'll come by the hotel."

Just as Sally leaned in to give Tomas another hug the door to the clinic opened. Tomas had his back to the door. A woman walked in and stood there observing Sally and Tomas standing very close together. Sally looked over Tomas' shoulder and then stepped back abruptly.

"Oh my God!" Sally exclaimed.

Tomas turned around, half expecting to see the missing doctor standing there.

"Iris," he said quietly.

"I hope I'm not interrupting anything," Iris said with a smile.

She disentangled herself from the warmth of his body. Noiselessly, she sat up and slipped out of the bed. Looking back at the sleeping man, she allowed herself a moment to study him. Even in sleep, she could see the worry and strain that played out on his face. He was relaxed though, his breaths coming in strong even waves.

Iris bent down and picked up her dress from the floor and slipped it on. Then she quietly left the room and walked outside. It was still early, barely dawn. Though the humans in the area were for the most part still sleeping, the birds and insects were singing loud and clear their salute to the morning light.

She stepped off the porch and headed down the path towards the back of the property which was butted up against a nature reserve. She left the property through a gate and immediately became enveloped into the moist, shrouded jungle. She was barefoot and the spongy moss covered ground was alive and responsive to her every step.

Yesterday was a blur. When she walked into the missing doctor's office and saw Sally and Tomas standing there together, she knew she had been right to come. The look on Tomas' face wiped out any hesitation that she had brought with her.

When she first saw his face, it was with furrowed brow and strain written all over it. As recognition became apparent to him, he lit up. His eyes danced, his mouth turned up in an uncontrollable smile, the biggest smile she had ever seen on his handsome face.

She walked for about an hour through the reserve holding onto the warmth and love that she felt having spent the night wrapped tightly around his body. The smells, sounds and colorful flora brought her back to the previous year.

But this time, instead of terror, she actually felt peace. She felt the nature of the place embrace her with its welcome. Though there was the stress of Tomas' current job, looking for another young missing woman, Iris was okay. She would help him through this. She would not be an added burden.

She walked back the way she came through the jungle reserve onto the property back to Tomas' cottage. When she got there, he was sitting on the porch. Two steaming cups of coffee and a plate of fruit were sitting on the table next to him.

She walked up the steps and he greeted her with a big smile.

"You weren't worried about me, I hope," Iris said.

"Iris, I don't worry about you. I know you," he responded.

She walked up to him and he took her hand and pulled her into his lap. She snuggled into him and kissed him on his neck. He wrapped his arms around her and they sat there quietly for a few minutes.

"You're barefoot," he finally said, noticing her bare muddy feet.

"Yep," she responded.

"Hm…seems like a nice cool shower might be in order here," he said.

"I might need a little help getting these feet washed," she responded teasingly.

"I think I can manage that," Tomas replied.

A little later while they were getting dressed, Sally pounded on the door to the cottage.

"Hey, you two! You remember we have a date for breakfast? I've been waiting out here patiently for the last ten minutes."

"Oops," Iris whispered to Tomas.

"Yeah, we're on our way out," Tomas yelled.

"Alrighty, then..." Sally muttered to herself. "I'm famished," she continued to no one in particular.

The three of them walked towards the main drag of town. The morning was already hot and humid. There wasn't the breeze that Iris was used to in Puerto Viejo, where the ocean played a big part in keeping the temperatures down.

"Oh, by the way, I invited that Michael dude to meet us for breakfast," Sally said. "He and his girlfriend are coming."

"I still find this all quite coincidental," Tomas said. "How Iris met his friend on the plane and his connections with this case. I'm looking forward to finding out who he really is and what his part in all of this is."

"Yeah, well I told you he works for a drug company that's looking into expanding into natural supplements. He had interviewed the doctor that was treating Simone Jenkins. The doctor kind of led him down the path of tracking down naturopathics. And somehow he ended up here," Sally explained.

"Well it's still a little suspicious to me," Tomas muttered.

"I have to agree," Iris chimed in. "Though he seems like an okay person to me. He was very gracious in offering me a place to stay for the night...and who would have guessed that he'd be headed this way the next day? Plus, I really like Anne."

They walked into the café and saw that Michael Turner and Anne were already sitting at a table set for five. They stood up and greeted the threesome. Anne gave Iris a hug and Michael shook hands with Tomas.

Tomas took in the striking good looks of the couple. Michael stood another four inches taller than Tomas' 5'10". He was classically handsome with green eyes and sensuous lips. Tomas surmised that Michael was well aware of his good looks.

Equally attractive was Anne. Tall and willowy, long flowing wavy hair and large clear blue eyes. She on the other hand had a somewhat self-conscious demeanor and seemed unaware of her penetrating beauty. Hm. An interesting couple. The woman was an innocent. The man...he wasn't quite sure how to peg him. He was a slick dude for sure.

They pulled up chairs and joined the couple at the table. Coffee was served and breakfast was ordered. Iris was sitting between Tomas and Sally, her thigh brushing up against Tomas'. Warmth flooded into her belly each time he pressed against her.

Tomas immediately started quizzing Michael.

"So, tell me just exactly how you came to be here, Mr. Turner."

"Please, it's Michael. Yeah, well, as I said on the phone, I was just transferred by my company to Costa Rica."

"What company?" asked Tomas.

"Biogenesis. It's a large pharmaceutical company with its headquarters in Seattle. But it has several different offices around the world. Not here, yet. That's why I'm here. To start making connections, feel out the area for potential. On top of that, I'm supposed to explore the feasibility of developing a natural supplements division. Using some of the local indigenous medicines. I was asked to connect with a doctor in San Jose who was working with our firm on some drug trials."

This all sounded a bit too pat for Tomas. Somewhat rehearsed.

"Dr. Olivera? Simone Jenkins' doctor?" Sally asked.

"That's right. Dr. Ferdinand Olivera."

"How did that lead you here?" asked Tomas.

"Uh, he told me about a couple of his patients that were being treated by a naturopathic. One in particular was experiencing a remission in her cancer. He wouldn't give me the name of the patient or the naturopathic. I did a bit of sleuthing and ended up here."

Both Tomas and Sally looked at Michael skeptically.

"And..?" Tomas asked.

"Tomas, Michael told me that Dr. Olivera's office had been broken into," Sally said.

"Yeah, that's right," Michael confirmed. "He said that his office had been broken into, charts strewn all over the place."

Sally looked at Tomas and said: "Do you think that has anything to do with Simone Jenkins?"

"Yeah, maybe that's how they found her. And finding her somehow led them here to Dr. Goetz."

As Iris sat at the table with Tomas on her right and Sally on her left, she skidded back in time and recalled a similar situation. Another lost woman. But then it was her daughter. Her heart started beating a little faster. She glanced over at Anne who met her eyes with a direct look. Anne raised her eyebrows at Iris in question.

Iris had told Anne about the previous year. Bits and pieces of it during the flight. She met Anne's gaze with a small smile conveying the message that she was okay. In that moment Tomas pressed against her thigh with his thigh as if to say, I'm here. Your daughter is safe and sound at home.

Just then Jeremiah Valencia walked into the restaurant. His face lit up when he saw Iris. She jumped up and gave him a big hug. He leaned over to Tomas and whispered something in his ear. Tomas stood and the two men walked away from the table and left the café.

A few minutes later, Tomas walked back in and sat back down.

"What's going on?" asked Sally.

"Jeremiah's leaving, taking our two guys back to San Jose. We've got another case that needs our immediate attention. I'm going to have to head back too. I'm sorry Sally. I'm not sure what our next steps are here. I think the local police, Hernandez and his crew, are going to have to continue on. They've got the two murders to investigate. Maybe along the way, they'll figure out what happened to your friend. I just don't have the resources to keep doing this."

Michael and Anne looked at each other. "Two people were killed? You think this is related to the missing doctor?" Michael asked.

"This is awful," Sally added. "I'm so worried about Leslie. Somebody's done something to her. And now with Miguel dead. God, maybe whoever did this was trying to get Miguel or Leslie to lead them to the Grandmother. I think it has to do with the Shaman and her healing herbs. Somehow it's all connected to that."

Tomas sighed. "Well it seems to be pointing in that direction."

"But who? Why?" asked Michael.

Anne looked at Michael. "Michael, you should know. Just think what your company would do to get its hands on some miraculous cure for cancer."

Tomas took in the pained look that crossed Michael's face. Guilt? "Well, then somehow, Hernandez will need to track down this 'Grandmother' you're talking about, Sally. Problem is one guide is dead and his brother is grieving; not likely he'll want to head up the mountain again. The family has a funeral to plan."

The group broke up after breakfast. Sally headed back to Leslie's office to close up and make arrangements for the cat. She told Tomas and Iris that she would be heading back to Puerto Viejo afterwards with a dejected tone in her voice.

Tomas planned to check in at the police station and let Hernandez know that he needed to get back to San Jose. Iris tagged along. Tomas wanted to fill in Hernandez on their possible theory. He also wanted to tell Hernandez about Michael Turner and how he had popped up in the middle of all this and that it would be a good idea to keep an eye on him and his girlfriend.

Michael and Anne stayed at the café and lingered over coffee a while longer. Both were silent as they toyed with the remains on their plates. Finally, Anne laid her hand on top of Michael's and looked directly into his eyes. Her blue eyes piercing deep into his green eyes.

"What do you think, Michael? I mean really, what do you think is going on?"

"I really don't know."

"Don't you think it's a little too coincidental? You being here? You being asked to see Dr. Olivera? His office broken into? His patient that was on the trials experiencing a remission? Her medicine gone missing? She also being a patient of the naturopathic who is missing? Doesn't take a rocket scientist to put this puzzle together. Really, Michael? What are you doing here?"

Michael looked at Anne with confusion and a bit of anger on his face.

"I'm not doing anything here, Anne."

"Seriously? If you don't know what's going on, then I'm guessing that someone is using you."

"What?! That's preposterous! I've got an assignment, a new job, that's all."

"A new job, here in Costa Rica. You're told to look up this doctor. You're told to check into natural indigenous stuff...Come on, Michael. Put on your thinking cap."

Michael sat there a few seconds, withdrawn. Then he abruptly stood up, pushing the chair back and walked out of the restaurant, leaving Anne there.

Anne thought for a moment, then paid the waitress and walked out. She looked down the block and saw Michael striding away quickly. Looking completely out of place in his slacks and white shirt.

She followed him staying a block back. At one corner she stopped for the traffic. She glanced at the cars waiting at the stop sign and saw a cute little blue convertible sports car. Something struck her about the driver. From the side she saw an attractive woman with short black spiky hair and big dark sunglasses. In the passenger seat was a man with a baseball cap on. Something seemed familiar about the couple.

They did not seem to notice her, so she slowed her pace down as they passed through the intersection. She looked up the block and noticed that Michael had disappeared. She kept walking up the sidewalk, looking into shops as she passed by them. Finally, she spied him in a tourist shop, just standing in the middle of it, hands in pockets, looking forlorn and lost. She walked in and stood by him for a few seconds. He turned and looked at her, almost looking straight through her as if he didn't recognize her.

"Anne," he finally said softly. "I'm sorry. I shouldn't have left like that."

"Hey, it's okay. It got a little tense there. I understand. Are you okay?"

"Not really. Sometimes I really ask myself, who am I and what the hell am I doing? I'm just going through the steps sometimes.....not really paying attention to the path I'm on. Really, you're right. I don't know why I'm here and why my company asked me to check in with Dr. Olivera. It all does seem bizarre. This missing doctor. The patient on remission. You know, it feels like Dr. Walker did send me here for something. Why me?"

"Michael, it's probably just crazy coincidence. You're a good product rep. You…you have flair and charisma. Maybe we're making this out to be more than it is…"

"Yeah, well tell that to that Vasquez guy. He looks at me like I'm a criminal or something. It's like I've been thrust into the middle of something and I don't know what!"

"Well, maybe we should head back to San Jose. Come on, let's put this behind us. We don't really have anything to do with this," Anne said somewhat unconvincingly.

Sally left the café and walked back to Leslie's office. She was very sad. Tomas had not been able to help after all. She ached with the thought that she might never see her good friend again. And somehow she felt that it was all her fault. That damned article! What had she been thinking?

As she approached Leslie's clinic, she noticed a young man standing in the doorway. She slowed down and watched as he peered into the windows and knocked on the door.

She walked up to him and asked, "Can I help you?"

He turned towards her and she gasped as she recognized a younger version of Miguel, the guide.

"Are you Miguel's brother?" She asked.

"Si," he responded, "I'm Alex. I'm going back up on the mountain. My brother cared deeply for la doctora. The least I can do is try to find her. Everyone is giving up on her. I cannot do that. I also need to find out if the Grandmother is okay. Everyone here is worried about her."

"What are you doing here?" Sally asked.

"I thought you might want to come with me." He looked at her directly not offering any further explanation.

"Won't I slow you down?"

"We will go slow and carefully. I know another route that my brother took me on last summer when he took me up to meet the Grandmother."

"Why do you want me to go with you?"

"Look, you don't need to…I just thought…" Alex trailed off and turned to leave. It was then that Sally noticed he had a backpack at his feet. He bent down and picked it up putting it on his back and started walking away.

"No, wait!" she said. "I…just let me grab some things. I'll come with you." She pulled a key out of her pocked and opened the door. "Come in, while I get ready."

She grabbed her backpack, which still contained her light sleeping bag. Got a water bottle and some protein bars. She looked at Alex.

"What else should I bring?"

"Good shoes, maybe a rain poncho. A first aid kit."

She hesitated. God what am I doing? But how can I not? She grabbed some more protein bars. Leslie had a stash of them in her office for sale. Well, she'd pay her back if and when Leslie was retrieved. She wrote a note on a piece of paper to no one in particular stating that she'd gone off with Alex to search again.

"Okay. Let's do this." As they walked out, she wondered if she shouldn't let the police know or Tomas. But they had all already given up. They'd think she was crazy and would likely talk her out of this. It was crazy. And yet she had to admit that she was annoyed and hurt that Tomas was giving up the search. Her knight in shining white armor was not quite that after all.

She hefted her backpack onto her back and they walked down the side street towards a small jeep parked there.

As Michael and Anne were walking back towards the hotel and his car, Anne stopped him and put her hand on his arm.

"Michael, see that little blue sports car at the corner?"

"Yeah. What about it?"

"Look at the couple in it. Don't they look familiar to you?"

The car was idling at the corner. Michael studied the backs of the couple. Something did strike him as familiar.

Just then an old little jeep pulled out of the street adjacent to the sports car, made a left turn and pulled into the main street and drove right by where Michael and Anne were standing. Michael got a glimpse of two people in the jeep and recognized the woman in the passenger seat. It was Sally Meza.

The sports car made a quick U-turn and seemed to be following the jeep. Anne pulled Michael into the doorway of a shop and watched the sports car go by. They got a good view of the couple in the sports car.

"Well, if I'm not mistaken, those are my neighbors. Mercy and Xavier," Michael said under his breath. "The woman looks different, different hair, but I got a good look at the guy, even with those dark glasses on and the hat. She obviously changed her hair. It's them, I'm sure."

"God, what are they doing here?"

"I don't know. But I'm going to find out. Come on!"

Michael started jogging back to the hotel and his car just a block away. As he neared his car, he yelled back over his shoulder, "I'm going to follow them!"

"Michael, wait!" But to no avail. Michael had jumped in his car and sped down the street.

Alex Puido drove the jeep with careful determination. Sally kept straining her neck to look behind them. "Someone's following us!" she exclaimed.

Alex did not respond. They had been on the road for well over an hour. Every once in a while, Sally would hear or get a glimpse of the car behind them. The road kept climbing, and was getting muddier and slippery.

"It's getting closer!" Sally worried and looked at the road ahead. It was getting narrower and steeper. Whoever was following them was gaining on them. Maybe it wasn't anyone to worry about, maybe just other travelers going up the mountain. Right. No, she knew in her gut that whoever was behind them was most likely foe not friend.

Just then, Alex swerved the jeep a hard left into the brush. She looked back and the trees closed behind them, completely hiding their presence. Alex stopped the car. They waited about five minutes before the car behind them went past. They waited longer as they listened for the car to turn around. It didn't.

They waited another ten minutes and just as Alex was prepared to start the car they heard another car coming up the mountain. It went past the place they were waiting and kept on.

Alex looked at Sally and shrugged. "No one ever uses this road. I wonder who that could be." He then started the jeep and put it into gear and continued on the path they were on. Going deeper into the woods on a barely discernible track away from the road.

"Do you know where we are?" Sally asked.

"Yes. Miguel took me this way once. Pretty soon, we will have to get out and continue on foot."

Michael Turner followed the blue sports car high up into the mountain, trying to stay a good distance behind them. They had to know he was there, though, as the noise from his car would travel a good distance and there hadn't been any other vehicle traffic coming or going. Well, he wasn't afraid to confront them, if needed.

But on second thought, he was probably being pretty naïve as he thought about the two dead bodies already in the mix here. Had they killed the guide and the police officer? What the hell was he doing? Why had he run off like this on his own? Hopefully they were too intent on following the jeep that Sally Meza was in and therefore not really aware of him.

But that hope was eliminated as he came around a bend, the road now a wet, washed out track. They had laid a trap for him. He slammed on his brakes and stopped just a few feet from the sports car. They were standing there, leaning up against the little car. Indeed, it was his neighbors. Xavier stood there with his arms folded across his chest, Mercy next to him with a gun loosely dangling in her hand.

They beckoned for him to get out. He put the car in reverse and pressed the accelerator. The car fish-tailed and crashed into the brush behind him. He kept pushing on the gas to no avail. Mercy walked over to the driver's side and told him to get out of the car. She dropped the gun to her side and smiled.

"Really Michael, we're on the same side here. Come on let's talk about next steps."

Michael opened the door and got up. He faced the two, shrugged his shoulders and made a feeble attempt at a smile.

"Maybe if you'd told me who you were in the beginning I

wouldn't have been chasing you up a mountain," he said in a joking way.

"Yeah, you're probably right," Javier said. "Truth is we're both working for the same people and are after the same thing."

"You work for Biogenesis?"

"Well…sort of."

"So, what are you doing up here?" Michael asked.

"Better yet, what are you doing up here"? Javier responded.

"Well, I saw you following some people leaving town, headed out of Bribri. What happened to them?"

"Got away."

"Too bad."

"Yep. It would make things a lot easier. Evidently there's a different road and we missed the turn off."

Mercy tapped the gun against her thigh. "So what to do now? What do you think, Xavier?"

Michael glanced at Xavier's hand, which was resting on the handle of a hunting knife strapped onto his belt. Mercy looked over at Xavier with the slightest raise of her eyebrows and a hardened glint in her eyes. She grasped the gun a little more firmly, and took a step towards Michael. Xavier had walked around the back of the car and Michael felt his presence closing in on him from behind.

"I'm pretty sure we could work something out here," Michael said. "We're both after the medicine."

He felt Xavier pause behind him and saw a slight softening of Mercy's gaze and a tiny shrug of her shoulders. He was taller and bigger than Xavier. His plays on the Lacrosse field, where speed and sudden twists and turns were needed, started playing across the landscape of his mind. He felt Xavier start to move closer and Michael determined that it was now or never that he needed to act.

He grabbed the handle of the car door and threw the door open towards Mercy, while taking a step backwards and purposefully falling onto Xavier who was just a couple of feet away. He landed on top of Xavier and then scrambled to his knees using an elbow to strike Xavier in the throat. He jumped to his feet and stumbled and crashed away as gun shots were flying towards him.

And then he ran as fast as he could through the trees with no sense of direction. He crashed through the jungle in a panic, as if he were drowning and desperate for a gulp of air. He kept on running. Occasionally, he'd hear his pursuers not too far behind him.

He continued, becoming out of breath and exhausted. He felt as if he had been running for over an hour. Most of the time he was climbing, occasionally the path would drop a foot or two and he would end up slipping and sliding and grappling to hold on to something like a wet tropical branch, some of which burned and cut his grasping hands.

He became completely disoriented in his location and time of day. It was hard to place the sun, as the jungle canopy shielded the light and sky from him. He came upon a small, rare sunny clearing, the ground soft and matted down. He slid down onto his knees and relaxed for a moment, embracing the sunlight and its warmth after the dark and smothering wetness of the entangled jungle-forest he was lost in. He listened intently for the sound of his pursuers.

He closed his eyes and took a few deep breaths. He was thirsty and once again berated himself for his foolishness. He was exhausted and scared and lost. And he was sure that Mercy and Xavier had not given up the hunt.

It seemed as if even the cacophony of jungle noises had momentarily silenced. He then felt a soft whisper of sensation on the back of his neck. He stood and slowly turned around examining the shield of jungle foliage surrounding the small clearing he was resting in.

Again, the soft breath on the back of his neck. He raised his hand and slapped at the back of his neck...imagining a mosquito or some other insect alighting on his vulnerable skin.

A dancing shimmer of color caught his eye and glancing towards the movement, he saw a large, beautiful and brightly colored butterfly float into the space, and then settle onto an outstretched limb of the foliage, its wings lightly fluttering in the gentle breeze.

Looking more intently at the butterfly, he moved closer to the foliage, teasing apart the different shades of green. In that green, something more familiar took shape and with a wildly beating heart, he jumped back in fright as he became aware that he was looking directly into the face of a young woman.

She searched his face with the most compelling eyes he had ever seen. One was as blue as the bluest, cloud-free sky; the other was a tawny, multicolored hazel-green. Her lashes were dark and lush, her skin was soft, clear and fair, her face framed by golden hair cascading down her back to her waist.

She put her fingers to her mouth gesturing him to be quiet and then beckoned him into the foliage. They stood there in stillness for about a minute, and then he heard the rustle of branches and stealthy footsteps. Eerily, the jungle noises quieted, the birds and insects stopped their racket as if they were waiting and observing.

She pulled him back a little further into the foliage, pressing her hand gently against his back, settling his jittery body into complete stillness. He felt her soft breath on his neck, measured and slow; calming his racing pulse, and ironically, he felt a peace flow over his body.

More rustling nearby. Then Mercy and Xavier stepped into the clearing. They both had rivulets of sweat pouring off their bodies. They stopped in the clearing and stood there for several minutes, looking at the ground and gazing intently into the foliage for any traces of human presence. Michael held his breath as it appeared that they were looking directly at him, their eyes searching and trying to decipher form.

Then the two intruders turned away and studied the adjacent foliage intently. They stood and looked around carefully for another full minute. Finally, Mercy beckoned to Xavier to follow, and they quietly moved out of the clearing in the direction away from Michael and the young woman behind him.

She kept her hand pressed firmly into his spine, holding him there, almost trancelike for what seemed like an eternity. Michael felt like they had stood in place for at least an hour, the already dark jungle had become even darker, and the air had become slightly cooler. He thought it could be evening.

Slowly, the jungle noises returned to their full crescendo. It had seemed as if all creatures had been holding their breath. Finally, the hand pressing against his back relaxed.

Michael turned slowly around to look at the young woman standing just inches from him. Without a word, she beckoned for him to follow her. He had no choice, he knew, because not only was he desperately lost, but he also felt the need to understand who she was.

Tomas and Iris had been on the road back to San Jose for about an hour. Neither of them speaking very much. Every once in a while, Tomas would lay his warm hand on Iris' knee with an assuring squeeze. She studied his profile as he maneuvered the curvy road up the Pali. He had a gentle, handsome face with deep dark brown eyes. He caught her examining him and twitched a slight smile.

"I wish I could have said goodbye to Sally," Iris remarked.

"Yeah, me too. I wonder where she went."

Earlier, before leaving Bribri, they had pulled up in front of Leslie Goetz's clinic. Iris wanted to let Sally know they were leaving, driving back to San Jose. She jumped out of the car and tried to enter the clinic. The door was locked, curtains pulled. No one answered her persistent knock.

Leslie's neighbor, Toni, had observed Tomas drive up and wanted to go out and speak to them, but she was busy with a customer. By the time she finished and stepped outside, Tomas was just pulling away from the curb. She waved, but couldn't get his attention.

She had seen Sally leave the clinic earlier. She had her backpack on, and strode right by her shop, intent on her destination. Unfortunately, Toni had been busy with a customer then, also. She hadn't seen that Sally was with someone. It bothered her a bit that Sally didn't stick her head in to say good-bye. She was probably on her way back to Puerto Viejo. But it really bothered her that everyone was giving up on Leslie.

"Well....." Tomas began.

"Yes?" Iris smiled.

"Am I going to be able to convince you to come home with me?"

"It won't take a lot of convincing. I haven't made any other arrangements," she said, smiling.

"How long?"

"I'm not sure. But I'll stay out of your way. I know you're busy."

"Not that busy," he said warmly.

Alex Puido and Sally Meza had been walking for over an hour. They came to a village high up in the mountains near a crashing waterfall. As they approached the village, two young men with hunting spears came out to meet them. Sally felt caught between the ancient tribal world and a new modern world. The two men were dressed in blue jeans, but barefoot and shirtless. Their hair cuts were short and spiky. Like one would see on young men in the city.

They gestured to Sally and Alex to stop. Alex talked to them in Spanish explaining their situation. Some small children came running out of their huts towards the group, laughing and giggling. One of them was swooped up into the arms of one of the young men.

Still holding onto their spears, they beckoned Sally and Alex to come into the village. A few old women and a couple of old men were sitting on a blanket grinding up some root on a stone. Several children were running around in some game.

The two young men sat on their haunches and drew a map of sorts in the dirt, pointing out landmarks to Alex.

Alex turned excitedly to Sally. "The doctor is alive. She's hidden up higher in a remote area. She was hurt and the shaman has been taking care of her. These two had found her at the bottom of a cliff and brought the shaman to see her. They then carried her far up into the mountain."

Sally teared up and breathed a deep breath of relief. "What about the Grandmother?" she asked. "Is she with Leslie?"

Alex turned back to the young men and asked the question. At his question, the old women and men stopped what they were doing, and the children stopped playing. They all looked up at Alex with deep sorrow.

One old woman uttered something under her breath that sounded like a curse to Sally's ears. They stood up and gathered the children and went back into their makeshift huts. Virtually turning their backs and closing their doors on the outsiders.

One of the young men answered. "The Grandmother is gone."

"Gone? What does that mean?" Alex persisted.

"She sacrificed her life for our shaman. It is what she chose. In order to protect the shaman and your doctor friend," the other responded. "There are some strangers, bad people, who are bringing evil onto our mountain."

"We think we have been followed up here," Alex said. "By these very same people you are speaking of. I think they killed my brother, Miguel," he added.

The two young men nodded in agreement and beckoned for Sally and Alex to follow them.

Tomas and Iris were two-thirds of the way back to San Jose and had pulled over to a look-out. They had stepped out of the car and were looking out over a vast green canopy of trees and jungle flora. It was a beautiful site. There was a gentle breeze at this altitude.

Iris breathed in deeply and leaned up against Tomas. He laid his arm across her shoulders and pulled her in. No words were needed. As they headed back to the car, Tomas heard his cell phone ringing. He reached in and noted the number.

"This is Vasquez," he said.

"Senor," the voice on the other end started. "We have a new development." It was Sergeant Hernandez from Bribri.

"What is it?" asked Tomas.

"The lady friend of the missing doctor, Sally Meza. Well it appears she went up the mountain with Alex Puido, Miguel's brother."

"What?! How did this happen?"

"The neighbor of the doctor's, the shop owner, well she went into the doctor's office and saw a note that Meza had left on the counter. The note said that she and Alex were going back up the mountain. That's all it said. Toni, the shop owner, said she saw Sally leave a few hours ago with a backpack on. She had been busy with a customer so didn't go out to talk to her, and just now went into the doctor's office to check on things."

"Well, what are you going to do about this?" Tomas asked.

"There's nothing I can do. I just thought you should know, her being a friend and all."

"You're not going to go look for her?"

Hernandez gave a big sigh over the phone. "Look, I don't have the manpower to traipse up that mountain again. These people are free to go up there if they want."

"Good grief, man. There've been two bodies so far. Someone is killing people. There's a missing woman!"

"There's too much territory to cover."

"Can't you call in some help? The OIJ?"

"I do have a call in." Hernandez replied. "You know better than anyone that people go missing in this country. It's expensive to call in the troops and search. I think that's why you're in the business you're in, right?" he added somewhat sarcastically.

"Yeah, I'm in the business....that being the operative word. I usually get paid," Tomas muttered under his breath, looking guiltily at Iris. "Alright, thanks for the information. Let me know if anything else happens, especially if Sally turns back up."

Tomas closed his cell phone and looked at Iris, who had obviously gotten the gist of the conversation.

"Oh, Tomas, we have to go back, don't we? I can help pay your expenses."

"I can't let you do that."

"Yes, you can. Now it's Sally. I owe her big time, Tomas. Really. We need to go back. Call Jeremiah. Call in the troops. Do whatever it takes. I'll hike up that damn mountain, if needed. Please, she risked her life for my daughter," she added softly.

Tomas looked at Iris, her furrowed brow, her big brown eyes pleading with him. "God damn it," he said under his breath.

Before they got into the car, Tomas called Jeremiah Valencia and asked him to come back to Bribri and to bring as many trackers as he could round up. In response to Jeremiah's query, Tomas explained the new development regarding Sally and also said that he would personally cover the cost. Jeremiah was given free rein to hire some help.

Truth was that Tomas had plenty of personal funds and though he wanted his business to succeed on its own, he knew that now it was a personal story as it involved two people he cared for deeply: Iris and Sally.

Xavier and Mercy were lost. They had lost the trail of Michael Turner and had been wandering around for over two hours. It seemed as if they were traveling in circles. They had not planned for this much time on the mountain and didn't have supplies with them.

They kept ending up near a large waterfall which always seemed to be the end of the trail. The roar of the waterfall was obliterating all other sounds. But Mercy had the uncanny feeling that they were being observed.

Xavier was a few feet in front of her once again approaching the waterfall. This time he moved up real close to it, the water drenching him. She came up close behind him and touched his shoulder.

He jumped and exclaimed, "Hell! Don't do that!"

She leaned in and said, "I think someone's out there."

He stopped and looked around. It was very hard to get his bearings with the crashing waterfall and the drenching mist. He couldn't see anything other than wet and green.

Mercy looked over his shoulder and noticed a small opening between the waterfall and the rock wall. She touched him again on the shoulder and pointed towards the opening.

"Maybe this is a way to the other side of the waterfall."

"You may be right. You stay here, I'll check it out."

"No! Wait! Don't leave me. There's someone or something out there. I can feel it," she whispered loudly.

"Okay, let's go together. Hold onto my shirt. And watch out, it's gonna be really slippery. A tumble down this waterfall wouldn't do either one of us any good."

"Yeah. I bet this is the same waterfall that the doctor fell into."

"Could be. But I'm so turned around, I don't know if it is.."

The two of them crept behind the falls and found themselves in a big cavern. They were able to go deeper into the cavern and further away from the crashing water. They could see that the path behind the waterfall to the other side was about 40 feet.

The water was roaring. They inched along. Mercy held tightly to Xavier's shirt. Finally they got closer to the end of the path and it became a very narrow space of only a few inches wide that they had to traverse before getting to the other side of the falls.

They took their time, creeping along the narrow path until they finally stepped out of the space behind the falls and found themselves on a trail. The mist was so heavy that they could barely see a few feet in front of them. Xavier stopped abruptly and held his hand back to stop Mercy.

Mercy looked over his shoulder to see what was stopping him and saw that a young man was standing there about five feet in front of them. He was shirtless, wearing jeans and was barefoot. And he had something in his mouth. She couldn't quite make out what it was.

Xavier had drawn his gun, but the young man had blown something out of his mouth, and whatever it was, it hit him in the neck. Xavier felt an incredible sting in his neck and slapped at it. Something was stuck on his neck.

Mercy watched in disbelief as Xavier tried to remove a large needle or quill out of his neck. He started to stumble, and she tried desperately to hold him up. But it was too wet and slippery and he slipped out of her arms, slipping to the ground and then tumbling over the rocks into the crashing falls.

She looked up at the young man and turned to run back behind the falls. She got through the little opening and the narrow trail and went as fast as she could behind the falls to get to the other side.

She looked over her shoulders and saw that the man with the poison dart was also behind the falls and following her.

He did not seem to be in any big hurry to catch up. She realized that she was trapped. She did not know her way down the mountain. Xavier was gone. And she knew she only had a few moments of her own life left.

She turned around and faced the young man. She could barely make him out, the mist was blinding. She lifted up her gun and took aim at his shape. Then she felt a piercing sting to her neck.

She slapped at her neck and felt darkness overtake her. She then slipped and fell out into the falls, crashing until there was only blackness and all went quiet.

Sally and Alex had followed the two young natives to a clearing near the falls. They could hear the loud road of water. One of them went ahead towards to the falls, while the other stayed with Sally and Alex and waited.

Only about 20 minutes had passed when the other young man returned.

"It is done," he said quietly.

"What?" asked Sally.

"The intruders are over the falls," he replied.

"Are they dead?" asked Sally.

He shrugged his shoulders.

"How did you know where they were?" Sally asked.

"We've been tracking them. We left them after we realized they were lost and rambling in a large circle, always coming back to the falls."

"They caused the death of the Grandmother and were continuing to look for the shaman. They brought this upon themselves," the other added.

By the time Tomas Vasquez and Iris got close to Bribri, dusk had begun to settle. Iris glanced up at the sloping flanks of the Talamancas admiring the purplish haze and mist shrouding the mysterious mountains.

She wanted to go up the mountain with Tomas and the search team. She was trying to devise a way to convince him that she could tag along. She needed to be there for Sally. Sally had been there for her deep in the jungle every inch of the way when they'd rescued Nina the year before.

They stopped first at the police station and talked to Sgt. Hernandez. When he learned that Tomas was planning to go back up the mountain with some of his own men, Hernandez relented and said he would accompany them, and could also bring along one or two men.

"It's too late to start out tonight," Hernandez remarked. "Let's meet here at 5 a.m. I'll have a jeep, and if you can get your hands on a 4-wheel, it would be best to have two vehicles. I think I can get us up to the first or second village. Maybe there we'll find someone to take us further."

"Sounds good," Tomas replied. "My guys won't be here until later tonight, and they'll be driving a 4-wheel that can handle the terrain."

"See you in the morning," Hernandez said. And then added, "And thank you."

"No, I should thank you," Tomas answered. "I understand the demands of this on your man-power."

Tomas and Iris then returned to the small hotel they had been staying in and checked in. He also reserved two additional rooms for Jeremiah and his trackers.

They unpacked, took a long cool shower and then decided to walk the town and find some place to have dinner. After dinner they walked back to the hotel and sat on the porch sharing a bottle of wine. They were quiet, both reflecting on the previous year.

Finally, after a big sigh, Iris took Tomas' hand and said, "I'd like to go with you tomorrow. Up the mountain to look for Sally. It's important to me."

He looked at her intensely with many different responses poised on his lips. He did not want anything to happen to her. He wanted to protect her.

But finally he squeezed her hand and said, "Okay."

Iris looked at him and thanked him with a big warm smile. They sat a few minutes longer in silence.

Then Iris sat up. "I wonder where Michael and Anne are. Do you think they headed back to San Jose?"

"Good question," Tomas replied. "I'm still curious about him."

And, as if on cue, a tall, slender woman was walking towards them on the path.

"Iris? Is that you?" Anne asked as she came closer. I thought you had left." She stepped up on the porch, looking lost and sad.

"What's wrong, Anne?" asked Iris. "Where's Michael?"

Anne glanced at Tomas, hesitating.

"What is it?" Tomas asked. "What's going on?"

"Michael chased after some people earlier today. He's been gone all day."

"What do you mean? Who did he chase after?" Tomas queried.

Anne looked at Iris. "You know those neighbors of his in his apartment building? The ones we had champagne with?"

"Yes, you mean Mercy and Xavier?" Iris responded.

"Yes, them. They're here in town; at least they were yesterday when we saw them. But Mercy had changed her hair. It's short and black now."

"That's weird," replied Iris.

"Why did Turner go after them?" asked Tomas.

"He saw them following Sally. She and somebody else were in an old jeep, heading out on the main road. Xavier and Mercy went after them. And then Michael ran back to our hotel and jumped in his car to follow them. It all happened so fast."

"Great, now we have another person on that mountain to be concerned about. What do you know about these two?" Tomas asked, looking at Iris.

"Not much really. Anne and I just met them the other night. Shared a glass of champagne. They're neighbors of Michael's."

Tomas turned to Anne. She shrugged her shoulders and said, "Yeah, it wasn't more than 20 minutes or so. Though I do recall them seeming very interested after Michael mentioned he was coming over here to Bribri to meet up with you, Tomas. They left pretty abruptly after that."

Tomas was quiet for a few seconds. "So, maybe they're up on the mountain, too. Looks like we might be missing out on this party. We better get this show on the road."

They said goodnight to Anne, went inside and prepared for an early departure in the morning.

Does anyone ever get found on this mountain? Tomas wondered. They'd been slipping and sliding, following muddy trails since the crack of dawn. They'd picked up a willing young teen to guide them after they had gotten to the second village.

Their new guide led them to a loud, roaring waterfall. The six of them followed the teen behind the waterfall and on a perilously narrow trail out to the other side. With him were Iris, Jeremiah and one of their trackers, Sgt. Hernandez and one of his men.

As they left the waterfall and the roaring behind them, they continued on a trail that at times became indistinct. The teen seemed to know though which way to go. Sometimes they bushwacked through thick brush until they came to a clearing and could see the trail continue out of the clearing.

About two hours from the waterfall, and with dusk becoming apparent, the teen guide suggested they stop for the night. A light humid drizzle fell; Tomas felt wet to the bone. He agreed and they set up camp. Dinner was protein bars and jerky, washed down with water. Nothing cooked. Couldn't have started a fire if they'd wanted to.

Iris laid a tarp down on the wet ground and spread her sleeping bag out on it. Tomas came over and pulled his sleeping bag out of its bag and laid it next to hers.

"Is this spot taken?" he asked.

"Not yet," she replied. "I love the places you take me to," she added.

"Yes, it's all part of my plot to get you to love this place so much, that you won't ever want to leave."

"Well, let me tell you, you sure know how to woo a girl," Iris responded with a smile in her voice.

He reached for her hand, and listening to the jungle noises, the insects' loud buzzing and other unidentified noises, Iris felt oddly at peace and safe. This is crazy she thought.

Somehow, they slept through the night. When Iris awoke, her hand was still intertwined with Tomas'. She looked over at him and saw that he was awake and looking up through the trees at the sun streams breaking through. She smiled at him and mouthed, good morning.

They sat up in their sleeping bags and looked around. Hernandez and his guy were sound asleep. Light snoring coming out of one of their bags. Jeremiah was sitting up in his bag, scratching his head. The guy he had brought along was just beginning to stir.

The young guide's bag was empty. Tomas followed the sound of some quiet conversation coming from the edge of the clearing. He got up out of his bag and followed the sound. About 30 feet away, the young guide was sitting on his haunches and talking to two other young men. They stopped talking and looked up at Tomas when he was about ten feet away.

The guide stood up and said, "They know where your friend is."

The two young natives had left Sally Meza and Alex at a very remote, tiny village on the edge of a steep cliff the night before. They told them to stay put until they returned. Sally hoped they would return with Leslie.

There were five huts in this village, and only young men and boys inhabited them. Alex explained that this was a base camp for hunting and fishing. Sally and Alex had slept out in the open. Surprisingly, Sally slept like a log, and woke up refreshed. She was so happy that Leslie was alive. She couldn't wait to see her. But she had to spend the day trying to be patient.

Finally, a few hours later, after an interesting time with Alex and the men and boys of the camp, which included eating some fine fish and some sort of bird for lunch, and then watching the men and boys tell stories and play games around the camp fire, Sally heard some voices coming up the trail into the camp.

The two young natives were walking back into the camp with a group of others trailing behind. Sally gasped when she recognized the tall, strong, handsome Jeremiah Valencia walking in, followed closely by Iris, then Tomas and three other men. They were all drenched in sweat and looked very weary.

Sally ran up to Iris and gave her a big hug. "What the hell?!" she exclaimed.

Iris responded with a big grin. "God, Sally, I'm so happy to see you. I was so worried."

"Hey, you know me. I'm indestructible."

Tomas walked up to the two women, dropped his gear on the ground and wiped his brow. He looked around and said to Sally, "Is Michael Turner here?" He asked, glancing around at the group of people encircling the new arrivals.

"No. Why?"

"Apparently he followed another couple up the mountain who were following you. Turner saw them taking off after you when you left town, and he then took off after them. At least that's what Anne said."

Alex walked up and said, "Yeah, we knew someone was following us. We were able to turn off on a well-hidden track and waited until they passed us. And then after a few more minutes, another car went by on the road. Maybe that was the man you speak of. After that we headed on down the road we were on."

Alex continued, "And, you should know," glancing at the two young natives that had brought them here, "evidently they ran into this couple – a man and a woman."

"What do you mean?" Tomas pressed.

"I cannot really say. Except I believe that they are no longer a threat. It is my understanding that this couple are the ones that killed my brother and are responsible for the Grandmother's death."

Iris had walked over and was listening. "Mercy and Xavier?"

Tomas thought to himself, I don't really want to hear this. He certainly didn't want Hernandez to hear any of this. He cut into the conversation just as Sgt. Hernandez walked up, redirecting it.

"So, do they know where Leslie Goetz is?" He asked nodding towards the two young natives.

"Yes!" Sally exclaimed. "Evidently, they found her at the bottom of a cliff and took her to a village doctor way up in the mountain."

"Well, then, let's go get her," Tomas pressed.

Alex stepped up and said, "They will bring her down. It's too hard to get there, and they really don't want us to accompany them. Said we would just slow things down. They're getting ready to take off now. We need to wait here."

Tomas sighed. He was torn. On the one hand, he was happy to not have to do any more traipsing up this mountain. On the other, he wasn't sure he could just sit back and let others do the work he was trained to do. But, it was their mountain, and he obviously couldn't find the doctor on his own.

"But what about Turner? He's up here somewhere, too. We need to find him."

Alex spoke to the two young men and relayed Tomas' concern. He turned to Tomas and said, "After they bring la doctora down to us, they will then find the man you speak of."

Tomas sighed again. Obviously, these two would be more adept at tracking a lost person on this mountain than he would. When all was said and done, he thought he'd have to figure out a way to put these two on his payroll for future jobs in this part of the country.

The two young natives left the village. Alex walked over to Tomas and his crew and told them they might as well get comfortable. It would be several hours before they returned, nodding up towards the higher flanks of the mountain, "It's a hard hike up there."

Dr. Zachary Taylor lay on the floor, looking up at the stripes of sunlight displayed across the ceiling. A calming sensation flowed through his body. He thought he had been laying there for most of the night.

And now he watched as sunlight filtered in through the windows. Birds were chirping. Soft music was playing somewhere.

He felt at peace. Faces of friends and loved ones flitted across the dreamscape of his mind. He rested on one in particular, Gretta. What a good friend, lover, confidente and supporter she had been in his life. Too bad they were both so driven in their career paths that they couldn't have made a life together. He regretted that.

He felt empty. So empty. Well, literally, he was. He recalled having spewed every possible element of stomach and intestinal contents out. Most of it reaching the toilet, but a lot of it ended all over the kitchen floor in the middle of the night.

He had attempted to rehydrate with some chamomile tea, but another spasm caused him to drop the kettle of boiling water all over him and the floor. He had fallen to the floor then in agony. He was sure he had passed out.

At one point, he must have come to and crawled into the sunroom, as that was where he was now. No pain, no grief.

The music became louder. The sound of the birds chirping seemed to be right in the room with him. He felt tender hands caressing his brow. A soft singing in his ears. Sounds of a waterfall.

He felt forgiven.

She was feeling so much better. She had no idea how many days she had been up here being cared for by the young shaman. They managed to communicate pretty well in Spanish and so Leslie guessed that she had been here for about a week. She was able to learn that this was the shaman who provided the ground up mushrooms to the Grandmother. Here she was face to face with this extraordinary young woman.

The shaman had taken such good care of her wounds. Not only had she kept her nourished and hydrated, she had set her sprained ankle and her broken clavicle. Leslie was sure that she had also suffered from a serious concussion, as there was still a pretty big lump on the back of her head. Plus, she was also still very dizzy and nauseated when she tried to stand up and move around.

No one else came to the dwelling. As far as Leslie could tell, they were very isolated and her tent-like shelter was the only structure. She could not figure out where the Shaman slept each night. Most likely, outside. She would disappear for hours at a time, but always tended Leslie's wounds and made sure there was food and tea for her to reach.

Somehow, Leslie needed to get down this mountain. Or at least get a message to somebody in town. Her friends must be worried sick. And then she remembered the two people that were responsible for her being in this predicament. Where were they? Were they still looking for her? And the more she thought about this, she wondered how did the young shaman get her to this place? Had she carried her?

Were they safe? Hidden well enough? Leslie wanted to get down the mountain, but she was also scared. Who were those people? Then she remembered that they were demanding to know where this shaman was. They wanted the medicine that meant so much to Leslie's practice.

Shame came upon her as she realized that she had brought all this upon herself and had most likely endangered the young healer. And worse of all, the Grandmother was dead. She had not been able to find out from the young woman, who called herself Zila, how the Grandmother had died. Zila would only shake her head no, when Leslie questioned her.

She pulled herself to sitting and scooted on her butt to the doorway. She pushed aside the cloth covering the opening and scooted out of the small hut. It was warm and she figured it was early evening. She wondered where Zila was. It seemed like quite a long time since she had seen her. Certainly not since early in the morning.

God, what if the young shaman never came back? Could she get herself out of here? Find her way down this mountain?

She maneuvered herself up on her knees, fighting down a wave of nausea. She sat back on her haunches, letting the dizziness pass. It was so quiet. Even the birds were silent. She sat there for a few long moments, stabilizing herself and letting the warmth soak into her bones. Her shoulder ached. She reached down to check out her hurt ankle which was still red and swollen. She wiggled her toes and was satisfied that here was only minimal pain.

Using her left hand to push off the ground she put her weight on her good foot and slowly rose up to standing. Another wave of nausea, but remarkably, it passed quickly. She slowly pivoted to look all around her.

She was in a heavily foliaged area with the hut situated in a very small clearing. The hut was built with branches and sticks and was covered with cloth and large palm fronds. It had protected her well from the elements.

As she looked around peering into the jungle, she sensed some movement in the periphery of her vision and heard a whisper of noise.

Was Zila coming back? Or was it something or someone else? Heart pounding, she gingerly stepped backwards until she felt the leaves and branches pushing up against her back. She squeezed herself into the brush, sinking into the foliage.

Just then Zila stepped into the clearing. But she was not alone. There was a man with her.

Zila stopped in the middle of the clearing, putting her hand out to silence the man. She stood there frozen for a few long seconds. She moved her gaze slowly around the space, peering into the thick foliage. Her eyes came to rest directly on the spot where Leslie stood.

Then, as if through some other unnatural force, she made direct eye contact with Leslie. Piercing through the elements to identify the human element of eyes within the green foliage.

Shocked, Leslie stepped out as if pulled by the intensity of the gaze of the young woman. Zila beckoned Leslie over and gently ran her hands over Leslie's wrap on her arm and shoulder and then knelt down to prod at the injured ankle. She stood up and slightly shaking her head in disapproval, she turned to the man.

Leslie stared at the man. She couldn't make sense of him. He was dressed in slacks and a white shirt – though they were dirty and torn in places. He looked at her with a half-smile and a shrug.

"I guess you're the missing doctor?" he asked.

"I guess I am," Leslie responded. "What are you doing here? Who are you?"

Just then, Zila put her fingers to her lips and shushed them. She had her head cocked slightly to one side and was listening intently. Not too gently she grabbed Leslie by her good arm and pulled her into the bushes while beckoning for Michael to follow.

She pushed and pulled the two of them rapidly deeper and deeper into the jungle forest, stopping every few steps to listen. All sound disappeared in the jungle except for the deep breathing of Michael.

They came to some large boulders covered in moss, when she stopped them again, shushing them, listening intently.

Zila pulled them behind one of the boulders into a dark, wet crack that was barely large enough for them to squeeze their bodies into. She pushed Leslie and Michael into the small cave about three feet and then indicated that they needed to stay there until she returned.

Leslie's shoulder and ankle hurt. She was crushed up against a man she did not know. They did not dare speak.

Michael's thoughts were a jumble. Had the two pursuers – Mercy and Javier – been able to follow them to this place?

After what seemed like an interminably long time scrunched up against a strange man's body, but probably not more than a few minutes, Zila reached into the crevice and beckoned for Leslie and Michael to disentangle and come out.

Her whole body ached. She had stomach cramps and felt nauseated. This was the first time in days that she had been upright. She was weak and as the man moved away from her body, he reached back his hand and pulled her out. She fell against him and he held her upright. Then he gently lowered her to the ground.

Leslie looked up as Zila approached her. Once again, Zila ran her hands over Leslie's body, touching, probing, massaging. She signaled for Michael to pick up Leslie and carry her over to the hut. He laid her down on the mat inside and Zila beckoned for Michael to step outside. Inside, she unwrapped the sling on Leslie's shoulder and the splint on her ankle. She took some pungent slimy ointment and massaged it into Leslie's hurting shoulder and aching ankle and then re-wrapped both areas.

She then took some cool broth and spooned it into Leslie's mouth. Leslie looked into Zila's strange eyes and said thank you for everything. Zila smiled and placed a cool hand on Leslie's forehead and lightly massaged her temples. Leslie fell into a peaceful sleep.

Zila stepped out of the hut, looking into the jungle, nodding affirmatively.

Michael jumped as two young men stepped into the clearing. Zila put out her hand to calm him.

Zila walked over to the visitors, indicating to Michael to stay where he was. He observed them in close quiet conversation which ended by Zila bowing her head to the two and inviting them over to Michael.

One of them spoke to Michael. "We will take you down the mountain. You have friends waiting for you."

"What about her?" Michael asked glancing toward the hut where Leslie lay.

"We will carry her down."

"How?" he asked.

"The same way we carried her up here."

Michael looked over at Zila. She was dismantling the make-shift hut around the sleeping Leslie.

The young men went over and began weaving together a flexible stretcher out of the materials, tearing the cloth into rope and tying the whole thing together. They then lifted the sleeping woman onto the stretcher. She barely stirred. Zila went over and smoothed Leslie's furrowed brow and laid her head on Leslie's chest for a few seconds then nodded to the young men.

They picked up the stretcher and beckoned Michael to follow. He looked back at Zila and said, "Thank you," not knowing if she understood. She looked directly into his eyes and nodded. Evidently, she was not going to join the troop and he understood why. The less modern humanity imposed itself upon this miraculous being, the better.

Anne Carmichael was at a loss. She felt stranded in Bribri. Everyone, including Michael, was evidently up on the Talamancas' flanks looking for the missing doctor. The strange couple from Michael's building were also hunting the doctor...she guessed. And why, she wondered? Who were they? What was their role in this strange drama?

God, she didn't know if she should hire a car and head back to San Jose on her own and just get on with her plans, or hang around town and do what? At a loss, she thought she would deal with her own immediate issues, which was her hunger. She hadn't eaten much in the last two days, ever since Michael had sped off in pursuit of Mercy and Xavier.

She grabbed her laptop and headed for an internet café. She wanted good coffee and breakfast and wanted to check her emails to see if her parents had been in touch.

Once she settled in with her breakfast order and a hot cup of steaming coffee sitting in front of her, she opened her laptop and checked her emails. Lots of them...wow, it had been a long time since she had gone days without being hooked into wi-fi; she almost regretted opening up her computer. It was nice to not be attached to the devices so constantly.

But, it was good she checked as she noted there were no less than six emails from her parents; three each from her mom and dad. She scanned the ones from her mom quickly. Her father was doing well; the treatment was working for the time being having brought his PSA numbers down to less than one; they were spending more and more time together, and Anne should relax and enjoy herself and not worry so much about her parents.

Then she opened her father's emails. They pretty much mirrored her mother's notes. All was well. He hoped Anne was enjoying herself, adding uncharacteristically philosophical comments about life being too short, she should live, love, and enjoy it to its fullest, as one never knew what was just around the corner.

That last remark was exemplified by a shocking bit of news. Dr. Zachary Taylor was found dead in his home just a day ago. The biomedical and pharmaceutical companies were in mourning for one of their greatest, provocative, and cutting edge researchers. Cause of death was unknown at this time.

This all seemed to deepen the mystery for Anne. Dr. Taylor was the one who had lobbied to get Michael to take the Costa Rica position. He was also the doctor who was having his controversial drugs trialed here. And, if Anne remembered correctly, one of the patients on the trial was also one of the patients that the missing naturopathic doctor had treated. The patient had had a miraculous remission from a deadly cancer. Man, she wished she could talk to Michael. She wondered what this meant for his job here, and what, if any, were the connections to Xavier, Mercy, the missing doctor, and the miraculous cure.

She decided she would stay in Bribri until Michael returned.

It looked like they were going to have to spend another night on the mountain. Dusk was setting in and still no sign of the two young men that had gone to retrieve the doctor. Tomas glanced over at Iris who was sitting in front of a fire with Sally in animated conversation. Iris' face was aglow and he thought she had never looked more beautiful or happy. What a surprising woman.

He couldn't begin to fathom what their next steps would be. Would she stay here in Costa Rica? What kind of life would they have together? All he knew was that he intended to find out. In that moment, Iris looked up and caught his eye and gave him a big smile.

He looked around the campsite. Jeremiah was in deep conversation with Sgt. Hernandez. Hm, he hoped Jeremiah wasn't looking for a different job. The man was his right hand, educated and sincere, but capable of being wily and ruthless if the situation demanded it.

Alex was sitting off by himself, staring off into the jungle. He was most likely grieving his brother, Miguel. But in truth, it was that grief that got him back up here and ultimately led to the deterrence of the two who most likely were responsible for this chain of events. Tomas didn't really want to pursue that train of thought. Where were Xavier and Mercy? At the bottom of a cliff? Buried? Under water? Or somewhere out in the world planning their next move?

What he really wondered, though, was who or what was really behind all of this? Was Michael Turner and his powerful pharmaceutical company the real culprits? He hoped he had an opportunity to put that question to Turner, if and when he was found.

Just then Alex stood up and walked towards the brush, as did a few of the young men. Tomas stood and looked over in their direction. In the twilight he was barely able to make out the newcomers. As they came closer, he recognized the two young natives. They were carrying a stretcher between them. He walked up and saw a sleeping women wrapped up in cloths on the stretcher. She looked amazingly at peace, with a smile on her lips, as if she were in the middle of a pleasant dream.

The two young men set the sleeping woman down. Another figure stepped out of the trees. As he came closer to the fire, Tomas recognized Michael Turner.

Sally got up and ran over to the sleeping woman. She got down on her knees and teared up. "Leslie! My god, Leslie!"

At that ruckus, Leslie Goetz opened her eyes and looked up "Sally?"

Acknowledgements

This is a work of fiction. While some of this story occurs in actual places, the names, characters, and incidents are the products of the author's imagination or are used fictitiously.

I would like to thank my daughter, Deshna, for her spirit of adventure. Our trips to Costa Rica were the backdrop for our journey of putting our stories on paper.

Costa Rica is a beautiful and exotic country. Yes, it might be easy to get lost in its dense jungles; but more likely, you can find yourself there, too.